PRAISE FOR *CA*

"Heat sizzles between these two . . . Anyone looking for inclusive romance should check out this breezy contemporary."

—*Publishers Weekly*

"This is a romance novel in which the plot outside of the relationship is also compelling, and that makes this book stand out."

—*Library Journal*

"Kianna Alexander writes an amazing story about two very determined women—in love, at odds, and risking a lot on a second chance."

—*Essence*

Can't Let Her Go

Millionaire Moguls

A San Diego Romance

The Southern Gentlemen

Back to Your Love

Couldn't Ask for More

Never Let Me Go

The Roses of Ridgeway

Kissing the Captain

The Preacher's Paramour

Loving the Lawman

The Roses of Ridgeway: The Complete Collection

Electing to Love

PHOENIX Files

Darkness Rising

Embrace the Night

Midnight's Serenade

The Phoenix Files Trilogy

Love's Holiday

Climax Creek

A Passion for Paulina

Seducing Sheri

Vying for Vivian

Adoring Ava

Persuading Patrice

Love and Life in Climax Creek: Volume One

Can't Let Her Go

KIANNA ALEXANDER

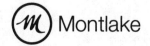

Montlake

Text copyright © 2023 by Eboni Manning

Published by Montlake, Seattle

www.apub.com

Amazon, the Amazon logo, and Montlake are trademarks of Amazon.com, Inc., or its affiliates.

ISBN-13: 9781542038454 (paperback)
ISBN-13: 9781542038447 (digital)

Front cover design by Faceout Studio, Molly von Borstel
Back cover design by Faceout Studio, Amanda Kreutzer
Cover illustration by Louisa Cannell

Printed in the United States of America

For the girls, gays, and theys . . . For the culture . . .
For the past, the present, and the future.
Love is love, and love wins. ALWAYS.

CHAPTER ONE

"You're all set, Trey."

With one hand on the snap closure of the black vinyl cape, Patricia "Peaches" Monroe opened it, pulling the cape away from her client's shoulders with her signature flourish.

Trey ran a hand over his head while checking out his reflection in the mirror mounted over her station. An approving smile on his face, he said, "You really hooked me up, Peaches."

"Like always, bro." After giving the cape a quick shake, she hung it on the hook near her mirror. "You know ol' Peaches gonna get that hairline right and tight."

The interior of Fresh Cutz Fine Grooming was bustling with activity, and she wouldn't have it any other way. She'd built the shop from the ground up, carefully overseeing every detail. She'd chosen the gray and cream paint on the walls, the sleek black textured-vinyl chairs with antiqued bronze finishing on the hydraulic base, and the black Formica countertops flecked with gold at each of the six barber stations. This place had existed in her mind long before it had in reality, and she loved to see it come alive each morning.

Trey reached for his wallet and handed over a few bills. "Keep the change, homie. You earned it."

"Thanks, Trey. I'll see you in a couple of weeks." She slipped the money into the front pocket of her black-and-gold apron and waved to him as he left. After taking a rag from the sanitizer, she wiped her chair down, well aware of the cacophony around her.

The buzz of clippers, the sports commentary blaring from the wall-mounted television, and the murmur of several conversations in progress were the background music for her task. The only places that came close to matching the noise level were the mall food court and the living room at her brother's house when her three nieces were hopped up on sugar—usually provided by her.

Once she'd allowed the sanitizer to dry a bit, she sat down in the chair, relishing being off her feet. She glanced at the two empty stations, where Zachariah "Stax" Stackman and Clyde, her part-time barbers, worked their shifts on Fridays and Saturdays. With today being a typical Wednesday, she was fully staffed with three other barbers and her shampooer slash receptionist. *Hell, the only reason I'm here today is for my regulars who won't let anyone else on staff cut their hair.*

Alonzo, her manager and the most experienced barber on her staff, called out to her from his station across from hers. "Yo, boss lady. You tired already?" His black slacks, apron, and charcoal-colored button-down covered a tall, slender frame. He had a salt-and-pepper afro, twinkling eyes, and a ready smile.

She chuckled, grasping the end of the plastic pick she'd stuck in her blond-tipped curls earlier. After running it through to the ends of her hair, she replaced it. "No need to be on my feet right now, so I'm taking a load off."

"Trey was the last client on your schedule today, right?" That question came from Kev, one of her newer barbers. His long dreadlocks were wound into a bun atop his head, and he wore black jeans and a long-sleeved navy T-shirt under his apron. Working the clippers over his client's nape, he added, "It's not even lunch and you're done for the day."

Looking between them, she said, "Yeah, I'm probably not gonna stay too much longer. Just until I tie up some paperwork in the office."

"The payroll?" Alonzo scoffed. "I took care of that this morning."

She leaned back in her chair, a bit surprised. "Once again, I'm impressed by your efficiency, Alonzo."

"That's why you hired me, right?" He returned his focus to cleaning his station, circling a sanitizer cloth over the dark countertop.

She scratched her chin. "I guess I'll just finish unpacking those boxes of products in the back room, then."

Evan, the only other female barber in the shop, looked up from her magazine. "Honey, Taylor's in there doing that right now. There was nobody checking in or waiting for a shampoo, so I sent them back there." She crossed one legging-clad leg over the other, tucking an end of her bone-straight, brown, highlighted hair behind her ear.

Peaches glanced at the reception desk for the first time in a little while and noticed Taylor's absence. "Damn. Y'all don't even need me today, huh?"

"We keep this place running like a well-oiled machine," Evan quipped. "You come and go as you like, and that's how it should be. You are the owner, after all." She shrugged. "Shops I worked before this, I rarely saw the owners, and even when I did, they weren't coming in to work on clients."

Peaches took a deep breath, inhaling the scent of Barbicide and hair oil. *I've worked so hard to get this place running and staff it with the best people. I think it might be to the point where it really does run without me. So what do I do next?* "You're right, Evan. I guess I just didn't expect it to happen so soon."

"This place has been an institution in South Austin for seven years now. Folks around here know that if they wanna look good, this is the place to get a cut." Alonzo eyed her as he walked closer to her station. "You've put in the time, boss lady. Now you can retire, let us run this place, and enjoy the profits."

"Retire?" She stared at him. "I'm definitely not 'bout to do that, especially not before you, old man." She punched him in the arm playfully.

He feigned injury. "Stop hating, Peaches. Don't you know sixty is the new forty?"

She rolled her eyes. "You tripping. Sixty is sixty, forty is forty, and I still got five years and some months before I hit that. I'm way too young to retire." She rubbed her hands together as she considered her options. "But I think I might have a better idea."

"You gonna tell us what that is?" Kev asked while trimming his client's beard.

She shook her head. "Nah. I'm gonna play this one close to the vest. For now, at least." As soon as the words left her lips, she shook her head. *"Close to the vest"? I really been spending too much time with Pops.*

Taylor strolled by then, pushing a supply cart filled with empty, flattened boxes. "I'm gonna take these to the dumpster."

"Thanks, Taylor." Peaches watched as her favorite "genderless enigma"—as Taylor was fond of calling themself—wheeled the cart to the door, then outside as Evan held the door open for them.

Kev's client left right behind Taylor, and a quiet fell over the shop, save for the talking head summarizing baseball on the television.

Alonzo broke the silence. "So . . . what is Taylor?"

Evan rolled her eyes. "You ask that question every few months, and the answer is always the same, Lon. They're nonbinary."

"I know, I know. But what was Taylor *at birth*?"

Peaches raised her hand. "You know I love you, Lon. You're like my bootleg uncle that can cut hair. But if you ask that question ever again, I'm gonna have to let you go."

His lips thinned. "Are you serious?"

"Absolutely. I don't allow clients, staff, or anybody in my presence to speak about Taylor that way." Their eyes locked, and Peaches held his gaze, just to make sure he knew she meant every word. "It's not that they need a defender. But they got one anyway, so don't try me, all right?"

Alonzo's gaze fled, but then he nodded. "My bad. I won't bring it up again."

The conversation ended just as Taylor returned with the now-empty supply cart. This time, Alonzo opened the door and held it so they could wheel it back inside.

Once everyone was back at their assigned stations, Peaches stood and gathered her small duffel. "I'm gonna head out for the day. I'll see y'all tomorrow."

Outside in the early-April sunshine, she inhaled deeply as she walked toward her cobalt-blue extended-cab pickup. After tossing her bag in the passenger seat, she started the engine and cranked up the volume on her favorite local hip-hop station, 100.5 "The Groove," as she pulled out of the parking lot.

She'd just merged into traffic on William Cannon when her phone rang. Her brother's name flashed across the screen on her dash, and she shook her head. *What the hell this boy want now?* Tapping the hands-free button on her steering wheel, she answered. "Hey, RJ. What you want?"

"Hey, sis." He paused. "Wait, why you answer like that?"

She was still a bit irritated by Alonzo's inexplicable curiosity about Taylor's undercarriage, but she didn't want to go into that with her brother. "Because, dude. Every time you call me, it's because you want something."

"What if I'm just calling to say hey?"

She rolled her eyes as she navigated through traffic toward her town house in Crestview. "That's a big-ass 'what-if,' RJ. So why not cut to the chase, okay?"

He sighed. "All right. I did need to ask you a small favor."

She waited while he got his story straight, saying nothing.

"I've been asked to work late tonight, and my sitter can't stay past five. Would you be able to watch the girls for a couple of hours? I should be home before eight."

She felt the familiar tinge of annoyance tighten her shoulder muscles, even as a smile touched her lips. She loved her nieces beyond measure, and though she didn't relish her brother's heavy dependence on her, she enjoyed spending time with them. "Sure, I'll come over and remind them why I'm the world's greatest auntie."

"Thanks, sis. I knew I could count on you. That's why I said yes to the overtime."

She cringed as she drove through Zilker. *I'm really gonna have to go upside his head.* "This is definitely a favor for the girls, not you," she teased. "But whatever."

"Just come over to the house a few minutes before five. I'll let Christina know to expect you."

"All right. So, how are you doing?"

"Swamped at work, but other than that, pretty good." He cleared his throat. "You?"

"You know me. I spend most of my time at the barbershop. Everything's good, though."

"I won't hold you. Thanks again for agreeing to watch the girls."

"You know I love them, bro." She blew out a breath. "I'll see you later, okay?"

"Sure." He disconnected the call.

She kept her attention on the road as she made her way home, but her thoughts were consumed by her relationship with her brother. He leaned on her for so many things, and that had been the case ever since they were children. She assumed some of it was natural, due to their five-year age difference. Still, that trend had continued into their adulthood and had only intensified when RJ's ex-wife, Tammy, divorced him two years earlier, leaving him with three young daughters to raise. Now he was an overwhelmed single father. And while she applauded the way he buckled down and did what he had to do to support his children financially, she wished he'd depend on her a little less.

After letting herself into the quiet confines of her home, she locked the door behind her. She dropped the duffel on the sofa and headed into the kitchen, where she washed her hands at the sink. A few minutes later, she was on the sofa with a turkey sandwich and a handful of plain potato chips, flipping through channels on the television.

While she ate, she debated activities she could do with her nieces later. *What are we gonna get into tonight? Should I try to keep the chaos to a dull roar? Or should I give them sweets and let them wild out?* Only time would tell; it really depended on her mood once she arrived at her brother's house.

During a commercial break, her gaze slid from the television down to the mantel and the smiling portrait of her mother, Ann-Marie. She sighed. *It's been two years, Ma. Sometimes it feels like you left us yesterday.*

A melancholy feeling took over as she contemplated her future. Her father, brother, and nieces all depended on her. It had taken so much work to get Fresh Cutz stable and profitable, and her commitment to her family had been a large part of why it had taken so long. They seemed to call on her for everything. But as the eldest daughter, it was expected that she'd always answer, no matter what. That was how it was supposed to be . . . right?

A second location would be a lot of work. Do I have the time, energy, and resources to pull this off . . . again?

—

Jamie Hunt grabbed the tray holding her lunch order from the counter at Awesome Burger, then carried it to a small table near the establishment's front window. From there, she had a decent view of the shopping center and could spend her lunch break engaging in some serious people watching.

She lifted her foam cup of iced lemonade and took a long sip before unwrapping her bacon cheeseburger from its gold-foil confinement. As she took the first bite, she heard someone calling her name.

Jerking her head in the direction of the sound, she cringed inwardly. Kendra, her coworker at Stellar Nails, waved with her free hand as she carried her own lunch tray in Jamie's direction. Around the shop, Kendra was mainly known for her inability to lower her voice beyond a strong stage whisper, and her penchant for neon, graffiti-style nail designs. "Hey, girl! Mind if I sit with you?"

So much for people watching. Plastering on a polite smile, she nodded. "Sure, come on over."

Kendra slid into the seat opposite her, their trays bumping together as she set hers on the small two-top table. "It's been a little crazy around the shop for a Wednesday, hasn't it?"

Jamie swallowed another mouthful of burger. "Yeah, it has. Having an entire sorority come in at once to get mani-pedis certainly did liven things up."

Kendra chuckled, folding a fry into her mouth. "At least they tipped well."

"True." She kept her reply short, hoping her unexpected meal companion would take the hint and ease up on the chatter.

"So, what are you getting into this weekend?"

"I don't really have any plans just yet," she admitted.

"I think I'm probably gonna swing by London's new shop, just to show some support, you know?"

"Is that this weekend?" She posed the question in a curious tone, even though she knew full well about the opening.

"Oh yeah, girl. It's opening weekend. She's having the WRNB come by, giveaways, all of that." Kendra bit into her chicken sandwich and chewed slowly.

Jamie said nothing, grateful for the silence as they both polished off their sandwiches. But before she could finish her fries, Kendra piped up again.

"You know, it's really cool what London is doing. The whole concept of the nail salon as a reflection of Austin's whole 'Keep it weird' vibe, the custom colors . . . hell, it's even got a really creative name."

"Yeah, I know." Jamie held up her fingers and made air quotes. "Austin-tacious Nails." Saying it aloud left a bitter taste in her mouth, but she tried to keep her face as neutral as possible. After all, no one but her and London knew that the name, as well as everything else about London's new shop, had been stolen from her. And frankly, for the sake of her sanity and her ego, she planned on keeping it that way.

"Hopefully the interior design and the setup lives up to the hype." Kendra dunked a fry in a puddle of ketchup and, while bringing it to her mouth, dropped a glop of red onto the front of the teal scrub shirt they both wore as a uniform. "Damn." She rolled her eyes, then ate the fry and stood up. "Let me get a wet paper towel and try to get this out before it makes a stain."

Taking the opportunity to extract herself from this rather uncomfortable conversation, Jamie stood and gathered her trash. "Okay. I'm gonna head back to the shop—I'll see you over there."

The two women headed in separate directions, with Kendra going to the restroom and Jamie taking her tray to the trash can by the door. When she stepped out into the muggy afternoon sunshine, she turned to her left and strolled down the breezeway toward Stellar Nails, four doors down from the burger place.

Once she was back inside the shop and seated at her table, she began to get a steady stream of clients: manicures and full sets, gel polish and dip powders. The work felt good, because it gave her a place to turn her mind, to keep her from spiraling into despair over the betrayal of someone she'd trusted with her dream.

The crowd started to taper off around five thirty, and her manager flagged her down. "You can go on home, honey."

After tidying her station and adding her implements to the sanitizer in the storeroom, she gathered her things and left the shop. She drove her white coupe from the shopping center in Highland to her apartment in the complex near Saint Johns Avenue and Guadalupe Street.

The solitude of the drive, and the quiet of her apartment, reawakened the thoughts in her mind. As she stripped off her scrubs and prepared to shower, she thought about London, about the loss of her dream, and about how she could finally release her anger and resentment over the whole situation.

She shook her head as she turned on the water in her tub/shower combination. *I'm tired of thinking about this. It's time to switch to something far more pleasant.*

Standing beneath the stream of steamy water, she let an image of Peaches form in her mind. The other woman was part of Jamie's five-person friend group, an amazing assortment of talented, intelligent queers. Out of all of them, Peaches had always stood out the most to her. The only stud in the group, she was fun loving, boisterous, and quick to crack jokes. She was also fine as hell, in the way only a woman in carefully coordinated, well-fitting masculine clothing could be. Peaches had a swagger, a certain vibe about her that had always appealed to Jamie.

And in recent months, that appeal had increased exponentially.

Jamie could clearly remember the moment she'd known her feelings for Peaches were deeper than friendship. It was at Peaches' birthday party several months back. As she'd sat there, half-drunk, watching a burlesque dancer give the birthday girl a rather enthusiastic lap dance, Jamie had felt a familiar yet misplaced emotion take over her mind.

Jealousy.

She'd frowned, questioning her reaction. *Am I trippin'? Is it the alcohol making me a little cray-cray?* By morning, when she'd awakened in Peaches' coat closet with a pounding head and a clear mind, she knew it was real.

Now she swiped her hand over her face to clear some of the water there, then lathered up with her favorite bodywash. Closing her eyes once again, she let her mind wander more.

Peaches stood across the room, dressed in one of those tailored suits she favored, smiling in her direction. Her full lips tilted into a smile, then parted. "Come here, baby."

Powerless to resist, Jamie slowly closed the distance between them, letting Peaches' strong arms encircle her. They stared into each other's eyes for a long, lingering moment. Then Peaches grasped her chin and pressed her lips against Jamie's. Every cell in her body caught fire as the kiss deepened, with Peaches' sure hands slowly caressing and circling Jamie's hips . . .

Only the cooling water and chill touching her skin drew her out of her rather enticing fantasy.

She's a good five inches shorter than me, and I know some studs have a complex about that. Please, Lord, let her be the type that's down to climb trees.

Hurriedly rinsing off the jasmine-scented suds, she turned off the water and stepped out, then wrapped herself in one of her big bath sheets.

She donned a pair of cutoff sweatpants and a white tee, then padded to her kitchen. She searched the cabinets and the refrigerator but found nothing of particular interest to her growling stomach. With a sigh, she flopped down on the couch, grabbed her phone from the coffee table, and dialed her best friend and neighbor.

Taylor answered on the first ring. "What up, girlie?"

"T, please tell me you cooked. Or at least you have an idea of something good for dinner."

Taylor laughed. "No, I didn't feel like cooking today. But I was about to order some takeout."

"From where?"

"That wing place three blocks over." They paused. "Why don't I just come over there and we'll order together?"

She smiled. "Sounds awesome."

"Cool beans. I'll be there in ten minutes."

Jamie disconnected the call and lay back against her couch cushions. *I'm so glad Taylor lives so close. Having my best friend live in the same complex as me is really top tier.*

While she waited for Taylor to arrive, she went to her social profiles and absently scrolled through the feeds. On one site, she stopped short at a picture posted half an hour earlier by her younger brother, Sean. According to the caption, her older brother, Shelby, had just made partner at his law firm, and the family was enjoying a meal at a fancy restaurant to celebrate his accomplishment. The image showed the smiling faces of her parents, Clarence and Bernadette; Shelby; her sister-in-law, Bethany, who'd been married to Sean for four years; and even her one-year-old nephew, Levi.

She frowned. *Literally the only person in the immediate family who isn't part of this little shindig is me.*

A knock sounded at the door, and she left her phone on the couch to let Taylor in.

"Hey, honey." Taylor grabbed her shoulder and gave it a small squeeze. "What's going on with you?"

As they returned to the couch, she handed her phone over to her friend. "Well, as you can see, I'm the only member of my family who's scrounging for a meal tonight."

Taylor cringed. "Well, damn."

"It's just another instance where my parents have forgotten my existence." She shook her head. "You'd think I'd be used to it by now, but somehow it still gets to me."

"Trust me, you're not the weird one in this situation." Taylor sucked their teeth. "Your parents are something else."

"Aside from that, I can't believe Shelby didn't tell me he made partner." She groaned. "Well, I guess he'll call his little sister eventually. But enough about my oddball family. What's going on with you?"

Taylor grinned. "Girl, a whole lot of nothing. You know me: I work, I eat, I sleep. When I'm not doing those things, I'm over here with you."

Jamie gave Taylor a playful punch in the side. "Come on, now. Why aren't you out here dating? I know you gotta be tired of this sex drought you've been in."

Stifling a giggle, Taylor admitted, "Yeah. It's gotten very much old. I've got a profile up on that flame app. So we'll see soon enough if anybody can handle a gorgeous genderless enigma like myself." Pointing an index finger at her, Taylor added, "Meanwhile, you haven't been getting much action yourself lately. I know because I'm always here . . . that means ain't nobody pulling up on you either."

Jamie laughed. "That's right. I guess my standards are too high . . . I'm just not feeling anybody on the apps or the social media sites lately."

Taylor's brow hitched, and they fixed her with a knowing look. "Let's be real. It's this secret crush of yours that's got you holding out for that good-good." Rubbing their hands together, they asked, "Are you gonna tell me who it is?"

Jamie sucked her bottom lip into her mouth.

Arms folded over their chest, Taylor declared, "If you want me to order these wings, you gonna have to spill the tea, honey."

Knowing her rumbling stomach wouldn't stand much more before it staged a mutiny, she sighed. "Promise not to laugh."

Taylor's hand shot up. "Scout's honor."

"You were never a scout."

"Okay then, pinkie swear. Or blood oath. Or whatever's gonna get you to tell me!"

She paused, taking a deep breath. "It's . . . Peaches."

Taylor's eyes grew as wide as Lady Bird Lake. "You're shitting me."

She shook her head. "No, I'm serious. Peaches is . . ." She licked her lips. "Just as delectable as the name suggests. At least, she is in my fantasies."

Taylor blinked once, then twice, then several times in rapid succession. "Well, damn. I didn't see that one coming." They paused, then cleared their throat. "How long have you been sweating her?"

"I don't even know. But I first noticed how serious it was at her birthday party last August." She recounted the events of that night, at least what she remembered. "That's how I remember things happening . . . though I was definitely drunk for part of it."

Taylor nodded. "Yeah, that all checks out. Since I'm always sober, I always recollect everything."

Jamie sighed. "I don't know if Peaches even knows I exist as a separate entity from our friend group. We've never hung out one on one. But I want her in ways I can't even describe."

Taylor grinned. "Well, since you finally spilled the beans, let me order this food. And while we eat, we'll talk strategy."

"You're going to help me?"

Taylor shrugged. "As much as I can. You're my best friend, and if this is what you want, I'm down to play wingman." They paused. "Or . . . wing-buddy, anyway."

CHAPTER TWO

Peaches pulled up to RJ's house a little after five that evening. After parking her truck at the curb to avoid blocking the babysitter in, she cut the engine, hopped out, and strode across the yard and onto the front porch. She rapped at the door and waited for an answer.

A moment later, Christina opened the door. A high schooler from the neighborhood, she'd been looking after the girls for a few months now. "Hey, Ms. Peaches."

She smiled. "Hey, Christina. How badly have my nieces traumatized you today?"

The young woman laughed. "They've been pretty good. Ella's a little . . . energetic, but that's how she always is."

Peaches chuckled, knowing her middle niece had probably given the teen far more trouble than she was willing to admit. "Well, at any rate, I'm here. So you can go on with your evening now."

"Thanks." Christina eased past Peaches onto the porch. "They just had dinner: meat loaf, mashed potatoes, and green beans."

Cocking a brow, Peaches asked, "You cooked all that?"

Christina laughed. "No, I just heated it up for them. Mr. Corbin brought in a bunch of those meals from the grocery-store deli." Stepping down onto the grass, she gave a wave. "Well, have a good night, Ms. Peaches."

As the young woman hit the sidewalk, Peaches entered the house and called out, "Where are my lil' girl bosses?"

"Come find us!" a small voice called out.

She recognized Ella's challenge, and as she shut and locked the door behind her, she let her gaze sweep over her surroundings. "Okay. But y'all know nobody's better at hide-and-seek than Aunt Peaches."

She crept deeper into the living room, glancing from her brother's boring gray curtains to his very basic black leather furniture, looking for any sign of the girls. Her gaze fell on the toe box of a small, sparkly pink sneaker, peeking out from behind the sofa. Jogging over there, she knelt and tapped the shoe. "Come on out, Reagan."

The littlest Corbin sister crawled out from behind the sofa, wearing a broad grin. "You found me, Auntie," she declared in her tiny three-year-old voice.

"Of course I did. I'm a beast at this." Peaches scooped the little one up into her arms and rested her small body on her hip. "Now, you come help me find your sisters, okay?"

Reagan nodded, her four pigtails bouncing in time with the movement of her head as she draped her arms around Peaches' neck.

As they moved through the living room into the open-concept kitchen, Peaches thought she heard a giggle. She stooped and used her free hand to open the pantry door.

"Dang!" Ella stepped out of the pantry, shaking her head. "How'd you find me so quick?"

"I heard you giggling, kiddo." Peaches looked at her niece's crooked superhero nightgown and wild hair and shook her head. "Girl, what's going on with that bird's nest on your head?"

Ella touched her head, her face showing a sheepish grin. "Dad put it in a ponytail, but the little thingy broke."

Peaches sighed. "Sheesh. I'll take care of it before you go to bed. Can't have you around here looking like Don King." She looked into the hallway that led to the bedrooms. "Where is Olivia?"

Ella shrugged. "I don't know."

"Well, go park it on the couch until I find her." She set Reagan down on the beige linoleum floor. "And take your little sister with you—Auntie's back getting tired."

While the two younger children dutifully took their seats, Peaches went down the hall in search of Olivia. She checked her niece's room first but, finding it unoccupied, moved on to the room shared by Ella and Reagan. Finally, she reluctantly opened the door to her brother's bedroom at the end of the hall.

Entering the black-lacquer tackiness of the primary bedroom, she found her niece on the floor, tucked into the space between RJ's bed and his nightstand. She had her nose in an open copy of *Ada Twist, Scientist*, and had a few more titles stacked on the floor nearby, but she looked up as Peaches got closer. "Hey, Aunt Peaches."

She grinned. "This was a pretty good hiding spot, especially since I try to avoid coming in here at all."

Olivia blinked, then stared up at her in signature ten-year-old confusion. "We were playing hide-and-seek?"

Laughing, Peaches said, "I'm gonna guess you weren't participating."

Olivia shook her head as she grabbed the edge of the nightstand and climbed to her feet, her book in hand. "Nah. I just came back here because Ella and Reagan were being too loud in the living room."

Peaches could only shake her head. In typical Olivia fashion, she'd ignored whatever weird stuff her sisters were up to, in favor of seeking out a quiet place to read. "I get it. But please don't make me come back in here. Your dad has terrible taste, and his bedroom is where style goes to die."

Olivia eyed her. "He was your brother before he was my dad, Aunt Peaches."

Peaches cringed. "Aw, dang, niece. Don't drag your poor aunt like that." She grabbed the girl's much smaller hand, leading her toward the

17

door. "Let's get out of here. If we stay too much longer, we'll both end up smelling like Axe Body Spray and bad decisions."

The confusion returned to Olivia's face, but she followed her aunt from the room.

Back in the living room, Peaches looked at her three nieces, seated in a row on the sofa. "Christina told me y'all had dinner. So what do you say to a little dessert?"

Bouncing with excitement, Ella shouted, "S'mores!"

"That sound good to y'all?" Peaches looked from Olivia to Reagan. Met with grins from them, she clapped her hands together. "Then it's settled." After reentering the kitchen, she opened the pantry and stepped inside. In the far-right corner, on the highest shelf, she spied her emergency dessert kit. She kicked the low metal step stool to the appropriate spot, then climbed atop it and pulled down the plastic basket. As she set it on the counter, she beckoned her nieces into the kitchen. "Come on, y'all. Help Auntie out."

Twenty minutes later, the four of them were back on the couch with their freshly made s'mores and glasses of milk. Peaches bit into hers, a smile touching her lips as she watched her chocolate-streaked nieces enjoying their snack. The television was tuned to Reagan's favorite cartoon, the classic nineties animated version of *Little Bear*, and for a while, peace settled over the room.

As soon as the s'mores were eaten and the milk glasses drained, though, Ella was on her feet. "Aunt Peaches, Aunt Peaches! Let me show you my new tumble from gymnastics!"

Peaches held up her hand. "Hold on there, sug. I totally wanna see it, but you just ate, so give it a minute before you turn your tummy upside down."

She pouted. "Okay."

"But you can grab that little vacuum out of the coat closet and suck up some of these graham cracker crumbs, though."

Brightening, Ella bounded to the closet and returned with the hand vac.

Peaches shooed the other two girls toward the designated play area beneath the living room window and watched as Ella turned on the vacuum and ran it over the couch cushions. "Thanks, sug. That way, your dad can't say we left a mess." She gathered up the glasses, then took them to the kitchen sink, gave them a quick wash and rinse, and returned them to the cabinet.

"Aunt Peaches, can I paint your nails?" Olivia asked. She and Reagan were having a tea party at the small table in the play area. Glancing from her niece's face to her own bare, rather uneven nails, Peaches nodded. "You can give me a whole manicure. But let me get your sister's hair looking decent first."

Peaches returned to the sofa and slid the girls' plastic tote filled with hair supplies from under the coffee table. With Ella parked on the floor between her knees, Peaches used a comb, a brush, some hair gel, and sheer determination to manipulate Ella's hair into a high bun. After adding a white bow to the front, she tapped her shoulder. "All done."

Ella got up and ran to the open area between the coffee table and the kids' table, where her sisters sat. "Okay, can I show you my tumble now, Aunt Peaches?"

"Go ahead."

Ella turned three tumbles, then stood and raised her hands over her head in triumph.

Peaches put her hand to her chest. "Girl, you're ready for the Olympics!"

"But is the Olympics ready for me?" Ella's broad grin reflected her pride in her own accomplishment.

Peaches laughed, as she often found herself doing when she spent time with her three young besties. "Probably not, but they just gone have to get ready."

Peaches read to the bleary-eyed Reagan and put her to bed around seven thirty. Then she got a much-needed nail trim and a coat of dark-blue nail polish from Olivia while listening with rapt interest to her grade-school gossip.

At eight thirty, she tucked the older two girls into their beds with a kiss and returned to the couch, where she checked her phone as she reclined. She opened a social app and went to her profile.

I haven't posted on here in months. The last pic is one Claudia took, from my birthday. She looked at the image, showing her with Aiko, Jamie, Taylor, and Claudia at Austin Beerworks, their mugs raised in toast. Claudia's incredible long-armed selfie skills allowed her to appear in the photo, on the left side of the frame.

Peaches' gaze lingered on Jamie, decked out in her UT Austin gear, her sleek hair hanging past her shoulders and a gleam of mischief in her eyes. Jamie and Taylor had dressed alike that night, but something about the way Jamie wore the outfit, paired with her statuesque frame, made it arresting and altogether feminine. She smiled at the memory of that night. *I gotta give Claudia credit. It was one hell of a party.*

The sound of a key turning the lock drew her attention, and she looked up to see her bedraggled-looking younger brother enter the house. Shutting the door behind him, he released a long sigh. "Hey, sis."

"Wow, I'm so excited to see you too, bro," she teased. "Is your face always that long when you come in from work, or is today a special occasion?" She swept her gaze over him, from the drawn expression on his brown-skinned face, to the slump of his broad shoulders, to the way his work clothes seemed to hang off his slender frame.

RJ rolled his eyes, loosening the tie at the neck of his blue short-sleeve button-up. "Sorry, Peaches. It's just been a hell of a long day. We have all this new equipment in the office, which is a good thing because it's more energy efficient."

"I would think that would matter at a power company," Peaches quipped.

"It does. Like I said, it's good." He flopped down on the couch next to her. "The thing is, while it's being installed, we have to transfer all our old data to it. And while I'm helping with that, I have to learn everything there is to know about it, so I can train other employees to use it."

Peaches cringed as she pocketed her phone. "I don't envy you that, bro. I'll stick to the clippers."

He blew out a breath. "How were the girls? Did they behave?"

"Sure they did. They were perfect little angels." *I'm not gonna tell him about that streak of nail polish on the couch cushion. He had a rough enough day. Besides, he won't even know it's there.* Standing, she reached in her pocket for her keys. "Reagan's out like a light. But I think Olivia is probably still up reading."

"I'll go look in on them in a minute." He slipped off his shoes, then kicked them under the coffee table. "Thanks again, sis. I don't know what I'd do without you."

"Fail spectacularly." She grinned, then rubbed her palm in several quick circles over his close-cropped hair. "Good night, dweeb."

"Night, sis."

He must really be tired—he didn't even bother with a snappy comeback. Usually he'd throw her some shade, like reminding her that he was a few inches taller than her five-foot-six-inch height and could reach high shelves without the step stool.

With a shake of her head, she let herself out, softly closing the door behind her. She crossed the front yard, climbed into her pickup, and started the engine. Moments later, she drove away into the warm spring night.

Thursday afternoon, Jamie left the nail shop and headed for the bank. A large party of women celebrating someone's birthday had come in, and their generosity had fattened her pockets nicely. It had been more than a week since she'd made a deposit, leaving her with far more cash than she felt comfortable carrying around.

I need to get this done today. Tomorrow she'd be attending Claudia's graduation party, and she knew she'd spend the better part of the day getting ready. Her friend had achieved the highest level of education of any woman Jamie'd ever met, and she planned on turning all the way up in celebration of Claudia's accomplishment. To that end, she'd taken Friday and Saturday off from work, because she anticipated needing a recovery day after the festivities.

As she pulled into the bank parking lot, she frowned when she saw the drive-through line wrapped around the building. Opting to use the walk-up ATM at the front of the building, she parked her car and climbed out.

She had to wait behind another person, but once they'd completed their business, she stepped up to the machine and quickly made her deposit. With receipt in hand, she turned and headed back to her car.

A familiar-looking gray sedan pulled up as she stepped off the curb. She stopped short, feeling the frown tugging at her lips. *Fuck. What is Mom doing here?*

Bernadette Martin-Hunt soon got out of the vehicle and strode into her path. Dressed in dark leggings, a flouncy white tunic, and a long beige cardigan, she had her favorite wide-brimmed hat pulled down over her head. The ends of her kinky-straight, jet-black wig peeked from beneath the hat brim. Behind the dark shades she wore, Bernadette's eyes assessed Jamie. "Well, hello, honey."

"Hi, Mom." Jamie started to move around her, toward her car.

Bernadette's hand flew out like the striped crossbar at a railroad crossing. "Hold on, Jamie. You're supposed to come over to the house to do my nails today, remember? You may as well wait until I finish up in the bank, and you can follow me home." She used the tip of her finger to adjust the shades. "After all, you visit so rarely, you could probably use the escort."

Jamie felt her ire rising. "Oh, no worries, Mom. I'm not coming over to do your nails, so there's really no need for me to wait around." She walked around her mother's extended arm to her car. "I was going to call you, but now I won't have to."

Bernadette followed her, shouting, "Jamie Carmen Hunt, how dare you take that tone with your mother?"

That seems to be about the only way to remind her I exist. Clearing her throat, she took a moment to gather her spiraling thoughts into something coherent. "Mom, I'm just informing you that I'm not doing your nails. I've said something you don't want to hear, and, respectfully, that's not the same thing as 'taking a tone' with you."

Bernadette pursed her lips so tightly they almost disappeared. "And do you mind explaining to me just why you aren't going to do my nails?"

"Sure. Because no one bothered to invite me to dinner last night." She folded her hands together, waiting.

Brow furrowed, her mom asked, "What are you going on about? What dinner?"

"Oh, I guess I wasn't supposed to know about it, but Sean can't stay off social media for more than five minutes." She paused. "That means he had his phone in his hand to take pictures but still didn't bother to call or text me."

"That's what you're talking about?" She waved her hand in a dismissive manner. "That was a last-minute thing. We hadn't planned on going out; it just . . . happened." She tilted her head and body slightly to the left, looking her daughter up and down.

"Nah. If there's more than one person involved, some kind of coordination had to happen."

She shrugged. "I suppose," she admitted. "But nothing complicated. We just agreed to meet and . . ."

Jamie felt her chin trembling and did her best to steady it. *I'm not about to let her see me cry.* "I'm not interested in hearing about the steps y'all took to gather everyone in one place and leave me out."

"Jamie, listen to yourself!" her mom screeched, both hands raised. "You're being unreasonable, and aside from that, you're making a scene?"

She shook her head. "No, I'm not. You're the one raising your voice."

Bernadette snatched off her shades and glared at her only daughter. Her voice dropped in volume, but the tone remained the same. "I can't believe you're behaving like this, in public no less."

Here we go again. Mom always does this kind of crap, and never admits to it. Honestly, I'm tired of it. "Five adults, all of whom have phones, sat down and celebrated Shelby's promotion, which I didn't even know about, and none of y'all could be bothered to send me so much as a stinking text." She hit the button to unlock her car doors, then opened the driver's side. "And when I mention it to you, and try to get you to understand how hurtful it was, you wanna tone police me."

"For goodness' sake, Jamie . . ."

"Save your dramatic exasperation, Mom. I'm going home." She shrugged, then lowered herself into the driver's seat and closed the door. Starting the engine, she rolled the window down. "I hope y'all enjoyed yourselves. But I'm not about to go out of my way for your comfort and benefit, when you wouldn't even reach into your purse for mine."

Bernadette opened her mouth, but before she could say the words, Jamie had rolled the window up. She backed out of the spot and drove away, leaving her mother standing there, open mouthed, on the sidewalk. She made it to the intersection before the tears came, and she was grateful to have escaped her mother's line of sight before emotion got the better of her.

By the time she got home and locked herself inside her apartment, the tears had ceased, replaced by anger. In her bedroom, she opened the drawer on her nightstand and pulled out the small green bag that held her stash.

She'd usually call on Taylor and see if they wanted to join her, but they were working late at the barbershop today for the start of the weekend rush.

Spreading her supplies out atop her mint-green comforter, she took a deep breath and began the ritual.

This was her way of coping with life's moments of stress and strain, her lifeline in a late-stage capitalist hellscape. *Some people take pills. Some drink. Some even go to the rage room, or the batting cage. Me, I get blazed.*

Once she'd ground her favorite strain, she added the tiny bits to one of her long prerolled cones, printed with metallic hot-pink leaves. After stuffing the cone as full as she could with a mixture of the sativa flower and dried lavender, she twisted the end to secure it.

She rested against the wealth of pillows at the head of her bed and lit the end with her trusty extendo lighter. With the first inhale, she could feel the calm entering her body, ushered in by the bud. The sweet floral flavor of the lavender provided a perfect complement to the spicy yet earthy flavor of the weed. Within a few minutes, the tension in her neck and shoulders loosened, and she sank even deeper into the pile of pillows behind her.

She exhaled through her mouth, watching as the smoke drifted and swirled around her, enveloping her within its hazy confines like an iridescent cocoon.

She got so deep in her enjoyment that when she heard a pounding sound coming from the front of the apartment, it took her a moment to identify its source. She narrowed her eyes. *Oh shit. Someone's at the door. Who, though? Taylor works late on Thursdays.*

After climbing to her feet, she made her way down the hall, into the living room, and to the front door. She peered through the peephole and felt her eyes widen . . . at least as much as they could in her current state. Opening the door, she said, "Shelby, what are you doing here?"

Instead of answering her question, her older brother took a deep inhale. "I know what *you're* doing . . . getting high."

She frowned. "What's your point?"

"My point is, I want some too." He offered a crooked half smile. "So . . . can I come in?"

She eyed her brother, still dressed in his professional lawyer attire of charcoal suit and white shirt with black loafers. The black-and-gray diagonal tie around his neck was undone, as was his top shirt button. With a sigh, she stepped back and allowed him entry.

Once she'd closed them both inside, he said, "Please tell me you have some more of whatever that is you're smoking."

"It's called Sunset Sativa, and yes, there's more." She gestured him toward the sofa, then perched on the arm as he sat down. "I'm not gonna give you any until you answer this question, though. Did Mom send you over here?"

He tilted his head to the left. "Yes and no. I mean, she told me y'all argued, and why. But I came here on my own."

"Fair enough." She left the room, and returned a few moments later with her tray and supplies. "I only made one for myself, so you gotta roll your own."

He picked up the empty cone and inspected it. "Well, this is girly."

She rolled her eyes. "You wanna smoke or not?"

With a wry chuckle, he went about the task, talking as he worked. "Listen, sis. I'm really sorry I didn't tell you about my promotion. Honestly, it just happened yesterday. The dinner was Mom's idea, and she insisted you wouldn't come."

Funny, she didn't ask me that. The men in her family seemed content to go along with whatever her mother said, at least as an alternative to arguing with her. "I appreciate your apology, Shelby. I would have loved to celebrate your accomplishment with you, but since you're here now, at least I can congratulate you in person." She gave him a playful punch in the arm. "Good on you, bro."

"Thanks, Jamie." He carefully tamped the ground bud into the paper cone before twisting it shut.

She watched as he lit it and took that first, tentative inhale. When he sighed on the exhale, she smiled. "It's good, right?"

"Some mighty fine cannabis you got here, sis." He coughed, using the side of his closed fist to beat his chest. "Mighty fine."

She eased into the spot next to him on the couch, enjoying the secondary contact buzz that his smoking was adding to her own high. Friendly silence settled between them for a while.

As he set aside the tray and blew one last smoke ring, Shelby said, "I know Mom and Dad would never agree with me. But I think you're the strongest one in our family."

She popped her lips, knowing what he was getting at. They didn't smoke together often, but whenever they did, the same topic came up. "Don't worry about it, Shelby. You'll know when the time is right."

"That's the thing. I don't know if it will ever be the right time." He paused, cleared his throat. "When could it ever be the right time to tell Mom and Dad that their perfect eldest son isn't perfect? That he exists so far outside of their expectations?"

She shrugged. "You don't have to tell them, bro. I'm the only one in the family who knows, and I would never, ever do that to you."

"I know, and I can't tell you how much I appreciate that." He let his head drop back against the cushions, his red-rimmed eyes focused on the ceiling. "I'm not hiding it from my partners—they all know I'm bi. But our parents? And Sean? That's a whole different story."

She let her own head drop, joining her brother in his visual assessment of the ceiling tiles. "What brought this on, anyway?"

"Last night, at dinner, Dad said it was perfect timing for me to finally get a wife, now that I'm partner." He blew out a breath. "There's an equal chance I come home with a husband, but I don't think they're ready to have that conversation with me."

"They're probably not." Jamie chuckled. "For now, don't worry about it. You may find a nice girl to bring home . . . or not. Let's just cross that bridge when we get to it, okay?"

He nodded. "Yeah. Okay."

Silence settled between them again, and Jamie's mind wandered. She thought about her brother's situation, but more than that, she thought about her own. Her parents knew she was a lesbian, since she'd come out to them at eight or nine. They already knew what a family would look like for her—whenever they bothered to give their only daughter a moment of thought, that is.

I guess being the oldest brings a whole different level of pressure.

Still, it would've been nice to know my existence has meant something to this family.

CHAPTER THREE

Damn, it's after five already? Fridays don't even go this fast when the barbershop is crowded.

Tucking her phone back into the pocket of her slacks, Peaches left the narrow confines of her galley kitchen and headed for her coat closet. After grabbing her white fedora from the upper shelf, she closed the door and went to the wall-mounted mirror above the console table. She watched her reflection and placed the hat on her head, adjusting it to the perfect angle. Satisfied, she padded to her bedroom.

Inside her closet, she flipped on the light and scanned her sneaker collection for the pair she wanted. She owned seventy pairs of sneakers, and wore them to nearly every occasion. She did have two pairs of loafers (one black, one brown), just in case the odd occurrence might call for something more formal, and a few pairs of fashionable but practical nonslips she wore at work.

She spotted her custom-painted Skechers with the UT Austin colors and carefully slid them from their clear acrylic box. After going over them with a slightly damp, fuzzy white cloth, she sat down on the small stool near the display and donned a pair of orange socks. Then she slipped her feet into the sneakers and laced them up.

After using a spritz of Bleu, her favorite cologne, she headed back to the front of her condo, checking her reflection one last time.

Let me get out of the mirror. This party isn't about me. It's about celebrating Claudia's amazing accomplishments—our girl has a PhD in pharmacology!

Oh shit. Her gift.

She returned to her bedroom long enough to grab the orange-and-white-striped gift bag holding Claudia's gift. Then, after retrieving her keys and wallet from the large seashell she used as a bowl by her front door, she left.

Outside, a warm, hazy April afternoon greeted her. She waved at Mrs. Cantini, the sweet little elderly woman next door, who was busy tending to her many potted plants. She climbed into her pickup and started it up, then adjusted her mirrors and backed out of her driveway.

She left Crestview behind, headed for the Chestnut neighborhood near the campus of UT Austin, where Claudia lived. Navigating through city traffic took her around twenty minutes, and she arrived at Claudia's remodeled historic bungalow shortly after the time on the party invite.

She parked on the grassy lawn, easing her truck into the space to the left of Aiko's SUV, and cut the engine. She got out with the gift bag in hand, then headed across the yard and up the two steps onto the wide front porch.

The screen door was shut, likely to make sure all the bugs remained outside, where they belonged, but the main door was open. She squeezed the handle on the screen door, then opened it and went in.

Claudia, the woman of the hour, entered the foyer as Peaches stepped into the house. She looked nothing less than regal in her long, fitted white dress, its high slit showcasing her bronzed leg. Her upswept hair highlighted the angular lines of her face. "Hey, Peaches!" She offered a bright smile and a tight hug. "Thanks for coming, honey."

"Wouldn't miss it." She stepped out of her friend's embrace and handed over the bag. "Congratulations, Claudia."

Her grin brightened. "Thank you! Come on in and get settled."

30

Peaches followed Claudia down the hall and to the left, into the living room. The room boasted gray hardwood floors, plush black furniture with silver accents, and metallic-silver wallpaper. White shag rugs adorned the floors, and various silver knickknacks occupied the whitewashed fireplace mantel and the shelves tucked into every corner. The other attendees were scattered around the room, and Peaches soon spotted Aiko, perched comfortably on one end of the sleek suede sofa. "What's up, A?"

Aiko looked up from her phone with a smile. She wore a white turtleneck, slim white jeans, and white loafers with an orange accent on the top and fringe. A gold belt encircled her waist; two thin gold chains were around her neck, her long, dark hair drawn back into a low bun. "Hey, playa. Look at you." She gestured to Peaches' outfit. "You dress up so rarely, sometimes I forget you can be stylish."

Peaches rolled her eyes, then took in her bestie's attire. "Meanwhile, I see you toned it down a bit. No vest today?"

She shook her head. "I don't own a white vest, and didn't wanna go looking for one."

Peaches laughed. "Yeah, I feel ya. This outfit is all the white stuff from my wardrobe." Sitting down next to her, she commented, "I thought Summer was coming?"

"She was, but she got roped into something at the community center." Aiko chuckled. "My baby can't help herself—she just has so much love for the community."

"It's a beautiful thing, really." Peaches thought back on Aiko and Summer's wedding. "How's married life treating you?"

She grinned. "It's amazing. We're just getting started, and knowing that is the best part. Waking up to her is the best thing ever . . . our moms are already talking about grandchildren. Can you believe it? We haven't been married a month yet. Not that I wouldn't have a baby with her. I know she'd be a great mom. I just love her so fucking much . . ."

"Yikes." Peaches laughed. "I really opened up the floodgates with that question, didn't I?" *I guess it's to be expected, my homie fresh off an island honeymoon.*

Aiko cringed. "Sorry, P. Didn't mean to get all mushy on you."

"No worries. I'm not a hater." Peaches leaned back in her seat. "I love seeing you this happy, real talk. You deserve it."

"Thanks." Aiko watched her intently. "You deserve it too, you know."

Peaches shook her head. "Nah. I've got too much going on right now. The barbershop, the fam. I barely have time for me, let alone a girlfriend."

Aiko shrugged. "I feel you. But sometimes these things just happen, regardless of how bad the timing might seem."

Peaches thought about that for a moment. "Fair enough. But seriously, the fam got me on call like an ER doctor. I just had to go over there a couple of nights ago to watch my nieces."

Aiko shook her head. "Really? What in the world your brother got going on now?"

"You know how RJ is. Always playing with half a deck. He had to stay late at work, and of course, his first instinct was to call me." She rolled her eyes. "I love my nieces. That's my lil' squad right there. I just wish their dad was a little more resourceful and a little less needy, you know?"

Aiko dragged her index finger along her chin. "Honestly, he's probably just gonna keep on asking you to do shit for him, until you say no."

Now it was Peaches' turn to cringe. "Damn, Aiko."

"My bad. I know it's not always that easy." She gave her a slap on the shoulder. "I'm gonna support you either way, P. Even if that means listening to you complain."

Peaches turned toward the sound of the front door opening. A moment later, Claudia reentered the room, with Taylor and Jamie close behind her.

Taylor strolled in wearing a pair of white denim cutoffs and matching jacket, a sequined white top, and tall silver boots. Peaches waved in their direction.

Jamie strutted in next, and Peaches found her gaze lingering far longer than normal. She wore a white tube minidress, with a round cutout strategically positioned just above her right hip. The cutout, and the knee-grazing hem of the dress, revealed an expanse of shimmering, golden-brown skin.

Am I tripping, or did she dust herself with glitter before she left home? Peaches' gaze dropped lower, to Jamie's shoes. The fiery-orange, open-toe stilettos on her feet had thin straps that encased the lower half of her long legs, crisscrossing upward from her ankles to her knees.

Peaches swallowed. *Damn. She look like ice cream on a hot day.*

"Yo!" Aiko snapped her fingers. "Didn't you hear Claudia? She said to go in the dining room for dinner." She was already on her feet, even though Peaches didn't remember her friend getting up.

Shaking herself free of whatever spell she'd fallen under, Peaches cleared her throat and stood. "Sorry. Zoned out there."

Aiko gave her a knowing glance. "Uh-huh."

In the dining room, they all took seats around Claudia's table. The lacquered black table, loaded down with food, seated eight, making it the perfect fit for their small gathering of seven. Besides Peaches and Aiko, Taylor and Jamie, their hostess had invited two more people.

"I want everybody to introduce themselves and tell how they know me, please. Let's go around the table." Claudia gestured to Peaches. "You can go first."

She cleared her throat. "I'm Peaches, and I've known Claudia since we took a class together in undergrad." She could clearly recall how chatty Claudia had been that first day of English Composition, becoming fast friends with both her and Aiko.

Listening as they went around the table, Peaches learned that the two women she didn't recognize were Vera and Sherri, classmates of

Claudia's from UT Austin's College of Natural Sciences. Vera had studied environmental science, and Sherri, nutrition and dietetics.

Once everyone had their say, Claudia gestured toward the many serving trays before them. "Y'all dig in."

Platters were passed around, and Peaches helped herself to a few items. Crab puffs, sliders, garlic-truffle fries, and tempura vegetables all ended up on her plate. When Aiko passed her a bottle of champagne, she filled her flute, then passed the bottle on.

The food was amazing, if a little rich. "Claudia wasn't playing when she said she'd be serving 'elevated appetizers.'"

Aiko chuckled. "Yeah. The food is great. A nice mixture of flavor, familiarity, and elegance."

"You sound like a true food critic," Peaches chided. "But you're not wrong, though."

Conversation flowed easily among the group for the duration of the meal. After everyone had finished eating, Claudia led them out to the backyard. The air was cool and breezy but still held a bit of humidity. Remnants of dusk remained, painting a thin line of orange at the horizon beneath the darkened sky. The trees overhead had been strung with white lights, the strands of small bulbs draped over the yard illuminating the space with a soft, intimate glow.

Their hostess started up some music, a classic Mary J. track from the late nineties, adding to the smooth, relaxed mood of the party.

Peaches sat with Aiko at the weathered gray wood picnic table, her back against the table as she observed the party. "It's nice out tonight."

"It is." She ran a hand over her hair. "Wow. I didn't know Jamie had moves like that."

Peaches' gaze shifted from the dazzling lights overhead to the even more dazzling sight of Jamie. Knees bent and palms on her thighs, her body moved fluidly, as if motion were its natural state. Taylor stood next to Jamie, egging her on.

Damn. She throwin' that ass in a parallelogram.

Peaches swallowed. Had she had too much champagne, or had she just taken leave of her good sense? She couldn't answer that any more than she could take her eyes off Jamie's heavenly body.

Aiko chuckled. "I probably shouldn't have called your attention to that, homie." She gave Peaches a nudge. "Roll your tongue up and put it back in ya mouth."

Shaking her head to regain her composure, Peaches looked at her best friend. "Tell me about your job. Now that you got that promotion, how are you liking it?"

"It's pretty awesome. I love that I get more creative control over projects, and not just the exterior stuff."

She nodded. "Word. I'm glad to hear it's everything you wanted." She paused, thinking about her own career conundrum. "I'm thinking about moving up too. Maybe opening a second shop."

"Wow, that's great." Aiko's grin reflected her excitement. "If you get a second location, I won't have to wait so long when I need a trim."

Peaches laughed. "Yeah, yeah." Turning her head slightly, she hazarded a glance in Jamie's direction.

Jamie was standing tall again, talking with Taylor and Claudia. And while she seemed fully engaged in her conversation, Jamie's eyes were locked on Peaches' face.

Peaches swallowed again.

"Yo," Aiko whispered. "Seems like Jamie's got her eye on you."

Peaches felt her tongue swipe across her lower lip. "Maybe so. I'm sure if she got something to say, she'll let me know."

⌒

Jamie held the eye contact with Peaches for a few more beats, then slowly let her gaze drop.

"You know, I feel like you're not really paying attention to what I'm saying," Taylor groused next to her.

"Sorry. I was a little distracted."

"Yeah, we could both see that." Claudia offered a dry chuckle. "Just be glad I'm not easily offended, girl."

She took a deep inhale to recenter, her fingertips grazing the clear quartz stone nestled between the cups of her bra. "My bad. Anyway, finish your story, Taylor."

As Taylor relaunched their epic tale of a date gone wrong, Jamie made sure to pay attention to her friend's every word. It wasn't easy, considering the glass and a half of champagne in her system and the ensuing warmth in her bloodstream, but she managed to take in the whole story. By the time it was over, she'd drained the last of her second glass. "So, I'm guessing you're not going to see him again, then."

Taylor scoffed. "Of course not. I mean, he got my pronouns right, but that's literally the least he could do. You know, baseline stuff. Other than that, the guy was a total bust."

She nodded. "I don't blame you. Stories like that make me glad I don't play on that side of the field."

Claudia sighed, long and heavy. "Well, girl, throw up a prayer for those of us who still gotta deal with men. It's ghetto out here, for real." She folded her arms over her chest. "They're either so insecure that they're intimidated by my education, or they're so full of themselves, they dismiss it altogether."

"You've got the broadest dating field of any of us, Claudia." Jamie gestured with her hands. "Expand your horizons, babe."

Claudia tapped one long, french-manicured nail against her chin. "You're right. As the resident pan goddess of this group, it might be time for me to switch things up a lil' bit." She was quiet for a moment. "But enough about our dating woes. Didn't you say you had something you wanted to talk to me about?"

"Yeah, I did." Jamie glanced at Taylor. "T, do you mind if I sneak off with our lady of the hour for a bit?"

"Nah, you're good." Taylor jerked their head in Aiko's direction. "It's high time I tease Aiko about her lack of vest, anyways."

As Taylor sauntered away, Claudia said, "Let's sit in the sunroom, where we can talk."

"Cool."

A few minutes later, Jamie sat nestled in the buttery-soft cream leather cushions of the sofa in the sunroom, with Claudia next to her.

"So," Claudia asked, handing Jamie a third glass of champagne while clutching another for herself, "what's up, girl?"

"I've been thinking a lot about my career lately, and the direction it's moving in. I think it's time for a change."

"Thinking about opening a shop?" Claudia set her glass on the polished-granite coffee table.

She shook her head. "No, not anymore."

Claudia's brow knit. "What? I feel like I missed something here."

Jamie tugged her left earlobe, feeling the tingling there. "Did you hear about a new Austin-themed nail salon that just recently opened?"

"Yeah, I did. Haven't had a chance to go over there, though." Claudia paused. "Wait. What does that have to do with . . ."

"That was my idea. The woman who opened that salon stole the entire setup and concept from me." Jamie let her gaze drop to her lap, feeling the betrayal rising inside her. "She was a coworker of mine, and I stupidly thought I could trust her."

"Trusting is never a stupid decision; using that trust against someone is." Claudia touched her shoulder. "I'm glad you told me about this because I'll never darken their door. Now tell me about this career change, because we don't dwell on terrible people with questionable morals over here."

Jamie chuckled in spite of her sadness. "Right. I had been thinking about going back to school, and this whole incident pushed me to make a move. A couple of months back, when I found out my coworker's plan to open the shop, I applied to a few colleges. I want to become a chemist, develop my own line of sustainable products that will have my clients' nails looking fierce, without the damage."

Claudia's eyes narrowed, her head tilting slightly. "Hmm. That's actually a really good idea." She held up her hands, moving her fingertips in a fluid, wavelike motion. "I love getting my full sets, but I have to take breaks so my nail beds can recover."

"Right. You understand where I'm coming from, then." She leaned forward. "I want to create something that has the same durability, versatility, and look as acrylic or gel, but won't require soaking off or drilling. The way I see it, my best bet is to go about this scientifically."

"I feel you, and I love the idea." Claudia grinned. "So, what do you need from me? A letter of recommendation or something?"

"Maybe later, but right now I just need advice." She leaned back against the cushion. "How do I choose a really good chemistry program? What do I need to look for?"

"Well, girl, I can tell you just about everything there is to know about the program at UT Austin."

She shook her head. "I know you can. But I don't want to go to school here."

Claudia's eyes widened.

Throwing up her hands, Jamie said, "Trust me, I'm not throwing shade at UT Austin. Most of our friend group went to school there, and I know the Longhorn pride runs deep among us."

She paused, trying to mold the jumble of thoughts in her head into a coherent statement. "You gotta understand, that comes with a certain level of pressure that, frankly, I don't want to subject myself to."

"I think I understand what you mean. My older brother was a star kicker for the football team, five years before I even arrived." Claudia tapped her index finger against her chin. "Even though I'm way more brains than brawn, and we're opposites in so many ways, I still felt like I was always competing against this specter of him whenever I was on campus."

"It's definitely similar to that. I want to branch out, somewhere I don't have a connection, so I can forge my own path."

"Seems like you've put a lot of thought into this." Claudia clasped her hands together and dropped them into her lap. "So, what schools are you considering?"

"I've narrowed it down to two programs out of the four schools that accepted me: Texas Southern, and UT San Antonio."

"They're both really good programs, so your process has been pretty solid so far." Claudia reached for her champagne. "What advice do you need from me?"

"I'm just having a hard time choosing between the last two schools."

"You're gonna go see the campuses in person, right?"

She nodded. "Absolutely. I'm road-tripping to San Antonio and Houston to gather all the information I can."

"And are you planning on attending classes in person?"

"Full-time, in-person classes. It's the fastest way to finish up my degree, and after so many years away from school, I really don't want to drag the process out any more than I have to."

"Hmm, let me think for a minute." Claudia tapped her fingertip against her chin, her gaze shifting to some faraway point. "I'd say it's important to look at notable graduates from each school's science department, and see what career field they've gone into, and what kind of strides or discoveries they've made."

"That's pretty good, I hadn't really thought of that." Jamie slipped her phone from the hidden inner pocket on her left hip and opened her notes app, typing up a few words to help her remember Claudia's advice. *Odds are, by the time I get home, I'm gonna forget.* The champagne was flowing through her bloodstream now, giving her a slight but noticeable buzz.

"Oh good, you're taking notes. I've got a few more tips." Claudia rubbed her hands together. "Also, you need to look at the science department's funding. Since research is an ongoing thing at a top-quality institution, you should be able to see a steady stream of grants, alumni donations, and even corporate funding coming into the department. If you can find that, you can expect the research labs to be well stocked with all the best materials." She paused. "That's another thing you should do, by the way. See their laboratories, in person. Ask to see the labs used by freshmen and the ones used by upperclassmen as well. That way, if there's any disparity between the two, you can ask the faculty about it right then and there."

"Wow. This is really good information." Jamie typed quickly to keep up with her friend's sage advice. "I'm gonna be super prepared going into my campus tours."

"Glad I could help." Claudia let her head drop toward her right shoulder, eyeing her intently. "This is going to be a major change, you know. Going from a customer-facing job to being a full-time student."

"You're telling me. It's been years since I left community college, but I still remember how grueling it was, taking a full class load for my associate in general studies alongside my nail technology classes." She blew out a breath as memories of those days played in her mind like an old highlight reel. "I pulled so many all-nighters. Just thinking about it makes me tired."

"Are you going to keep working while you go after your degree?" Claudia asked.

She shook her head. "No. The silver lining to this whole stolen-business-idea debacle is that now I can put the money I saved for buying and outfitting my new shop toward my living expenses. I should be pretty well covered, as long as I can finish up my degree in four semesters or less." She scrolled back through the notes she'd tapped into her phone, making sure she'd gotten it all down. "If I can snag a scholarship or grant, that will make it even easier."

"Awesome. Well, it sounds like you're on the right track with this." Claudia's expression grew wistful. "I just wish you were going to school locally, so you'd be closer."

Jamie picked up her friend's hand, gave it a squeeze. "Same. But no matter what school I end up choosing, I'll only be a quick drive down the highway from Austin. Don't worry, I still plan on bugging the hell out of you, every chance I get."

Claudia laughed. "Well, that's both distressing and comforting."

They talked for a few more moments, with Jamie listening as Claudia outlined the itinerary for her celebratory cruise. When Claudia excused herself to help one of her classmates find the bathroom, Jamie sat alone on the sunroom sofa and downed the rest of her champagne. Claudia's obvious sadness about her moving to a new city had ignited an unexpected sense of melancholy in her. So, she swung by the kitchen counter and poured herself another glass of champagne, then another. As the fifth glass of bubbly settled into her body, she felt the characteristic warmth of comfortable tipsiness take over. Her mind went just a bit fuzzy, as did her vision, but her mood improved tenfold. Feeling the grin spread across her face, she sauntered out the back door.

Noticing her walk was a bit wobbly and off kilter, she grabbed the handrail as she descended the four stairs from Claudia's treated-oak patio onto the soft grass. Her eyes fell on Peaches, who stood off to the side of the yard beneath a willow tree. Holding an amber bottle in front of her, she appeared to be deep in thought.

Squaring her shoulders, Jamie marched across the yard. Her heels sank a bit in spots where the soil was loose and moist, but that didn't deter her. She ended her trek when she came face to face with her slightly bewildered-looking acquaintance.

"Hey, Jamie. What's up?" The words dripped from Peaches' lips, her voice smooth and dark like warm maple syrup. Her brow was slightly hitched, an indication of her confusion.

It was all Jamie could do not to drool. She didn't know if it was the champagne, or the smell of Peaches' expensive cologne, or both that had reduced her brain to mashed potatoes, but at any rate, it took her a moment to form a coherent phrase. "I . . . um . . . you look nice tonight."

Peaches grinned. "Thank you. So do you." Her gaze raked over Jamie's body, like a slow, purposeful touch. "Very, very nice."

A tingle raced down her spine like an electric current. She inhaled deeply, taking in even more of the heady fragrance Peaches wore. She couldn't place it well enough to identify it, but she did pick up some earthy notes, as well as a hint of musk. "Oh my God. You smell like a stack of money. What cologne are you wearing?"

Peaches' tongue darted across her lower lip before she asked, "So, you like the way I smell?"

"I just said I did." Jamie giggled, then stifled the sound with her hand once it had reached her ears. "So what are you wearing?"

A low chuckle escaped Peaches' lips. "It's Bleu by Chanel. I wear it a lot. I guess you could say it's my signature scent."

Jamie swallowed, her eyes connecting with Peaches'. "Look, I know this might sound crazy, since we don't see each other much . . . ya know . . . one on one."

"I'm listening."

"I just wanna say, I find you extremely fucking attractive." She hiccuped, then covered her mouth once again. Her cheeks grew hot, and she felt like an awkward teenager. "Sorry. That came out a little intense. But the sentiment remains. I really wanna get to know you better."

A mischievous twinkle shone in Peaches' dark eyes. "No need to apologize. I don't mind the intensity at all. I can appreciate you saying exactly how you feel." Peaches took a single small step toward her. "But I have to ask you something."

"H-hmm?" She hiccuped again. *Sheesh. These damn hiccups won't let me be great.*

"Are you sober right now? I mean, like, fully aware of what you're saying?"

Jamie sucked in her lower lip. Releasing it, she said, "Yes to the second thing. Not so much . . . on the first thing."

"That's what I thought." Peaches placed a hand on her shoulder, gave it a squeeze. "Baby, I can't tell you how flattered I am. But I'm gonna need you to catch me when you're sober if you want me to take you seriously."

Even in her altered state, Jamie could feel the indignation rising inside her like fire in her belly. It wasn't an outright rejection, but still, not being taken seriously, when she meant every word she'd said, had her quite perturbed. "Fair enough." With a terse nod, she turned to walk away. Apparently, she made the turn a bit too fast, because she lost her balance before she could complete the revolution.

Peaches grabbed her arm, steadying her a nanosecond before she went careening face-first into the loamy grass. "You good, baby?"

Offering another terse nod, she slipped her arm out of Peaches' grip before slowly, carefully, picking her way across the yard and back into Claudia's house.

CHAPTER FOUR

"Damn!" A chilly breeze blew over the Colorado River, making Peaches grasp the open halves of her black windbreaker jacket and snatch them closed. She'd worn the jacket with matching pants and a white tank with the black longline sports bra underneath. "I don't know why I let you talk me into doing this, especially on one of my extremely rare Saturdays off."

Striding along next to her on the Butler Trail through Zilker Park, Aiko grinned. She was clad in a pair of gray leggings and a matching long-sleeved tee, along with all-black sneakers. "Come on. After all that partying and rich food last night, you've gotta admit it's refreshing to take a morning walk. Right?"

Peaches groaned aloud. "Maybe. But next time, I'll take my refreshment the way the good Lord intended. Fresh from the coffeepot."

"I don't know why you're complaining," Aiko said with a laugh. "You've been able to keep pace with me the entire time. Besides, there's a reason we're walking—I usually run when I come alone."

"Well, my knees and I can appreciate that you didn't ask me to run." Peaches reached her arms over her head, stretching a bit as she walked. "At least it's nice weather today."

"Sunny, midsixties, barely any humidity." Aiko released a sigh, her easy smile and relaxed posture indicating her contentment. "A perfect spring day to get some outdoor exercise. And after this, we'll grab something light for brunch."

Peaches shook her head. "Nah, bruh. It's nine a.m. on my Saturday off, and you got me out of bed doing physical activity. We eating something heavy for brunch. You owe me that much, at least."

Aiko laughed again. "All right, all right. I'll let you pick the brunch spot." She paused the flow of words without halting her steps. "So, what was all that last night with you and Jamie?"

Peaches swallowed. *Claudia's gathering was such an intimate one, I guess I shouldn't be surprised someone noticed us standing off to the side together.* "Yeah, about that."

"I'm listening." Aiko eyed her expectantly. "So, give me the details."

"I was standing off to myself, finishing up a bottle of pale ale, when Jamie walks over." She scratched her jawline. "Well, 'walk' might not be the right word. She was a little unsteady on her feet. It was subtle, but noticeable."

"Cool, cool. Now tell me what y'all said to each other—I saw your mouths moving, but I wasn't close enough to hear what was said."

Peaches chuckled. "Calm down, nosy. Anyway, I asked her what was up. She tells me I look nice tonight, and I'm flattered, so I thank her and tell her she looks very nice too."

"Knowing you, you laid that praise on pretty thick."

"Nah. I could see she was a little tipsy, so I kept it light. Anyway, after that, she says I smell like a stack of money . . ."

"Lemme guess. You asked her if she liked how you smelled."

She cringed. "I couldn't help myself. You know how I get when the cologne is doing its job. So I tell her what I'm wearing. Then she proceeds to tell me that she wants to get to know me better, and that she finds me, and I quote, 'extremely fucking attractive.'"

Aiko came to a dead stop in the middle of the trails, and grabbed Peaches' forearm. "You're bullshitting me."

She shook her head. "Nope. Real talk, shawty was coming on very strong."

"Well? What did you say to her?" Aiko's eyes were wide.

"I told her I was flattered, but essentially, I couldn't take her seriously because she wasn't fully sober. I'm not saying she was drunk, but she definitely wasn't operating at peak capacity, ya know what I mean?"

Aiko's eyes returned to their normal size but remained fixed on her face. "Okay. I applaud you for taking the gentlewoman's route. But what happens next? You can't just leave this hanging in the air between you, not after she approached you so boldly."

She shrugged. "Why can't I? Like I said, she was tipsy. She may not even remember much of the party, let alone her conversation with me. And I'm not about to risk the potential embarrassment of being the one to bring this up."

Folding her arms over her chest, Aiko asked, "So, you're just going to pretend it didn't happen, then?"

"Yep. We don't really see or run into each other outside of the larger friend group, so it won't be hard. Logistically, at least." *What will be hard is trying not to think about Jamie, the scrumptious way she looked in that dress, and everything she was trying to offer me. Aiko doesn't need to know that, though.* "Basically, I'm putting the onus on her. If she's serious, she'll seek me out. And if she's as serious as she claimed, it won't be long before she does."

"You sound awfully cocky, playa." Aiko shook her head. "This is a side of you I've never seen. I know how much you love tall, elegant femmes, and Jamie definitely fits that type. It's hard to believe you're willing to just sit back and wait for her to make a move, instead of your usual approach."

Peaches tilted her head to the left. "And what would you say is my usual approach?"

"Getting out your gear and climbing her like a tree." Aiko snorted.

Before she could reply, a small group of cyclists approached. They stepped apart, allowing the three bikers to pass safely between them. "We can't just be standing here in the middle of the trail."

"Yeah, let's head for the trailhead." Aiko began walking again.

Falling into step next to her friend, Peaches said, "I feel like you were making a subtle joke about my height with that tree-climbing thing."

"Oh, it was subtle? Then I should have just called you short out-right." Aiko elbowed her playfully.

Peaches elbowed her right back. "Stop hatin', Aiko."

"I'm not a hater. It's just odd to me the way short studs love to latch on to tall femmes. It's almost a meme at this point."

She rolled her eyes. "Whatever." *Yeah, I've thought about it a time or two. But it's never seemed like a good idea.* "Don't act like it's not the same with you slender stems and your obsession with thick and curvy femmes."

Aiko's hand went to her chest. "Well, shit, bro. You got me on that one. My baby thicker than a Snicker, and I wouldn't have it any other way."

"Exactly." A satisfied smile tugged at her lips in response to her friend's admission.

They reached the trailhead and the parking lot beyond, and headed to Aiko's car. Inside the cabin of the vehicle, they stashed their water bottles in the cup holders and buckled their belts.

"Where to for brunch, Peaches?"

"Bouldin Creek Cafe, please. I'm gonna need some fuel so I can handle my errands today."

"The vegetarian place?" Aiko's brow arched. "I thought you said you wanted something heavy."

"Listen. They have great omelets, and they serve alcohol . . . not to mention they're woman-owned. So yeah, that's where I wanna go."

"Gotcha." Aiko backed out of the parking space and pulled out of the lot. As they got underway, leaving the rolling green hills and streams behind them, Peaches stared out her window. The azure-blue sky above held barely a cloud, and seemed to stretch on endlessly above her.

Even though her eyes were focused skyward, she could still see Jamie, standing there looking like a five-course meal, with that glimmer of desire dancing in her hazel eyes.

I keep thinking she wasn't serious, or that it was just the alcohol talking.

But what if I'm wrong? What if she was serious, and she decides not to approach me again? I did reject her, even though I feel like I did it politely.

What if that was my one and only chance with her, and I blew it?

"You all right over there, Peaches?" Aiko asked from the driver's seat.

She nodded. "Yeah. Just trying to calculate how many calories I burned, so I can replace every single one of them at brunch."

Aiko shook her head and laughed. "You're a mess."

"True, but that's what makes me so lovable." At a moment like this, humor was her saving grace. There was no way she'd admit how Jamie, who'd been just another member of the homie squad thirty-six hours earlier, had her nose wide open. Nope, that simply wouldn't do.

After a search for parking, the two women entered the café and took seats at the bar. Peaches browsed the menu while absently drumming her fingertips on the polished wood.

"You drinking today?" Aiko asked.

"Nah. I'll just do a coffee." She shook her head. "I think I had enough last night. Besides, I need something close to a clear head so I can tie up some loose ends around my place."

"Same. I'm overdue to prune and deadhead my orchids, plus Mom and Summer both have lists of things for me to take care of." She held the back of her hand to her forehead, feigning exhaustion.

"Married life getting to you, playa?"

"Nah." Aiko chuckled. "You know I'm always gonna look out for Mama. And as for Summer, she could ask me to hot-tar the roof bare-handed, and I'd do it. Anything for my baby."

Peaches couldn't help smiling at that remark. Seeing her best friend so happy and in love made her feel so good inside . . . and also, just a little sad that she didn't have that for herself. *I wonder if there's a life like that in the cards for me . . .*

The waitress took their order of an iced mocha and the café's signature omelet for Peaches, and an iced matcha latte and a veggie tofu scramble for Aiko.

They spent the next hour or so chatting over their meals and drinks before Aiko drove Peaches back to her place in Crestview. "I'd hang longer, P, but duty calls."

As she stepped out of Aiko's SUV into her front yard, she waved her off. "It's cool. You know I understand. I'll see you later."

With a wave, Aiko drove off down the road.

Once inside her town house, Peaches kicked off her white-on-white cross-trainers and tucked them into their designated plastic shoebox in her closet. Then, after tucking her sock-clad feet into a pair of old but comfortable house shoes, she made her way to the kitchen and spent about fifteen minutes tidying. Oftentimes during the week, she'd be in and out of the space and didn't always put things where they belonged, so she found that this weekly tidying ritual helped to keep her home from falling into utter chaos.

She was just about to move on to cleaning the half bath in the front of the town house when her phone rang. After shifting her cleaning caddy to her left hand, she reached into her right pocket and answered the call without looking at the screen. "Hello?"

"Peaches, it's your papa."

She held in her chuckle, wondering why he felt the need to announce himself that way whenever he called her. "Hey, Pops. What's up?"

"What are you doing?"

"Right now?" She set the caddy down on the closed toilet lid, then grabbed the glass cleaner and gave the oval-shaped wall mirror a liberal spritzing. "Cleaning my guest bathroom."

"Uh-huh. Nice to know you're doing something domestic."

She rolled her eyes, but said nothing.

"Anyway, your brother needs you. Says he can't get the girls' hair together, and he's taking them to church tomorrow."

She let out a long sigh. "I just did Ella's hair the other night, and the other girls were pretty put together then. How has that been undone so quickly?"

"Your guess is good as mine, Peaches." He paused. "Listen. Just go over there and help him out. You do hair for a living anyway."

She set down the cleaning caddy and stripped off the rubber gloves. Resting her fingertips against her temple, she said, "I'm a barber, not a hairdresser. My expertise doesn't really apply here, unless one of the girls wants a fade."

"That's not funny, Peaches." His tone was gruff. "I know you like to forget you're a woman, but there won't be no such behavior for my precious granddaughters."

She winced. "Yikes. You could stand to turn down the homophobia by like five notches, Pops."

He grunted. "You know I don't mean nothing by it. Look, just go on over there and do something with your nieces' hair."

"Yes, sir," she acquiesced. "Anything else you need?"

"Yes. Pick up my medicines from O'Keefe's drugstore. I've got four prescriptions waiting over there."

"Okay. I'll try to get over there before they close." She didn't bother asking about the payment, because she knew she'd have to open her wallet to pay his copays . . . again.

"See that you do—I need my medicine." He yawned. "All right. Just drop 'em by here on your way to your brother's. Love you."

"Love you, too, Pops. But it's my day—"

He hung up before she could finish her sentence.

She tucked the phone away, feeling the familiar tension setting into her neck and shoulders. She hadn't taken a Saturday off in about three months. And now, instead of getting her house in order for the coming week, she'd be playing personal errand girl to her father, and hairdresser to her nieces.

You'd think RJ would have learned to make a decent ponytail by now, after raising three daughters all this time.

It was painfully obvious that his ex-wife, the girls' mother, had done most of the domestic and child-related tasks when she was around. Still, it was past time RJ learned.

Jamie groaned as she rolled out of bed late Sunday morning. After a night spent cycling between staring at her ceiling and sleeping just deeply enough to have unpleasant dreams, she felt an equal amount of exhaustion and frustration.

Parked on the edge of her mattress, she swiped a hand over her tired eyes, then stretched, the hem of her nightshirt rising around her hips. Standing, she trudged to the bathroom.

When she returned, she opened her bottom dresser drawer and grabbed a pair of ratty sweatpants. After pulling them on to cover her bare ass, she jammed her feet into her rubber-ducky slippers, then tied an old black bandanna around her cornrows.

When I feel shitty and restless like this, there's only one thing to do. Stress clean.

She went to the hall closet, then opened it and squatted down. While the four wide, built-in wire shelves held extra linen and her winter gear, the floor of the closet was reserved for two large plastic dishpans, filled with cleaning supplies. After sliding both pans out, she ferried them to her kitchen counter and left them there before returning to the closet to grab the broom, mop, and the fluffy duster hanging on the inside of the closet door.

With all her gear assembled, she stood in her kitchen and took a deep breath.

Her mind went back to the events of Friday night again, predictably, and she cringed. *Ugh.* It seemed no matter how much she tried to think of something else, literally anything else, her conversation with Peaches kept replaying, over and over.

I guess I had enough champagne to make me walk sideways but not enough to make me forget our conversation ever happened. Go fucking figure. The last two nights she'd slept terribly, and while she was no expert on dream interpretation, she couldn't help drawing a parallel between her extreme embarrassment and the constant barrage of nightmares where she experienced similar emotions in a myriad of ways. *It seems my mind likes to come up with creative ways to torture me.*

Deep in the recesses of her brain, a thought of breakfast erupted. The ball of tightness in her stomach made her force that thought away and opt instead for a drink. After grabbing a water bottle from her cabinet, she filled it with ice, water, and a squirt of lemon juice from the little plastic lemon she always kept in her fridge. She closed the lid, then gave the bottle a shake and took a long swig before setting it aside.

She went to the console in her living room and opened up her record player. She didn't know anyone else her age who owned one, but she appreciated sound quality more than she did the convenience of streaming apps, at least for the music she loved most. She reached into the wooden storage bin on the console's lower shelf and pulled out her copy of Sean Paul's early-aughts album *Dutty Rock* and placed it on the turntable. As the familiar, silly introductory interlude began to play, she went back to the kitchen for the stuff she'd need to tackle her bathroom.

In the bathroom, she sang along to the music as she sprayed, scrubbed, and wiped down every visible surface. She used an old toothbrush to clean the caulking around the tub and sink fixtures, and got a surprising amount of Golden Honey number four foundation off the sink faucet. While she swept and mopped the blue-and-white-tiled floor, she alternated between shaking her hips and moving the cleaning tools across the floor.

She returned to the kitchen to change out her tools and began cleaning that room. Everything got wiped or scoured, including the counters, the appliances, and the double sinks. Beads of perspiration formed around her hairline, and she dabbed them away with her shirt-tail, trusting her headscarf to do the rest. She grabbed one of the two chairs from her dining set, then slid it beneath the ceiling fan in the center of the room. Her duster, even combined with her five-foot-eleven height, didn't reach the very top of the fan fixture. The apartment's high ceilings had been a selling point for her, but they made tasks like this one a bit of a pain.

She climbed up on the chair seat, steadied herself, and began vigor-ously polishing the brass fittings with the fluffy duster. After tossing it to the floor, she grabbed the old pillowcase she'd sprayed with a generous amount of citrus furniture polish, and slid it over the fan blade closest to her.

A pounding knock sounded at her door, startling her enough that she nearly fell off the chair. Regaining her balance, she stepped down carefully and went to the door, stopping on the way to turn down the volume on her music.

She checked the peephole, then swung open the door. "Taylor, why you banging on my door like the feds?"

Standing on the doorstep dressed in medium-blue skinny jeans, a gray-and-white tee with Queen Latifah's face and the word "UNITY" in block letters, and a pair of white sneakers, Taylor laughed. "I tried the regular knock, but obviously you couldn't hear me over the island rhythms you're blasting." Shaking their head, Taylor slipped inside the apartment.

As she closed the door, Jamie asked, "What's up?"

Taylor eyed her up and down. "Girl, the better question is, What's up with you? You look a hot mess—sweating and bedraggled. What in the world you got going on?"

She sighed, looking down at herself. "I've been cleaning."

"It smells like pure bleach in here." Taylor, with brow cocked and head tilted to the left, stared at her. "There's cleaning . . . then there's whatever intense shit you've been doing."

Jamie drew a deep, cleansing breath, inhaling the fumes of several different cleaning products. Releasing it, she said, "Yeah. So I might have been stress cleaning because I slept like shit and needed an outlet that didn't involve committing a crime." She paused. "But let me crack a window and let some of the fumes out."

Taylor winced. "Uh-oh. What the hell happened?"

"It's pretty intense, or at least it feels that way to me."

"Well, I wanna hear all about it." They paused. "But not until after you take a shower and put on some decent clothes. It pains me to see you looking like this."

Jamie glanced at the kitchen and noticed the tiny bit of paint she'd scrubbed off the wall just above her stove. *Yikes.* "Yeah. Hang tight while I do that."

Taylor parked it on the couch and pulled out their phone. "Take your time, honey."

She went back to her sparkly-clean bathroom, shrugged out of her sweat-dampened clothes, and turned the shower on. Once the temperature reached her preferred heat level, which a former lover had referred to as "just below boiling," she stepped beneath the steamy stream and sighed.

The hot water relaxed her body as she scrubbed away the results of her overzealous cleaning jag, and when she stepped out a bit later, clean and jasmine scented, she felt renewed . . . physically, anyway.

She returned to the living room with her long water-wave lace-front wig firmly in place and wearing one of her favorite dresses. The bright-orange, halter-style maxi dress, imprinted with a batik-like white floral pattern, made her feel like a proverbial goddess. She'd paired it with flat white sandals that bared her toes, but not her heels.

Taylor grinned as Jamie approached the sofa. "Yasss. Now that's the Jamie I know and love."

She smiled, in spite of her less-than-stellar mood. "Is there a reason I had to get dressed?"

"Yeah, duh. I'm taking you out of here. You obviously need some fresh air and a distraction." Taylor paused. "Let me guess. You haven't eaten, have you?"

Jamie sucked her lower lip. "No . . . but I'm definitely hydrated. I had a whole bottle of lemon water."

Taylor's headshake was slow and a bit judgy. "Girl, this is why you need a friend like me. Let's grab something to eat, and then hit the mall. On the way, you can tell me what's got your thong in a bunch."

"How'd you know what kind of panties I'm wearing?"

"Are there any other kind?" Taylor asked with a completely straight face.

Jamie snorted. "Let's get out of here."

Soon, they were outside and seated in Taylor's fiery-red two-door coupe. Jamie snapped her seat belt into the buckle and flung up the same silent petition to the ancestors that she sent each time she rode with her lead-footed bestie.

"You know, I can see you over there with your eyes closed and your lips moving," Taylor remarked. "You do that every time you get in my car."

Opening her eyes, Jamie twisted her lips into a crooked smile.

Eyes narrowed, Taylor groused, "I know you not praying. Bish, I done drove you around plenty of times and ain't crashed once."

Eyes darting around the cabin, anywhere but on her friend's face, Jamie said, "Yeah, but you got a heavy foot, Taylor. I be clinging to the dashboard."

"But did you die, though?" Cranking the car, Taylor grinned and revved the engine a bit before zipping out of the parking lot and into the early-afternoon traffic on Saint Johns Avenue.

By the time they pulled into the drive-through of a local coffee-house for a quick bite, she'd adjusted to the initial shock of her friend's driving. They ordered muffins and iced coffee, and as they pulled back out into traffic, Jamie took a sip of hers.

"So, now that you've got a little something on your stomach besides the water, tell me what's going on. I was at the shop all day yesterday, regretting my decision not to take the day off. If I wasn't so exhausted when I got home, you know I would have called you."

"It's cool. I know how busy Saturdays are at the shop." She let her head drop back against the supple leather of the headrest. "I got a little tipsy at Claudia's party, and liquid courage led me to do something I hadn't planned on doing."

"And what was that?" Taylor's gaze remained on the road, but their concern was evident. "I mean I drove you home, but you were basically asleep the whole ride. It's a wonder you were able to carry yourself upstairs to bed."

She purposely waited until they were stopped at a red light to speak, then blurted out, "I told Peaches I'm attracted to her."

Taylor's head made a very slow pivot to the right, revealing a wide-eyed, open-mouthed stare.

Jamie blinked a few times.

The light changed, and Taylor proceeded through it. "I'm glad you said that while I was stopped. Girl, what the fuck?"

"C'mon. I know I told you I was kinda feelin' her."

"Yeah, but I thought that was a secret you was gonna take to the grave. You said yourself it would probably make things weird with the squad." Taylor navigated into the parking lot of the shopping center and began the search for an open parking space.

"It still might. I just couldn't stop myself from saying it. It was definitely out of character, but in that moment something just came over me."

"Blame it on the alcohol, like Jamie Foxx said, girl. That's the only good explanation we got."

She nodded as they finally pulled into an empty spot about a half a mile away from the nearest entrance. "The fact that I dimed myself out to her isn't even the worst part."

"I'm guessing she reacted badly to your lil' declaration?"

"Not badly, per se. Just condescendingly."

"Give me the CliffsNotes version, and try not to retraumatize yourself too much." Taylor cut the engine and swiveled in the seat, facing her.

Jamie closed her eyes as she recalled the almost pitying look on Peaches' face. "I complimented her outfit, she complimented me back, so it started off well enough. But when I told her how I felt, she totally dismissed me. Said she couldn't take me seriously while I was tipsy."

"How many glasses of champagne did you have?"

"Five."

"Then you absolutely were tipsy." Taylor appeared thoughtful. "I can tell you didn't like her response, and I'm sorry it made you feel a way. Tell me about her tone, though."

"I felt like she was talking down to me, like an adult telling a kid they're mistaken about something, know what I mean? It's the second time this week someone has dismissed my feelings, when I cared enough to be honest with them."

Taylor looked confused for a moment; then recognition crossed their face. "Oh yeah. Mama Hunt."

Jamie nodded. "Yeah. It makes me wonder if my feelings are invalid, or at least misplaced."

"Uh-uh, girl. Don't let nobody gaslight you, because your feelings are absolutely valid." Taylor drained the last of their iced coffee. "Let's look on the bright side of things, shall we?"

"What bright side?" It was a genuine question, as she didn't see how having her emotions crumpled up and tossed aside like a used gum wrapper—twice—could have a silver lining.

"First, with Mama Hunt, you stood your ground and didn't let her steamroll you into validating her mess at your own expense."

Jamie leaned back and looked up, considering Taylor's words. "Okay, that seems about right. What about with Peaches? Where's the good in that?"

"Peaches may have come across dismissive. But from what you told me, she wasn't cruel or egotistical about it. She didn't laugh in your face, or try to put you on blast and embarrass you." Taylor paused, staring out the windshield for a moment. "Actually, when you think about it, she behaved in a very chivalrous fashion. She respected you enough not to take advantage of your inebriation, and instead asked you to be reflective."

Jamie blinked several times, staring at her friend. "Sometimes you say some really wise shit, Taylor. It's hard to believe you're the same person who belts Weird Al songs at the top of their lungs."

Taylor laughed. "Okay, first of all, Mr. Yankovic is a genius, and you will respect his craft in my presence. Second of all, I'm right and you know it."

"You're absolutely right, and even though I hate it, I'm mature enough to admit that."

"Good." Taylor opened the driver's-side door. "Then let's get our butts in this mall and shop."

They entered the mall, and Jamie made a beeline for Lady in Lace, a boutique lingerie shop.

Following her inside, Taylor asked, "Girl, what you about to buy in here? More thongs?"

Jamie chuckled. "Yeah, but I need a little something extra today." Her eyes fell on a gorgeous french-cut teddy, its delicate lace dyed a deep crimson red that she knew would look amazing against her skin tone. "You made a good point about Peaches. I'm thinking I need to pursue this, but with a little change in tactic."

Taylor's grin reached Cheshire cat level in a nanosecond as they glanced between the teddy and Jamie's face. "Fuck. Yes."

CHAPTER FIVE

Peaches began her day well after eleven on Sunday morning. As she sat up in bed and stretched her arms over her head, she let out a yawn. *That was just enough sleep to make up for getting up early yesterday.*

After a quick shower and morning routine, she slipped on a pair of loose-fitting black basketball shorts bearing a white stripe down the side and a white tank top. Barefoot, she made her way to the kitchen and fixed herself a quick meal: a grilled ham-and-cheese sandwich, a handful of plain potato chips, and an ice-cold can of grape soda from the fridge.

When she'd finished eating, she returned to her closet and searched her shelves for a pair of sneakers. *I know just the pair I need to dust Aiko's ass on the court. Now where are they?* She climbed onto a step stool and started shuffling boxes around in search of her trusty cloud-white Adidas Dame 8s with the metallic-gold trim. After locating the box on the uppermost shelf, she reached up and swiped it down.

She caught the box as it fell but missed the thin strips of paper that fell with it . . .

She stooped to investigate after stepping down from the stool with the shoebox in her arms. She flipped over the strips . . . and frowned.

The strips were printouts from a photo booth. Beneath a thin layer of dust were images of her hugged up with her ex, Denise. She sighed, shaking her head. *I thought I got rid of all these. Since I missed these, I'll fix it right now.*

She left the closet with her sneakers and the photos. After pausing to lace up the shoes, she carried the strips out the back door, onto her patio. There, she placed the glossy ribbons of paper atop a pile of hickory chips in her cast-iron firepit. A few moments later, she watched the regrettable images melt away in the dancing flames.

Once she'd safely doused and covered the firepit, Peaches donned her sunglasses and left the house, headed south out of her neighborhood, toward the Clark basketball courts at UT Austin's Caven Lacrosse and Sports Center.

By the time she arrived, she found Aiko lounging against the fence surrounding the courts, all four of which were empty.

"Hey, Peaches." Aiko, dressed in a blue T-shirt and matching cutoff sweats, had the bright-orange ball resting against her hip. She straightened as Peaches approached. "I was beginning to think you weren't coming."

"And miss out on embarrassing you on the court?" she scoffed. "No way."

Inside the fence, Aiko gave the ball a few solid bounces against the court surface. "Heard from Jamie yet?"

Squatting into a defensive stance, Peaches shook her head.

Aiko offered a curt nod as she continued to bounce the ball. Half a second later, she took off running toward the basket.

Peaches took a wide step to her left, sticking out her arm.

Aiko twirled around it.

Peaches spun, following her friend and darting around her for the block. Arms raised, she jumped . . .

. . . then cursed as the ball soared over her head, crashing into the backboard before falling through the net.

"Swish." Aiko winked in her direction.

Rolling her eyes, Peaches watched the ball as it fell. It made a single bounce before she snatched it and sprinted for the hoop on the opposite end of the court.

She was lining up her shot when Aiko slapped the ball out of her grasp.

Peaches cursed.

Aiko laughed. "Get your head in the game, P."

Try as she might, Peaches did not adhere to her friend's admonishment.

Forty minutes later, she was sitting on the court's sun-warmed surface, her back resting against the fence. She was drenched with sweat, despite the absolutely trash game she'd just played.

Aiko joined her, sitting next to her before folding her long legs in front of her. "Damn, P. Why you let me beat you like that?"

She offered a wry chuckle. "Trust me, that wasn't my intent."

"You must be thinking hard about something else, playa. I've beat you before," she quipped. "But you only made one basket the whole game."

"I know the stats. Thanks for the commentary, Barkley." Peaches rolled her eyes. "You right, though. My focus is elsewhere." She told her friend about the photos she'd found.

Aiko whistled. "Whew. Talk about a blast from the past."

"And not the good kind either. Felt kind of good to burn them, though."

"I bet." Aiko paused. "You know what? I think I've got an unfair edge over you today."

"And why is that?"

"Because I'm knee deep in newlywed bliss, getting the goods day and night," Aiko teased. "Meanwhile, I know you're in a drought."

She blew out a breath. "Don't remind me. Besides, don't coaches always say that fucking before a game weakens your athletic abilities?"

Aiko laughed. "That may be true for men, but not for us. My baby got me feeling like Mario after a power-up."

"Yeah. While you're over there with your Princess Peach, I'm just at the crib by my lonesome." Peaches made an exaggerated sad face.

"On the real, though, P. You said that after Denise . . ."

Peaches held up her hand. "Don't say her name."

"Sorry. After . . . your ex . . . you said you wanted something real, something that transcended the physical."

"I know. That doesn't make waiting for it any easier, though."

Aiko cleared her throat. "Have you ever considered that Jamie might be your chance?"

Peaches cringed. "No. Of course not."

"I mean, she might not be Mrs. Right, but at the very least she can maybe help you . . . scratch that itch." Aiko gave her a quick elbow jab and a knowing look. "We're all adults, P. No harm in testing the waters."

"I'm not even gonna entertain that thought," Peaches insisted. "No, I'm sticking to my guns. I'm not reaching out to Jamie. Like I said, if she's for real, she will reach out to me."

"You know me, I'm not one to push," Aiko responded.

Peaches' phone chimed then. She slipped it from her pocket, swiped the screen, and read the text message silently. All the while, she could feel her friend's gaze on her face.

"Well?" Aiko's tone was expectant.

Knowing her friend wouldn't leave her alone until she answered, Peaches recapped the message. "Jamie just texted me. She wants to meet up for frozen yogurt tomorrow."

"Boom."

Peaches stared at her phone screen for a few moments, considering her response. After a few silent moments, she tapped out a reply.

How about we meet at Menchie's at 7?

Jamie responded a few moments later with a heart-eyes smiley face.

Pocketing her phone again, she turned toward Aiko. "All right . . . I set it up."

Aiko gave her a playful slap on the back. "See? That wasn't so hard, was it?"

Jamie spent the better part of Monday morning doing back-to-back clients. Mondays at the nail salon were a mixed bag; some weeks they had barely any customers and spent the day tidying up and gossiping. Today wasn't one of those days.

While her butt remained firmly planted in the chair at her station, her mind wandered elsewhere. She couldn't stop thinking about Peaches, and about meeting up with her at day's end. *My curiosity is running wild . . . this is my chance to really talk to her, one on one . . . find out what makes Peaches tick.*

"Yikes. Ease up on my cuticles, honey," groused her client.

Jamie cringed, setting aside her orangewood stick. "Sorry about that. Let me add a little oil to them." She opened the small glass vial, then applied some of the citrus-scented liquid with the dropper and worked it in.

By the time she'd finished applying the woman's french-tip gel manicure and sent her on her way, it was just past twelve thirty. When her manager released her for lunch, she didn't hesitate to tuck away her tools and implements, grab her phone and purse, and head outside.

She sat down at an outdoor table with a shake and fries from Awesome Burger, and as she munched, she looked at her phone. *I need to go ahead and make the call . . . putting off talking to him isn't going to make it any more enjoyable.*

With a sigh, she dialed her father's number.

Clarence Hunt answered the call on the third ring. "Hello, Jamie."

"Hi, Dad." She sipped from her milkshake, noting his tone, the same dry one he always used when he answered her calls. "Are you busy?"

"Not at the moment." He paused. "Is there something you need?"

"Yes, actually." She folded a fry into her mouth. "I wanted to get Uncle Cordell's number from you."

He cleared his throat. "I can give you my brother's number. But do you mind telling me why you want it?"

Here we go. "Don't you remember, Dad? I told you I'm going back to school."

"I don't remember you saying that." The confusion in his tone validated his words. "If you are going back, though, I certainly hope you'll study something more lucrative and intellectual than what you're doing now. At your age, there's no time for playing around anymore."

"Sheesh, Dad. Not even bothering to hide your disdain today, huh?"

"You know I'm only speaking practically," he insisted. "You already went to school once, and wasted time on this nail thing. The economy is always in flux, and you know people cut back on nonnecessities during downturns. I mean, look at your brother. A good lawyer is always in demand, no matter what the economic situation looks like."

She drained the last of her milkshake. "Dad, as much as I love hearing you talk about how Shelby's job is way more important than mine, I only get an hour for lunch. So can you just give me Uncle Cordell's number, please?"

"Sure. But you know he won't be back on campus until the spring, right?"

She blinked a few times. "No, I didn't know that. I applied to UT San Antonio partly because he teaches there, in the department I want to join."

"You want to study science?"

"Yes, Dad. Chemistry, in particular." Wanting to steer the conversation back in the proper direction, she added, "Why isn't Uncle Cordell going to be on campus in the fall?"

"He's gone on sabbatical. He's in Atlanta, working on a vaccine trial with the CDC. An assistant professor has taken on all his organic chemistry classes and labs in the meantime."

"I see." She tapped her chin, considering this new information and how it might affect her decision on where to study. "I'll take the number anyway. Even if he's not on campus, he can still give me helpful info."

"Okay, hold on." After a few moments of silence, he said, "I just texted you the number."

Rather than give her father a chance to prolong the conversation any further, she said, "Okay, thanks. Gotta go. Love you."

The moment he returned the sentiment, she disconnected the call. In many ways, she got along slightly better with him than she did with her mother. Still, his tendency to bend to his wife's whims rather than risk an argument kept their relationship from becoming closer.

Back at her station, Jamie went about the rest of her workday, doing her best to keep her focus trained on her clients. As the end of the day approached, she found herself feeling restless, anticipation buzzing through her bloodstream.

She left the nail shop and headed straight home to change out of her drab uniform into something more appropriate for her meetup with Peaches. Deciding to keep it simple and stylish, she slipped into dark denim jeans, a fiery-red tank top, and flat-soled red sandals.

While she stood in the mirror, running the brush through her hair, her phone rang. She grabbed it from her dresser and answered. "Hello?"

"Hey, Jamie. It's Peaches."

"Oh, hey!" Realizing she sounded too excited, she dialed it back before continuing. "I'm gonna leave my house in like five minutes. If you get to Menchie's before me, just grab us a good table."

Peaches sighed. "About that. I'm not gonna be able to meet up tonight."

The hairbrush poised in midair, she frowned. "What? Why?"

"I have to pick up my nieces from dance and take them home. My brother got called into work and won't be home until late."

"Damn. Foiled by some kids."

"You're not hating on my nieces, are you?"

She offered a dry chuckle. "No way. I love kids. Got a nephew myself that's almost two." She blew out a breath. "I'll admit I'm disappointed, though."

"So am I." Peaches paused. "We're gonna have to try it again, soon."

"Yeah, we should." Glancing at her reflection, she took comfort in knowing that Peaches couldn't see her pout.

"I'm really sorry about this, Jamie."

"No worries. I get it, duty calls. I'll reach out to you again soon, though."

"I'm looking forward to it." Peaches chuckled. "You know what they say about the third time."

She laughed in spite of herself. "Bye, Peaches." Shaking her head, she disconnected the call and kicked off her shoes.

Welp. Won't be needing those.

CHAPTER SIX

Tuesday morning, Peaches was at the gym just down the street from her town house, getting her workout in before going in to the barbershop. Gripping the designated spot on the handles of the elliptical machine so she could monitor her heart rate in real time, she put effort into pushing the long handles back and forth while her feet rotated the large pedals. *I need to focus more on my upper body—don't wanna get those dangly arm-fat bat wings.*

After finishing a thirty-minute stint of cardio, she moved on to weights: triceps presses and kickbacks, biceps curls, and shoulder presses. By the time she ended her workout, she was sweaty and a bit ripe. She headed to her truck, since she hated using public showers, and drove the short distance back home.

She took a quick shower to wash away the postworkout grime, then dressed in one of her black-and-gold Fresh Cutz button-down shirts and a pair of clean, pressed black slacks. At the mirror in her bathroom, she ran a few drops of oil and a dab of moisture cream through her curls, then fluffed them with a plastic pick. *Roots getting kinda long . . . might need to touch up my color. Should I keep it blond, or go red?*

Leaving the question of her hair color for later, she went into her bedroom and grabbed her phone off the dresser to check the time. It was almost nine: she needed to get a move on so she could get to the shop by ten.

She put on a pair of black socks and a pair of black Stacy Adams loafers. Slipping a gold Bulova men's watch onto her left wrist, she went to the kitchen for a quick breakfast.

Seated on her sofa with her plate of scrambled eggs and wheat toast and a mixed-fruit protein smoothie, she ate the meal in contemplative silence. A glance at the mantel over her fireplace landed her gaze on the photograph centering the decor there.

It was an image of her mother, Ann-Marie, smiling as she stood at her station in the beauty shop she used to work at. Seated in the chair was Peaches, who was about five at the time. Looking at her younger face, she could remember the day well. She'd just discovered that her mother was pregnant with RJ, and she wasn't too pleased about no longer being the only child. The expression on Peaches' small face, a crooked half smile that looked less than genuine, was a result of that news, as well as the rather girly pigtailed hairstyle her mother had just manipulated her hair into.

She shook her head as she thought of that day. Part of her wished she could go back to that time, not just because of the comparably carefree nature of childhood, but also because it would mean seeing her mother's face again. Ann-Marie had been the central pillar of the Corbin family, and ever since her untimely death two years earlier, Peaches had felt as if her family were collapsing in on itself in her absence.

Damn. I miss you, Mama.

The pain of the sudden loss of her mother had dulled with time, but not nearly as much as she would have hoped. Most days, it was just a quiet undercurrent, a single note continuously played but drowned out by the busyness of everyday life. But there were moments when that single note became a symphony of grief, the sound and fury of it overtaking everything else, leaving her paralyzed in a heap of sobs. In those moments, she sought the solitude of her room, or of the nearest body of water, where she could mourn on her own until the storm passed.

It's April. Mom's birthday is coming up. The date was just a few days away, and it stood as a bittersweet reminder of all she'd lost when Ann-Marie had collapsed in the kitchen that cold winter day. She'd been just shy of fifty-two, claimed by heart disease, the same silent, insidious killer that had stolen so many other women from their family and friends.

Next to that photograph was one of Olivia, Ella, and Reagan, all dolled up for last year's Easter services. Of the three of them, Olivia looked the most like Ann-Marie; she'd inherited her grandmother's eyes, along with her high cheekbones and facial shape.

Shaking herself free of her inner monologue, Peaches carried her dishes to the sink, giving them a quick rinse before tucking them into the dishwasher. With her keys in hand, she pocketed her phone and wallet and headed to work.

She entered Fresh Cutz at seven minutes past ten and greeted her staff as she headed for her station near the back. "Morning, y'all."

Taylor, seated at the desk, responded in kind, as did Evan and Alonzo, who were typically the only other barbers to come in on Tuesdays. Kev usually joined them Wednesdays and Thursdays as business picked up; then it was all hands on deck for the weekend crowd.

"Hey, boss lady," Alonzo called out from his comfortable perch in his barber chair. There were no clients in the shop, and he seemed to be enjoying the downtime. "Remember when I said you should retire?"

"Yeah, I remember that." Peaches reached for her apron on the wall hook near her station and slipped it on.

"Well, I take it back."

She chuckled as she tied the strings around her waist. "Oh, I can't wait to hear the explanation behind that."

"I'm finna tell ya. It was a madhouse in here Saturday." He shook his head slowly. "Folks was waiting outside when I came to open up. Soon as I got the doors opened, they start lining up at the desk."

She glanced to Taylor, who nodded a confirmation.

"Al's right," Evan added. "It was wall-to-wall people in here for most of the day. All the chairs full, waiting area full, people standing by the door." She spritzed her station mirror with glass cleaner. "Between everybody working, we cut forty-six heads Saturday."

Peaches grinned. "No shit?"

"No shit." Evan scrubbed the mirror with a paper towel. "Hell, I did six undercuts before noon."

Peaches couldn't hold back her laugh. "Damn. What was happening in Austin over the weekend that made everybody need a fresh cut all at once?"

"There was a hip-hop show at the Erwin Center Saturday night. Megan Thee Stallion, Slim Thug, Scarface, and some other acts."

"That's quite a lineup . . . a lot of the heavy hitters from around these parts." Peaches now understood why the shop had been slammed with clients all day. "Well, I'm sorry y'all had to go through that, but it's very good for the bottom line. Besides, the place is still standing, so it looks like y'all handled it well."

"Just barely," Alonzo quipped. "I was so tired when I got home, I passed out on the couch. Didn't even make it to the bed, and slept right through early service Sunday."

Evan laughed. "Same, though I did manage a shower before falling asleep on top of my covers." Seated now, she was scrolling through her phone. "Have y'all heard about this mess with that high school up in the country parts?"

Peaches frowned. "Nah. What you talking about?"

"Girl. This high school in Port Nestes, or some mess like that, has a slur as their mascot. The cheerleaders wear fringed dresses and war bonnets, run around doing tomahawk chops, talking about scalping folks."

"I saw that mess on Twitter," Alonzo declared. "Don't make no sense to be carrying on like that, in this day and age. Ain't no excuse."

"Nope." Evan shook her head. "It's some racist bullshit, really and truly. And because the school is out in the fucking sticks, nobody would know about it, but somebody took video of the cheer squad at a pep rally and uploaded it to the internet."

Peaches shook her head. "See, shit like that gives the whole state a bad name. I'm gonna need them to get their heads outta their asses and stop broadcasting their ignorance like that."

"For real. Hopefully, being shamed in public will get them to change their ways." Evan set her phone on her station as the bell above the door rang, announcing the arrival of the day's first few clients. Taylor quickly checked them in, until there was a customer seated in each barber's chair, along with two people waiting in the front of the shop.

"Morning," Peaches said as she swung her cape over the young man seated in her chair. "What's your name, and what can I do for you?"

"Steve. And let me get a trim." He ran a hand over his tall fringe of curls, shaped into a box. "I wanna keep the shape but clean it up a bit."

"Okay, Steve, I can take care of that." Assessing his hair and head shape, she settled on a drop fade and a sideburn taper. She opened her drawer and grabbed her clippers, attached the proper comb guide, and got to work.

After finishing up the fade work, she used her shears to neaten up the ends of his hair, restoring the box shape. When she was done, she used a fluffy brush to dust the fallen hair off his neck and shoulders, then handed Steve a hand mirror. Rotating the chair so he could see the full picture, she asked, "What do you think, Steve?"

He smiled, nodding as he regarded his reflection. "Thanks. Looks great."

"Awesome." She unsnapped the cape and tossed it over her arm, accepting the two bills he handed her. "You need change, my man?"

He shook his head. "Keep it. You did great work, and I'll be back."

"Glad to hear it." She smiled at Steve, waving as he made his way to the front of the shop and out the door.

On his way out, Steve paused to hold the door for someone entering.

"Thank you," said a soft, familiar voice.

Peaches stared as Jamie sauntered into the barbershop, and it was all she could do to keep her jaw closed.

Jamie's dark, waist-length waves were parted on the right this time, a departure from the center part she normally wore. Her eyes obscured by sunglasses, she was dressed in a bright-white crop top, its single long sleeve covering her left arm while leaving her right shoulder, arm, and lower abdomen exposed. Glittery black script lettering across her pert breasts read "Foxy," and Peaches couldn't agree more. A pair of cutoff black denim shorts clung to Jamie's full hips, the fringe grazing her midthigh. Peaches' gaze traveled down the length of her long, shapely brown legs, capped in a super-clean pair of all-black Nike Tanjun sneakers. She carried a plastic bag in one hand and a paper sack in the other.

Jamie smiled as she shifted the bags to one hand, then lifted the glittery silver-framed sunglasses and rested them atop her hair, her wrist full of silver bangle bracelets jangling in time with the movement. Those dark, shimmering eyes now in view, she looked around the shop before her gaze met Peaches', lingering for an extended, silent moment.

Peaches swallowed. *Gaht damn.*

Jamie's glossy lips parted, and she offered a simple greeting. "Hey, y'all." She eased over to the reception desk and spoke to Taylor, setting the plastic bag in front of the shampooer slash receptionist. "I brought you lunch, friend."

"Thank you, boo!" Peaches could easily hear Taylor's gratitude over the low hum on Evan's clippers.

Jamie leaned in and lowered her voice, and despite a concerted effort on her part, Peaches could no longer hear what was being said. But she could see Taylor nodding and gesturing in a rather animated fashion. *Why do I feel like those two are up to something?* While Peaches didn't know much about Jamie, she did know that her friendship with Taylor was just as tight as the one Peaches shared with Aiko, if not more so.

Grabbing a broom to avoid getting caught staring, Peaches began sweeping up the hair from the cut she'd just finished.

As she stooped to guide the hair into the dustpan, her back to the reception area, she could feel someone approaching her station. There were a lot of smells in the shop: hair products, disinfectant. But she smelled something new, something she didn't usually smell at work.

Expensive perfume. It was floral, clean, and altogether hypnotizing. After tossing the hair clippings into the trash bin beneath her station, she stood and slowly rotated her body.

Jamie was standing on the edge of her chair mat, a soft smile on her face and the paper sack in her hand. She spoke loudly enough to be heard over the surrounding sounds. "Hey, Peaches."

"Hey, Jamie. How are you?" Peaches was barely keeping her composure in front of this tall, voluptuous, delicious-smelling femme, but she'd be damned if she let it show.

"I'm good." She held up the bag. "I brought you something."

"Oh, really? How nice." Peaches took the offered bag, finally able to make out the logo stamped on it.

"A lil' bird told me you like the red velvet cupcakes from Sweet Tooth Bakery, so I thought I'd bring you one."

"Thank you." Peaches set the bag down on her station counter before her clammy hands could soak it in sweat. "I love those cupcakes, so I appreciate this gesture."

Jamie shifted her weight a bit, her right hand coming to rest on her hip. "I'm glad. But I've got something else for you, and I promise, it's much, much sweeter than what's in that bag." She paused, hit her with the bedroom eyes. "I'll have to give you that in private, though."

Alonzo wolf-whistled. "Oh shit, boss lady."

Peaches could hear similar reactions from everyone present in the shop, and she felt like she was ready to pass out. *I ain't no lightweight by any means, but . . . this a whole lotta woman, even for me.* She rolled her eyes at the buzz traveling through the shop but returned her full focus to Jamie. "So . . . what you said Friday night . . ."

"I remember everything. And I meant every word." She took another step, closing the distance between them. "If I'd gotten to see you yesterday, I would have told you then."

With Jamie's tits just inches away from her lips, Peaches swallowed again. "Yes, ma'am."

Jamie felt her lips stretch as her smile widened. "I'm glad you understand me now. And now that we've gotten that out the way, I've got a proposition for you."

Peaches swiped the back of her hand over her forehead. "When you come at me like that, I'm likely to agree to just about anything you ask, baby."

"Good." She sucked in her lower lip. "I'll be taking a little road trip this weekend. I'll be leaving Austin Friday, and I'd hate to have to travel alone."

Peaches leaned her upper body forward, the motion slight and barely perceptible. "Where you headed?"

"Houston and San Antonio." Jamie fluttered her lashes just a bit, even though she could sense she was about to get her way. "I'll be taking tours of two college campuses."

Peaches appeared thoughtful for a moment. "Sounds . . . interesting."

"I'm glad you think so. Because if you agree to come with me on this road trip, by the time this weekend is out, you'll be absolutely, unequivocally convinced about my feelings for you. Let's just say . . . I can show you better than I can tell you." She maintained visual focus to let Peaches know she had her full attention. Yet she didn't need to look around to know that every eye in the barbershop was on the two of them, and every ear tuned to the frequency of their conversation.

Peaches closed her eyes for a moment, mouthing a single word that escaped her mouth on an exhalation. "Fuck."

It's nice to see the calm exterior cracking just a little bit. "Is that an offer, or just a reaction to what I said?" Jamie asked.

Peaches opened her eyes, both hands coming to rest on the back of her barber's chair, and met Jamie's gaze with a smile. "I'm certainly not gonna back down from such a strong, public challenge. You want a road-trip buddy? You got one."

Jamie couldn't stop the grin from spreading across her face. "Excellent. I'll text you all the details and logistics."

Peaches nodded. "I'll look out for it."

"I don't want to hold you up—I know you have other clients coming in." Jamie tucked the phone away again. "But I appreciate you hearing me out. Have a good day, Peaches."

"Oh, I will." Peaches' tongue swept over her lower lip.

Jamie strolled away, knowing Peaches' eyes were on her ass, just as she'd intended them to be when she'd chosen this outfit. As she stepped out of the barbershop and back into the spring sunshine, the air was thick with moisture and fragrant with the blooming of various trees and flowers.

She exhaled.

Before that breath could escape fully, Taylor came careening out the door behind her.

Hearing the bell, Jamie sidestepped to avoid a collision. "Taylor, what are you—"

"GURL!" Taylor exclaimed, arms in the air, wide eyed, a broad grin on their face. "I can't believe you just did that! In front of everybody!"

Jamie giggled. "I had to make myself plain. Besides, I told you I was gonna make sure Peaches had no choice but to take me seriously."

"I know. But damn, I ain't know you was gonna do all this." Taylor's arms dropped to their sides, and they shook their head, blowing out a breath. "We ain't used to this type of excitement around the barbershop. Other than the occasional political or sports discussion that goes off the rails, we keep it pretty chill around here."

"I see." Jamie often conversed with Taylor about work, but this was the first time she'd heard the vibe described that way. "I've been in enough barbershops to know how they talk, so I'm glad the atmosphere is more peaceful here."

"They gonna be talking about this for weeks," Taylor insisted. "I know because I'mma keep bringing it up. Go, best friend!"

Laughing, Jamie high-fived her bestie.

A few clients passed them on the sidewalk to enter the barbershop, and Taylor turned. "Let me get back to work. Thanks for the excitement, girl."

"You're welcome. I'm just glad I got my point across."

"That, you did." Taylor waved before prancing back into the barbershop.

Shaking her head at her friend's silliness, Jamie returned to her car and got in. On the drive back to her apartment in Heritage Hills, she turned over the details of the last hour in her mind. She'd gotten up, showered, eaten, and dressed, all the while thinking about what she intended to do.

Lucky for me, everything went pretty much as I planned it. I can't really tell if I caught Peaches off guard, because she looked pretty calm throughout. Sure, Peaches had been sweating a little, but so had she. It was an unseasonably warm, humid day. Beyond that, the interior of the barbershop was also stuffy, and she'd noticed sweat beading on just about every brow in the place.

I was worried I might be coming on too strong, but she seemed to take it in stride. She remembered the moment she'd entered the shop. Seeing Peaches, standing in the back, smiling and talking with the other barbers, had given her pause. Peaches was Fine, with a capital *F*. Her fresh-pressed work clothes, the fashionable shoes, the gold watch glittering on her wrist . . . those things only added to the visual appeal.

What she really liked about Peaches, though, was her build. She wasn't particularly tall, but height wasn't a box Jamie needed to check for someone to be attractive. Peaches was solid, a big body. Broad shoulders, strong-looking arms, and that little extra bit of weight that let you know she could hold her ground in a windstorm without getting blown over. It was obvious she worked out, but she did it in a way that didn't make her too bulky. Something about that body type, athletic but not too muscular, solid but not overwhelming . . . it just melted Jamie like butter in a hot skillet.

I wanna know what it feels like to be in those arms . . . I wanna know the power in those hips. She licked her lips. *I bet she can blow my back right the fuck out. I just need to confirm it . . .*

The forty-minute drive from Fresh Cutz back to her apartment went quickly, dominated by her thoughts of Peaches, and what her next steps would be now that she'd locked her crush into a road trip. *I'd better make sure everything is in place.*

Once she'd gotten inside her apartment, she went to the fridge for her water bottle. She took a swig, then sat down on her couch and placed the legal pad where she'd been keeping notes related to both colleges on her coffee table. And while she knew she should focus on the task at hand, her mind kept drifting back to the fine-as-fuck barber.

There's so much I want to know about Peaches. What's her favorite color? What's her family like . . . has she had any serious relationships? Hell, what are her moon and rising signs? I know she's a Leo, but that's it. She thought back to Peaches' rather raucous party last year, and how much fun it had been. She grabbed her phone and sent Peaches a quick text, asking the time and location of her birth so she could get a more comprehensive astrological view of her.

Rather than stare at the phone waiting for a reply, she put the device to use, flipping pages until she located the number for student affairs at UT San Antonio. After going through a few automated menus and a very helpful receptionist, she was finally routed to the person who could confirm the date and time of her campus tour.

While she was talking to the university employee, her phone buzzed against her ear, indicating an incoming text. She held off on checking it until she'd completed her call. She looked at the screen and read Peaches' reply. With the information in hand, she plugged it into her favorite astrology website.

Oh, she's an Aries moon with a Cancer rising? Well, that explains why she couldn't back down from my challenge. Jamie giggled to herself. She wanted to dig deeper into Peaches' full chart, analyze all her houses and planets. Maybe they could discuss those little tidbits on their road trip. Putting that thought aside, she located the phone number for her contact at Texas Southern and made another confirmation call.

The designated meeting spot for the Texas Southern tour had been changed, so she jotted down the details of the new location on her legal pad as she ended the call. She pulled up the GPS function on her phone, flipped to a new page, and planned a tentative route for the trip.

Friday: UT San Antonio
90 minutes' drive
Tour Time: 4PM
Contact: Karla
Location: UTSA Student Union Building, UTSA Circle
Saturday: Texas Southern
3.5 hour drive
Tour Time: 3PM (leave San Antonio by 11AM)
Contact: Tashaun
Location: Sterling Student Life Center

Satisfied that she'd gotten all the important details down, she closed the pad, then tucked it and her ink pen into the brown portfolio she kept them in. Then she fired off a quick text to Peaches, filling her in on the itinerary. Checking the time, she headed for the kitchen to grab a quick sandwich before leaving to do her evening shift at the nail shop.

Tuesdays weren't terribly busy at Stellar Nails, at least most of the time. Still, business usually picked up later in the day as people started to get off work, so she often worked a short four-to-nine shift to help with coverage.

Seated at her station, she took a few moments to arrange all her tools to her liking. She was expecting five clients today, back to back. That meant her shift was fully booked . . . as long as all her clients kept their appointments. Since they were all regulars, she had no expectation of anyone flaking on her at the last minute.

"I'm fully booked with fill-ins," Kendra said, her tone upbeat. "What about you?"

"One mani with gel polish, and four acrylic full sets." Jamie slid open the center drawer on her table, moving things around until she found the vinyl roll containing her freshly sanitized metal implements. "Should be an interesting shift."

"Right. I'm hoping someone will let me try out that new glow-in-the-dark glitter polish on them."

Jamie nodded, knowing the product she was talking about. "I've used it once. It does have pretty good color payoff. Smells awful, though." The polish gave off a strong chemical odor, one she could still clearly recall more than a week after using it on a client.

"Really? What did it smell like?"

"It's hard to describe, but it's kinda metallic or industrial." The odor had made her curious about what was in the stuff, so she'd checked the label, which had revealed little to nothing. "The label should give more useful information. People are putting this stuff on their bodies, and they should know what's in it."

Kendra shook her head. "Girl, you be thinking way too hard about that kind of stuff."

"Maybe." Still, she couldn't shake those kinds of thoughts. She felt like she was at a crossroads in her career. She'd been doing nails for more than a decade now, and while she loved the creative aspect, her perception of the work was changing.

She truly enjoyed sculpting and embellishing a unique look for each client, using her artistic skill to create a visual interpretation of a concept and, at times, the client's personality. Yet there were things she wanted to change. The long days trapped in a mask that barely filtered out the acrylic dusk particles, the way her hands and wrists ached from overuse, how her own nails sometimes went ragged and neglected as she focused on those of her clients. Something had to give, because passion was quickly being replaced by frustration. And having London steal her idea, essentially rendering her exit plan from the manicure table moot, had only made the feeling worse.

She looked up with a smile as her first client of the afternoon took a seat at the table. "Hey, Kathleen." She threw up her hand to stop the older woman from setting her purse on the floor. "Hold on, honey. Put your purse on the hook."

Kathleen laughed as she course corrected. "Sorry, Jamie. I forget that every two weeks!"

"No worries, honey." It was hard to explain her culturally developed aversion to setting a purse on a floor, and she wasn't sure if Kathleen, a white woman of a certain age, had any frame of reference for it. Still, she did her damnedest every week to keep the sweet but oblivious older lady from dooming her financial future, even though it meant repeating herself.

She cared about her clients, and as she began the process of removing the old, cracked polish from Kathleen's fingernails, she thought about how her impact on their lives could be even greater if she moved to the technical side of the nail business.

As their nail tech, she could make their hands look pretty and raise their confidence. But as a chemist, she could still do that while also protecting their health and their consumer rights. From her extensive real-world experience, Jamie knew all the ways nail products could be improved upon.

And she planned on tackling as many of the problems as she could.

CHAPTER SEVEN

Wednesday evening, Peaches left the barbershop just after five. As she drove the familiar streets, she put in a call to Spencer Hart, her accountant. He'd been managing her business finances ever since Fresh Cutz had opened, and she trusted him to be brutally honest with her, no matter what.

"What's up, Peaches?" Spencer's familiar voice filled the cabin of the truck. "You just caught me. I'm about fifteen minutes from calling it quits for the day."

"I know you don't mind a quick call with one of your best clients, Spence," she teased.

"Of course not, honey." He chuckled. "So, to what do I owe the pleasure of this lil' chat?"

"I want you to look over the books and see how feasible you think it would be for me to open a second barbershop." She brought the truck to a halt at a red light.

"Oh, really? I haven't heard you mention that in a while. What brought this on?"

Now it was her turn to chuckle. "Let's just say my employees gave me a not-so-subtle nudge in that direction. Can you draw up two sample balance sheets for me? One that approximates costs in the Austin metro area, and one for the Houston area?"

"Sure thing." He paused. "Why Houston?"

"I've got a connection down there. A college classmate who works admin for a local Realtor."

"Okay, gotcha. Give me about a week to draw it up, and I'll bring it by your office. How does that sound to you?"

"Sounds great. Thanks, Spence."

"No problem."

Ending the call, she pulled into the parking lot of Byrd's Academy of Dance in Hyde Park, and she cut the engine of her truck. The parking lot was pretty full, but luckily she managed to grab one of the last parking spots that could accommodate the wide body of her truck.

Tonight was the night of her nieces' dance recital for their ballet classes. RJ was supposed to be here, but once again he was working late. Luckily, the mother of one of the girls' dance friends had stepped in to drop them off after school at the dance academy so they could prepare for their recital. Being the world's best auntie, Peaches had come straight here from the barbershop without even stopping at home to change. Her brother's work schedule allowed very few social outlets for the girls outside of school, and they really seemed to enjoy dancing, so she supported them any chance she got.

Using her key remote to lock the truck as she walked away from it, she headed for the double doors at the entrance of the one-story brick building. The lobby was brightly lit, and the walls, painted a shade of soft peach, were filled with photographs of various dance classes with their instructors. Many of the images featured the familiar face of Danielle Byrd, the owner of the school. From years of attending recitals here, and listening to the chatter of her nieces about the beloved Ms. Byrd, Peaches knew she was a world-class dancer and a master ballerina who had traveled with the famed Alvin Ailey American Dance Theater before founding the school.

The recital was due to start within five minutes, and very few people still remained in the lobby, making it easy for Peaches to cross the space and head for the short hallway that led to the small theater where performances were held. The inside of the theater was just as crowded as the parking lot indicated, and Peaches stood in the back, her eyes scanning for a seat. Spotting one open near the middle of the third row, and realizing that was probably as close as she could get to the stage, she strolled down the aisle and sidestepped her way to the seat, excusing herself as she went along.

The house lights were brought down a couple of minutes later, and Ms. Byrd herself walked out to the center of the stage from the wings, illuminated by a single spotlight. A petite Black woman in her early forties, she wore dancer's attire: a long-sleeved black leotard, a black circle skirt, black tights, and ballet flats. A black silk scarf was tied in a bow around her close-trimmed curls.

After a smattering of applause, she began to speak. "Welcome to our nest, dance fans. We are so excited to show you all the new ballet techniques we've been working on at every level of study. Tonight you will get to see four different performances, one from each of our different age categories of dancers. First will be the Ducklings, then our Mallards, then our Flamingos, and lastly, our Swans. Again, thank you so much for your support in joining us, and we hope you enjoy the show." Grasping the edges of her skirt, she gave a small curtsy, then disappeared offstage once again.

Peaches felt the grin tilting her lips as the first class, the Ducklings, meandered out onto the stage. They were wearing the cutest costumes, with leotards, leggings, slippers, and frilly tutus all in a soft shade of yellow. On their heads were headbands with dangly, star-topped antennae. Offstage, someone cued up the music for Tchaikovsky's "Waltz of the Flutes," and their little bodies began to move mostly in time. Peaches kept her eyes on Reagan, who was positioned just to the left of center on the stage. For the next ten minutes, she and everyone else in the auditorium were treated to perhaps the most adorable dance ever performed in public. It had been a long and unusually busy day at the barbershop, but by the time the little Ducklings teetered off the stage, Peaches felt her mood had improved tenfold.

During a brief pause in the show, the dance instructors came out to make a background change for the next class. Once they were finished, the Mallards came out onstage. Ella was in this group, dressed just like her fellow dancers in a mint-green ballet outfit with matching slippers. Each dancer in this class carried with her a small lace-trimmed parasol in a pastel shade, and Peaches stroked her chin as she wondered what their performance theme was. As soon as the music started and she heard the familiar strains of the old tune "Singing in the Rain," she understood the presence of the parasols. The Mallards danced in front of a projected image of falling rain and a cluster of papier-mâché trees and bushes. Ella played a starring role in this number, doing a small solo toward the middle of the song. When Ella began to dance by herself, Peaches began loudly clapping and hooting up until the moment her niece made eye contact with her. While twirling her parasol, Ella gave Peaches just the slightest glare, causing her to turn the enthusiasm down a notch.

The house lights came up for a brief ten-minute intermission then, and as people began to leave their seats and roam the aisles of the theater, Peaches remained in place, her mind wandering back to yesterday's pleasant yet shocking interruption of her workday. Of all the things she might have expected to happen on a sleepy Tuesday at the barbershop, having Jamie come in, dressed like some tall Nubian goddess, to proclaim her feelings for her in front of everyone present wasn't one of them. *Shawty got me. I was caught off guard in 4K.*

A few days earlier, she'd been wondering if Jamie's slightly tipsy declaration had any merit. That was no longer an issue, because Jamie had made herself crystal clear, in the most bold and public manner possible. Now she had a new problem. She'd agreed to Jamie's out-of-left-field request to go with her on a road trip this coming weekend. Honestly, she didn't know how she felt about the upcoming trip. She still had a lingering worry that if she started a romantic fling with Jamie, it would make things super weird among their friend group should things go sideways between them. Still, there was no way she could have turned her down, not in front of everybody who'd been watching and waiting for her to answer.

The house lights dimmed again, keeping her from going any deeper into her ruminations. When the stage was illuminated, the Mallards had been replaced onstage by the Flamingo class, clad in hot pink. While none of Peaches' nieces were in this group, she still enjoyed their performance, set to the tune of a vaguely recognizable early-aughts pop song.

Olivia's class, the Swans, was the last to come onstage. Dressed in black-and-white ballet costumes, each young girl had a pair of gossamer fabric wings attached to her back. As they took their positions onstage, crouching as they awaited their musical cue, Peaches sat forward in her seat in anticipation. *Oh, this is gonna be good.*

Deniece Williams' classic eighties song "Black Butterfly" began to play over the speaker system, and the young women began a beautifully choreographed routine. Peaches watched in amazement as Olivia glided across the stage, much like the butterfly described in the lyrics of the song. She'd been watching Olivia dance ever since she'd first begun at the age of four, and to see her growth from where she'd begun to where she was now was truly a proud moment for Peaches as an aunt.

After the recital ended to thunderous applause from the audience, Peaches took her place in the long line of parents, friends, and others awaiting their little dancers on the side of the stage. Once Reagan, Ella, and Olivia appeared at her side, she immediately launched into enthusiastic praise. "You girls are just amazing. I'm so, so proud of you."

"Thanks, Auntie Peaches," Ella said as the four of them walked up the aisle toward the exit. "I didn't see Dad in the audience. Did he have to work late again?"

She sighed. "Yes, your dad did have to work late again, yet again. But that's why you have the world's greatest auntie as backup."

Reagan, who was clutching Peaches' right hand, looked up at her with those sweet, precious, beaming puppy-dog eyes. "Auntie, can we have frozen yogurt? Please?"

"Now you know your dad doesn't like you to have frozen yogurt this late in the evening." Peaches could see the pout forming on her young niece's face as she paused for dramatic effect. "However, your dad's not here, and you girls did an amazing job onstage tonight, so of course you can have frozen yogurt."

The girls let out a brief cheer, and Peaches grinned with mischievous satisfaction as she loaded them into her truck and drove them a couple of blocks down the road to a local frozen yogurt joint. Within twenty minutes of leaving the dance school, the four of them were seated on a bench outside the small establishment, each of them holding a paper bowl loaded down with frozen yogurt and toppings.

It always get so quiet when Black folks are eating something good. Peaches let her mind wander as she enjoyed both the fruity frozen treat and the company of her young nieces. Eventually, though, her mind wandered back to the situation at hand with Jamie. She still didn't know what to do. Part of her wanted to back out, but the other part of her knew that if she did, she'd never live it down with the other barbers at the shop. Hmm. *Time to seek some wise counsel.* "Hey, girls. Auntie needs some advice."

"What's up, Auntie Peaches?" Ella posed the question around a mouthful of frozen yogurt.

"Okay, so yesterday at work, a really pretty girl came in and told me she liked me in front of everybody."

The girls immediately oohed in unison, eliciting a chuckle from Peaches.

"So, do you like her back?" That question came from Olivia.

She thought about how to phrase the answer to that one. "Technically, yes. I mean, we're already friends."

Olivia appeared confused. "Then what's the problem, Auntie?"

"Well, like I said, she told me in front of everybody that she likes me. And she made it very clear she meant as more than a friend."

"Oh. So you mean she wants you to be her sweetheart." Ella's tone was a bit teasing.

"Yes, that's definitely what she wants. As a matter of fact, she asked me to go on a road trip with her this weekend."

Reagan, who'd been quietly enjoying her gummy-worm-laden concoction this entire time, finally spoke. "You gonna go, Auntie?"

Peaches swallowed. "I kind of said I would . . . but now, I'm not so sure I should go."

Olivia began shaking her head slowly. "Auntie, if you promised her you would go, you should keep your promise."

"I know, I know. I'm just a little nervous about being with her all by myself, since we're usually together in a group. I just don't know how things are going to turn out."

"Come on, Auntie," Ella said. "I know you're not scared. You're always telling us to have courage and try new things."

Children have a very funny and inconvenient way of reminding you of things you forgot you said. "I know, Ella. But I think this is a little different."

"How is it different?" Olivia set her empty yogurt bowl beside her on the bench. "Remember when I told you I wanted to skip the Flamingo class and try out for the Swans? And you told me the only way I would know if I could do it was if I tried?"

Peaches crunched on a mouthful of yogurt and nuts. "Yeah, I remember saying that."

"A lot of people in the Mallards class with me said I couldn't do it. But I decided to listen to you, Auntie. And I'm glad I did, because now I'm the youngest Swan in the whole class. And I'm just as good as everybody else."

Yikes, I feel called out.

"Olivia is right, Auntie," Ella added. "You told her to try something that might have been hard or scary, and it went well. Now you gotta do the same thing."

"Yup," Reagan added sagely.

"Well, looks like I'm going on a road trip." Peaches chuckled, shaking her head. The girls made good sense, and she just couldn't argue with them, especially not since they'd taken her own advice and given it right back to her. "Thanks for your help, girls."

"No problem, Auntie," said Olivia. "Let us know when you get back if you got yourself a new sweetheart."

Laughing, Peaches stood and helped the girls clean up their mess before loading them in the truck and taking them home.

〜

When Jamie left the nail salon around nine Wednesday night, instead of driving home, she returned to Claudia's house in the Chestnut neighborhood near UT Austin. Claudia had texted her, asking her to come by after work and pick up some things she thought might be useful for her new life as a chemistry student.

Thankfully, by the time Jamie hit the Monarch Highway, the evening rush of people leaving their jobs in the city and heading to their homes in the suburbs had cooled off a bit. It took a little less than twenty minutes to reach Claudia's driveway.

As she eased her car into the empty spot next to Claudia's small SUV, her hostess appeared in the doorway, dressed in a sleeveless white tunic and a pair of fluid, wide-leg black pants. Offering a wave, she said, "Hey, girl, come on in. I've got lots of goodies for you."

Amused and slightly curious as to what exactly Claudia planned on giving her, Jamie got out of the car, then closed and locked it behind her as she headed for the front door.

The inside of Claudia's house smelled of floral and citrusy aromas, making Jamie curious as to what her friend had been doing before she came. "Have you been spraying something?"

"Yeah, I have," Claudia said with a laugh. "Lemon furniture polish. Mama always taught me to clean up before you have a visitor."

"Same, but my mama was more partial to Murphy Oil Soap. According to her, it works better than any of that 'fruity stuff,' and it'll clean just about anything."

Claudia chuckled. "I've never used that stuff, but my granny and my aunties swore by it. Maybe it's a generational thing." She appeared thoughtful for a second before waving her toward the couch. "Anyway, just sit on down. What I'm about to give you will make your life a whole lot easier once you start classes."

Jamie took a seat on the sofa and tossed one leg over the over, brushing some lingering acrylic dust off the front of the soft scrubs-like pants she'd worn to work.

Claudia walked to the coat closet in the hallway and returned shortly, pulling a large wheeled plastic crate behind her. Parking the crate next to the sofa, she gestured to its contents. "There you go, my friend. A treasure trove for the chemist in the making."

She leaned over, peering inside the full crate. On the top of the pile was a thick three-ring binder. She picked it up and read the block letters printed on the front aloud. "Cheat Sheets. What's in here?"

Claudia grinned. "I'm glad you asked, girl. What you have in your hands is all the foundational concepts of chemistry, distilled down to their most basic form—diagrammed, color coded, and laminated."

She opened the binder, and her eyes widened when she began to peruse the contents. "Wow. You weren't kidding." There was the periodic table of elements, a glossary of chemistry terms, and a page filled with numerical data, including the melting, boiling, and sublimation points of various substances. Much of the data was neatly handwritten, with important points underlined or highlighted. "Damn, Claudia. This is some hell of a resource."

"I know." Claudia's self-satisfied smile said it all. "That's how your girl maintained a 3.95 GPA all the way through undergrad. And now that you're about to embark on the journey of scientific enlightenment, it's only right that I pass it on to you."

Jamie nodded, setting the binder aside to go through the rest of the treasures. She lifted a medium-sized white file box, then opened the lid and peeked inside. "Is this a lab kit?"

"Yep. Fully stocked too. That damn thing set me back three hundred bones, so I held on to it." Claudia perched on the arm of the sofa as she rattled off the contents. "Let's see. There's a lab coat, two pairs of goggles, some beakers, stirrers, a Bunsen burner, graduated cylinders . . ."

"Wow. And there's still more stuff in here." She eyed the books on the bottom of the crate but didn't pick them up. "Textbooks?"

Claudia nodded. "Yeah. Those are all the ones I held on to from my core classes. Check with your profs to see what they use, but they might come in handy."

"I'll definitely take a look at them," Jamie promised. "I remember from community college how expensive textbooks are, and how the publishers make a 'new edition' every semester by updating one chapter, to force us to buy new ones."

"Girl, that saga continues to this day. It's a whole mess." Claudia shook her head. "Anyway, now you should have everything you need to get you started."

Jamie blinked back the tears forming in her eyes as she placed all the items carefully back into the crate. "I can't thank you enough for this, Claudia. This is an incredible gift, and your support means so, so much to me."

Claudia leaned closer, draping an arm around her shoulder. "I know your family is less than stellar, babes. But trust and believe, your squad is always here for you."

Jamie leaned into her embrace. "You're the best."

Claudia gave her a squeeze. "I've got one more thing for you."

She stared. "You can't be serious. You've already given me so much, and I don't think anything else will fit in this crate."

Laughing, she said, "No, not another physical thing. More of a heads-up."

"Okay, I'm listening."

"So, you know I've been working in the field for a few years now, since I graduated undergrad."

She nodded. "Yeah. You always say your job is amazing."

"It is, for the most part. Working at a place like Divine Skin is pretty cool, and I love knowing I'm helping develop the next level of antiaging skin care products." She paused. "It's a medium-sized company, so I don't feel the pinch of working for a mom and pop, or the facelessness that comes with working for a huge corporation."

"Right. So far, all I'm hearing is good things, but . . ." Jamie eyed her friend. "I feel you're about to tell me something that's not so great."

"Yeah. So most of the people at the company, from the CEO down to the people working in the laboratory with me, are white women." She paused, her lips stretching into a half smile, half cringe. "It's been . . . not great at times."

"Oh, snap." Jamie leaned in. "What happened?"

"There were a lot of rude comments, off-color jokes . . . you know, your typical microaggressive bullshit. As time went on, and they began to see me more as a colleague, things did improve."

"So, what do you think changed things for you?"

"Two things. One, they could clearly see that I knew my stuff. And two, I had a few come-to-Jesus meetings with some particularly bothersome individuals." She folded her arms over her chest. "Look, the industry doesn't have a lot of people who look like us, and that's across the board. When you hear calls for more Black women in STEM, trust me, it's because we're sorely needed. You've got to go in there, be professional and respectful, but still demand your respect, sis."

She took a minute to absorb what she'd heard and turn it over in her mind. "I gotta admit . . . hearing this is a little unsettling. Still, it only solidifies my decision to go back to school and become a chemist. Time to kick down some doors for the little Black girls coming behind us."

With a slow nod, Claudia said, "Yes, girl. That's what the fuck I'm talking about."

Jamie chuckled, then stifled a yawn. "Sheesh. I'm beat."

"Let me help you load this stuff into the car."

Outside, Jamie popped the trunk as Claudia put down the telescopic handle. Then the two of them worked together to lift the crate into the trunk. Once it was closed inside, Jamie gave her friend another tight hug. "Thanks again, girl."

"Listen, you're very welcome. And now I don't have to keep storing it all, so, two birds." She winked, then waved as she returned to the house.

A few minutes later, Jamie pulled out of the driveway, headed home with the bounty. She stopped off at the grocery store and bought a premade chicken Caesar salad and some black grapes for dinner, because she knew she didn't have the energy or the desire to cook.

She was headed across the grocery store parking lot, plastic shopping bag and keys in hand, when her phone started ringing. Grabbing it from her pocket as she approached her car, she answered it without checking the screen. "Hello?"

"Hey, Jamie."

She stopped dead, the plastic bag dangling from her wrist and the key extended toward the lock. The voice was immediately recognizable, since she'd been hearing it in her dreams for weeks now. "Peaches . . . hey there."

Peaches cleared her throat. "I hope I didn't catch you at a bad time."

"No, not at all." She looked around, remembering where she was and what she'd been doing. After using the key to unlock her door, she slid into the driver's seat, placing the bag with her dinner on the passenger seat. Closing herself in, she continued, "Just leaving from a quick store run. I'm . . . glad you called."

"I had to," she admitted. "I've been thinking about you."

Heat bloomed in her core and rose up her torso until it warmed her cheeks. "Funny. I've been thinking about you too. But since you called, why don't you tell me what's on your mind?" She stuck the keys in the ignition but didn't start the car.

"Mmm." The sound seemed to rumble up from low in Peaches' throat before traveling through the speaker. "First, I wanna say I was really flattered when you came into the shop the way you did yesterday. No woman has ever approached me so boldly."

"Sounds like I caught you off guard," she teased.

She chuckled. "You did . . . but I held my own. I just wanted you to know that I really enjoyed your approach."

"I'm glad. I could tell I would need to make a splash if I was going to get you to take me seriously."

"Oh, you definitely got me, baby. I know you meant what you said . . . you effectively removed any doubts I had about your interest." She paused. "Listen. I feel like we should make an effort to get to know each other a little better. You and I have never hung out alone, just the two of us."

She sucked on her bottom lip. "You're right, we haven't. Don't tell me you changed your mind about the trip. We're leaving in two days."

"No, no. I'm gonna go with you. After all, I did say yes."

"That's right. And I expect you to keep your word."

She laughed. "Geez. You sound like my niece."

"Huh?"

"Nothing. Anyway, I was gonna ask if you wanna go out to dinner tomorrow night. That way, we can meet up, chat a little bit. You know, find out some things about each other before we're trapped in a vehicle on the highway together."

She giggled. "You make a good point. We probably should hang out. Name the time and place, and I'll be there."

"Do you like Mexican food?"

"Sure."

"How about we meet at Fonda San Miguel, around seven thirty?"

"Sounds perfect." She smiled, knowing that if this were back in the day, she'd be lying across her bed, twirling a phone cord around her index finger. "I'll be there."

"All right, bet. I'll see you tomorrow night, baby girl."

Jamie's eyes rolled back in her head at the sound of the pet name coming out of Peaches' mouth. *It's not the first time I've been called that, but when she says it . . . holy fuck it's sexy.* "Good night, Peaches."

"Good night."

Disconnecting the call, she sat there in the parking lot, clutching her phone in her hand as she let out a teenage-girl squeal. Then, taking a deep breath to compose herself, she set her phone in the cup holder, started the engine, and drove herself home.

CHAPTER EIGHT

Standing in front of the mirror in the women's restroom inside Fonda San Miguel, Peaches looked at her reflection. She did a slight turn so she could see her outfit and appearance from several different angles. Wanting to match both the vibe of the restaurant and the vibe of the date, she'd chosen a casual yet upscale look: a long-sleeved solid-black tee; color-blocked slim-fit sweatpants in black, red, and white; black-on-red Fila Fazal sneakers; her favorite gold wristwatch with a diamond face; and a twenty-two-inch Cuban-link gold chain with a lion's-head pendant. She reached into her right pocket, grabbed the small bottle of cologne she'd brought with her, and gave her neck a final spritz. Looking good and smelling good always went hand in hand for her, and even though this thing with Jamie was very new, she wanted to make the best possible impression.

As she ran a hand over her curls, she noticed someone standing just to her right in her peripheral vision. Glancing at the person behind her in the mirror, she saw a petite, rather confused-looking woman with short curly brown hair and bright-red lips, her blue eyes wide. The woman stared at her for about two beats too long, and Peaches immediately knew why. Raising her hands, palms up, Peaches made a gesture as if cupping her breasts, all while meeting the woman's gaze in the mirror. The woman's mouth dropped open, and she darted out of the bathroom, the door swinging shut behind her. Shaking her head, Peaches tucked away her bottle of cologne and pushed her way out of the restroom back into the restaurant waiting area.

Peaches crossed the terra-cotta tile floor of the entryway, headed for the tall table in the center of the space. The table was currently unoccupied and, because of its positioning, provided the best view of the double doors at the entrance. Taking a seat on one of the polished wooden stools, she laid her phone on the colorful tiled surface of the table. Before she had fully settled into the leather cushion seat, her phone began to ring, the vibration rattling the device against the table. She picked it up and answered the call. "Hey, Aiko, what's up?"

"Hey, playa, just checking in with you. I guess you're getting ready for your trip by now, huh?"

"In a way," Peaches admitted. "I'm at Fonda San Miguel, waiting for Jamie."

"Oh, snap." Aiko chuckled. "So, whose idea was this little date?"

"Mine. I just thought it made sense for us to talk and get to know each other a bit better before we got on the road."

"That actually does make sense, especially after the way she ran up on you at work like that . . ." Aiko paused. "I guess you were right when you said she would come to you if she was really serious."

"Yeah, I guess I was. But who knew she'd come on so strong?" Peaches rested her elbow on the table, her chin in her hand. "I just wonder if she's going to keep that same energy this entire weekend."

"What's the matter, homie, worried you can't hang?" Aiko laughed. "After all these years fishing it, maybe it's time you take it."

"Hardy har-har." Peaches rolled her eyes but decided not to dwell on all the possible meanings behind that statement. "Get off my phone, bruh. She'll be here any minute."

"All right, I'll let you go. May the force be with you and whatnot."

"You're a mess. I'll talk to you later . . . bye." She disconnected the call and tucked the phone back into her pocket. Drumming her fingers on the surface of the table, she alternated between watching the door and observing the small crowd of people around her. The low sofas behind her had a few people sitting on them, and both patrons and staff moved through the area, headed to and from the dining room. She'd purposely chosen this time to meet here, knowing that it fell perfectly between the early-dinner and late-night cocktail rush.

The heavy wooden door swung open with a creak, and Peaches swiveled on the stool to look in that direction. Jamie strode in, wearing a royal-purple crop top with three-quarter-length sleeves, closely fitted dark denim flare-leg jeans that showed the curvy lines of her thick thighs and hips, and a pair of bejeweled purple ballet flats. Her long hair was back in its usual style, center part, dark shiny waves hanging down to her waist. Silver bangles jangled on both her wrists as she walked toward the table where Peaches sat.

She's so fine, she makes my eyes hurt. Peaches swallowed, doing her best not to drool. "Hey, Jamie. You look amazing."

Jamie offered a soft smile. "Thanks. I wasn't sure what to wear, so I kept it casual since that's kind of the vibe of the restaurant." She stood there, her gaze traveling up and down Peaches' body. "I like your 'fit too. Very stylish."

"I appreciate that." Peaches took a moment to enjoy the little stroke to her ego, then stood. "Do you mind sitting at the bar? Or do you want to ask what the wait is for a table?"

"Let's see what the hostess says." Jamie started walking toward the hostess stand.

Peaches followed, and then asked the uniformed hostess standing there, "What's the wait for a table for two?"

The hostess picked up the walkie-talkie clipped to her waist and spoke into it, inquiring with one of her coworkers about vacant tables. "Actually, I do have one open table for two right near the bar. Would that be okay?"

"That would be fine," Jamie answered.

The hostess grabbed two menus, then led them through the space and into the dining room before stopping at a small round table directly across the aisle from the bar. Setting the menus down on the table, she said, "Here you are. You two enjoy."

Peaches thanked the hostess, then pulled out a chair for Jamie to sit down.

Jamie eyed her as she lowered herself gracefully into the seat. "Well, this is refreshing."

She grinned. "Oh, I'm all about chivalry." Moving around to the other side of the table, she took her own seat across from her gorgeous companion. "So, how was your day today?"

"It was a little hectic, honestly," Jamie said, picking up her menu. "I had a hard time getting out of the nail salon, even though I already told my boss I was leaving early today so I can get ready for my trip. As soon as I wrapped up that last manicure at a quarter to seven, I was out the door. Luckily, I don't live that far from my job, so I had time to go home and change real quick before coming here."

Peaches looked at her, taking in her flawless, barely there makeup and the glossy pink tint of her lips. "If you rushed getting ready to come here, it doesn't show at all. You're absolutely stunning."

Jamie's gaze dropped, and she sucked her lower lip into her mouth ever so slightly. "I see you have good taste. I like that."

"I'm just getting started." Peaches could feel the heady sensation of budding desire rising inside her. This was where it began, with flirtatious words and lingering stares. And with a woman like Jamie, Peaches knew where it would end . . . multiple orgasms.

A waiter approached the table then, carrying a tray. Setting a glass of ice water in front of each of them, he asked, "Are you ladies ready to order, or do you need a few more moments to look at the menu?"

"I need a little bit more time," Jamie said.

"No worries." The waiter took the tray under his arm and left them.

Peaches perused the menu, trying to decide what she wanted to eat. Doing so while sitting across from Jamie proved to be more difficult than she had anticipated. The interior of the restaurant was filled with various delicious aromas: spicy jalapeño, savory grilled meats, and fresh citrus. Yet, even above all those smells, she could still detect the faint hint of roses, jasmine, and sandalwood rolling off Jamie's body. *Whatever perfume she wears has got my hormones doing flips. I can barely think straight.* She tried to train her mind to focus more on the menu and less on how long it had been since she'd enjoyed the soft curves of a woman's body.

"What do you think you'll have?" Jamie asked, glancing at her over the top of her menu.

Damp drawers . . . that's what I'll have. Peaches cleared her throat. "I don't know. It's been a while since I've been here, so I'm trying to refresh myself on the menu." It was true, she hadn't been here in a while, but it was Jamie's proximity that was making it hard for her to focus more than anything. *If I can't handle sitting across from her at a table in a restaurant, how the hell am I going to handle riding in a car with her?* Taking a deep breath, she did her best to mind the menu instead of her date.

Thankfully, by the time the waiter returned, both of them had settled on their meals. Jamie ordered the seasonal salad and the tortilla soup, and she requested Ancho Relleno San Miguel.

"Anything from the bar, ladies?" the waiter asked.

They both answered in unison. "Numero Uno Margarita." On the heels of that, they both stared at each other in stunned silence.

With a laugh, the waiter took each of their menus. "Okay, then. Two house special margaritas, coming up." Still laughing, he walked away.

"I see we have similar tastes in adult beverages," Peaches said, her tone mirthful. "Hopefully that bodes well for us taking this road trip without strangling each other."

"That reminds me," Jamie said. "I plugged your information into my astrological charting site."

She felt her brow furrow. "I'm not seeing the connection between the margarita and my sign."

"Not that. I mean, when you mentioned the road trip, it reminded me of why we're here. To get to know each other better before we go." She took a sip of her water. "So I figured your chart was a good place to start."

"I'm a Leo. What more is there to it than that?"

She laughed. "Oh, honey, that's just your sun sign—it goes way deeper than that. You're an August Leo, which isn't exactly the same as a July Leo. And since I already knew your sun sign, I knew there's no chance you would have turned me down when I came to you in the barbershop."

Confused, Peaches asked, "Why do you say that?"

"Leos are very sure of themselves, and they never back down from a challenge." Jamie placed her hands on the table, lacing her fingers together. "Now, when you gave me your other information, I found out all your astrological business. But the main thing is I know you're an Aries moon and a Cancer rising . . . those two with your sun sign make up what we refer to as your 'big three.'"

"So that's why you asked for my birth time and place." Staring at Jamie's perfectly french-manicured nails, Peaches wondered exactly what would be revealed about her based on her "full chart." She said, "Okay, then, your turn. What's your sign?"

"I'm a Capricorn sun—my birthday is January seventh."

"I'll admit, I don't know a whole lot about astrology. But I feel like I'm going to learn some new things about that this weekend." Peaches leaned back in her chair, maintaining eye contact with Jamie. "I want to know some other stuff about you. Let's start with some basics: favorite color, favorite food, favorite movie."

"Let's see: yellow, the baby back ribs from Stubb's Bar-B-Q, and *Clue*."

Peaches felt her brow hitch with surprise. "*Clue*? You mean that wacky eighties movie based on the board game, with Tim Curry?"

She nodded, grinned. "Yes it's goofy, and silly, and the plot is all over the place. It even has all those alternate endings to throw you off. I think it's one of his better performances and is super underrated. I love that movie—it's definitely a comfort watch." She tilted her head slightly to the right and said, "Okay, same questions."

"Easy. Orange, the chicharrones at Joe's Bakery, and *Eve's Bayou*."

She appeared impressed. "*Eve's Bayou*. That's a classic."

"Yeah. I saw it when I was like ten or eleven. It's really good storytelling, and both Jurnee Smollett and Lynn Whitfield gave fantastic performances." She could still clearly remember the first time she'd seen it, and how she'd thought about it for days afterward. "It's definitely not in the 'comfort watch' category, but it's a really good movie."

"I think having a favorite movie like that shows that you have some depth to you."

The waiter returned, carrying the tray laden with their food. After he'd set the plates on the table, along with their drinks, silverware, and napkins, he left them to enjoy their meals.

Jamie spooned up some of her tortilla soup and groaned with pleasure. "The food is always so good here. And so nicely presented."

While Peaches knew that groan had been initiated by the spicy soup hitting Jamie's taste buds, she couldn't help being enticed. Turning her focus to her own plate, Peaches used her knife and fork to cut a piece of her ancho. The first bite was loaded with seasoned chicken, almonds, and capers, accentuated by the creamy cilantro sauce.

They ate in silence for a few moments before Jamie spoke again. "Listen, I know my approach was a little unorthodox. But I really do like you, and I'm curious to see what might happen between us if we become more than friends. I'm glad you agreed to go on this trip with me."

Peaches felt warmth spreading through her chest and a smile tilting her lips. "Even if it was my Leo nature that made me say yes, I'm glad I did too. I'm willing to give this thing a shot." She raised her margarita glass in salute. "Here's to whatever crazy-ass adventure lies ahead for us."

"Cheers." Jamie lifted her own glass and tapped it against Peaches'.

Once they'd finished their meal, Jamie walked with Peaches to the parking lot in front of the building. As Jamie trailed behind Peaches, their fingertips cupping, she realized she wasn't ready to go home yet.

Giving Peaches' hand a small tug as they stood on the asphalt in the shadowy parking lot, she said softly, "I don't want this to be over yet."

Peaches smiled. "Wanna come sit in my truck and keep talking?"

Nodding, she let herself be guided to the pickup truck, where Peaches had backed into a parking space so that it faced Fonda San Miguel's ornate entrance. The huge vehicle, an extended-cab model in a shade of rich blue, barely fit between the lines.

Peaches opened the passenger-side door and gestured her in, then closed the door behind her. Once she was in place in the driver's seat, she asked, "So, Jamie, how do you like my ride?"

"This thing is massive." She settled into the leather seat, marveling at the amount of space she had to stretch out. "Is it as terrible on gas as I think it is?"

Peaches laughed. "It's not great, but it's not too bad either. It gets like seventeen city, twenty-four highway."

She cringed. "Meanwhile, my little midsize sedan gets like twenty-two, twenty-eight." She paused. "I was planning on driving us, but will you be comfortable riding in a car? It definitely doesn't have this kind of interior space."

Peaches scratched her chin. "Honestly, I'd probably feel cramped."

"What do you want to do, then? We're leaving tomorrow morning, and renting a car seems like too much hassle at this point." Jamie stared straight ahead, watching as a young family exited the restaurant, the parents shepherding their small children across the lot to the family minivan.

"I don't mind driving, if it's cool with you."

"Yeah, okay. I guess all this leg and head room will come in handy while we're going down the highway." She pulled out her phone and typed out a message. "I just sent you my address."

"Got it," Peaches said as her own device vibrated. Looking Jamie's way, she asked, "I'm assuming you already have rooms reserved in the two cities?"

Jamie nodded. "Yeah. I did that a couple of weeks ago." She paused, thinking about the type of rooms she'd booked, both in San Antonio and in Houston. "I . . . uh . . . booked king rooms at both hotels." When she'd initially planned the trip, she expected to be traveling alone. And even after she'd gotten it in her head to ask Peaches to accompany her, she hadn't made any changes.

Was that forgetfulness? Or wishful thinking?

Silence fell between them for a moment.

"I think I'm okay with that," Peaches said. "After all, king-sized beds are pretty big, so personal space shouldn't be an issue. Right?"

"Right." Jamie couldn't contain the short burst of nervous laughter that erupted from her throat. *Why am I acting like this? I've never had a problem going after what I want. And I want Peaches. BADLY.*

"I'm gonna let you take the lead on . . . you know, whatever happens in the room." Peaches tilted her head, stroking the V between her thumb and forefinger over her chin. "I can sense that's what you're used to, and I'm okay with that."

Jamie nodded, taking note of the earnest expression Peaches wore. "I appreciate that." Her nerves were getting the better of her, for whatever reason, so she changed the subject. "What time are you gonna pick me up? Since you're driving now?"

"I looked at the little itinerary you sent me. I'm not exactly a morning person—that's why I'm rarely at the barbershop before ten—but I don't think we'll need to pull out too early."

"Right." Jamie thought about the schedule she'd jotted down on the legal pad. "I think we should be good as long as we leave by eleven. That way, if we run into traffic or any other delays, we should still get there on time."

"Sounds good. That gives us time to stop off for gas or snacks or whatever too." Peaches smiled in her direction.

As she gazed into Peaches' eyes, Jamie couldn't help thinking about all the things the word "whatever" could entail. She turned her head a bit, looking into the truck's expansive back seat, then quickly turned around again.

"It reclines," Peaches announced, as if she could read Jamie's mind. "I'm not saying . . . I'm just, you know, saying."

Jamie swallowed. "Useful information." Taking a deep breath, she fought the dizzying effects of Peaches' cologne. "It's getting late. I probably should go home, so I can make sure I have everything together for the trip."

"Yeah, me too. Gimme a minute, I'll let you out." Peaches opened her door and climbed out of the truck.

Jamie smiled as she watched her walk around the front of the truck. Soon, Peaches appeared at the passenger-side door and opened it. Gesturing dramatically toward the darkness, she said, "You may step down, milady."

Jamie laughed as she stepped onto the running board. The worn soles of her ballet flats betrayed her, and she tilted forward, crashing into Peaches.

Peaches' arms wrapped around her waist, steadying her. "Damn, baby. You good?"

She couldn't help noticing how solid Peaches' frame felt against her own, or how strong her arms felt. *Oh shit.* She buried her face in Peaches' shoulder. "I guess the margarita hit," she said, hoping her light chuckle would conceal her embarrassment.

Peaches maintained her hold on Jamie's waist as she helped her back to solid ground. "Can you drive home?"

"Absolutely." She straightened and looked into Peaches' eyes. Immediately, she knew she'd made a mistake. Licking her lips, she said softly, "The only thing I'm drunk on right now is you." The words flew out of her mouth before she had a chance to stop them.

Peaches' expression changed then, her brown eyes taking on a dark, sexy gleam. "Shawty, if you keep tempting me like this, there will be trouble."

"Sometimes I like trouble," she teased. "What kind are you offering?"

Peaches reached out and dragged the tip of her index finger along Jamie's jawline at an achingly slow pace as she spoke. "The kind where you can't get out of bed . . . the kind where your legs are too weak to carry you . . . the kind that will make you beg . . ."

Jamie growled, wrapping her hands around the back of Peaches' head and drawing her face closer. Closing her eyes, she pressed her lips against Peaches'.

Peaches responded by holding her tighter, forcing their bodies even closer together. Jamie's tongue darted out, and Peaches opened her mouth, allowing their tongues to twirl and stroke against each other in a passionate dance.

By the time Jamie eased away, she felt hot and breathless. Sweeping her tongue over her kiss-swollen lips, she straightened up. "You're right. Let me carry my ass home."

Peaches grinned. "I'll walk you to your car."

They walked over a few spaces to where Jamie's sedan sat. "I'll see you in the morning, Peaches." She unlocked her door.

"Eleven o'clock sharp. I'll be there, baby." Peaches moved past her to open the driver's-side door.

"You're gonna have me spoiled," Jamie said as she slipped behind the wheel.

"That's the plan." With a wink, Peaches closed her inside the car and walked back to her truck.

Jamie started the engine of her car, taking several more deep breaths to steady herself before pulling out of the parking space. As she sat at the road, looking both ways before entering traffic, she heard the rumble of Peaches' engine.

After leaving the parking lot, she turned left onto North Loop, with Peaches following behind her at first. But as she crossed the intersection at Woodrow Avenue, she continued straight as Peaches made a left turn.

The drive home was a short one, under ten minutes, and that made Jamie appreciate Peaches' choice of restaurant even more. Walking up the stairs to her apartment, she could still feel the tingle on her lips, left behind by the kiss she'd shared with Peaches. *Who knows if she can really make me weak in the knees? All I know is I wanna find out the hard way.*

She entered the apartment and locked herself in before kicking off her shoes and tossing them in the basket by her front door. Heading straight for the bedroom, she stripped off her clothes and took a hot shower, her mind drifting off into fantasy as she stood beneath the steamy water.

This time tomorrow night, I could be in the shower with Peaches . . .

After her shower, she threw on a pair of cotton pajama pants and a cami, then dragged her suitcase out of the closet.

She was tossing in clothes and toiletries when her phone went off, indicating someone texting her.

She grabbed the phone off the bed and looked at the screen, hoping it was Peaches. She cringed when she saw the text was from her younger brother, Sean.

Hey, J Bird, can you watch Levi this weekend? Bethany's doing a livestream from a convention and wants me to come with her.

She considered not responding but knew he'd just keep pestering her until she did. First, I hate that nickname. Second, no I can't watch Levi. She sent the text and went back to her packing.

A few minutes later, the phone buzzed again. Rolling her eyes, she read the new message. Aw, come on sis. You sure you can't watch your nephew?

She fired off a response. No way Sean. I told you I have my college tours this weekend, and it's rude of you to ask on such short notice anyway.

You were serious about that? I thought you were joking when you said you wanted to go back to school.

She wanted to scream. *Just like everyone else in my family, with the possible exception of baby Levi, he either ignores everything I say or doesn't take it seriously.* Instead of shouting her anger aloud, she sent her most succinct, and final reply. Good night, Sean.

Putting the phone on Do Not Disturb so she wouldn't be aware of any further messages her annoying little brother might send, she turned her focus back to making sure she had everything she needed for this trip.

If everything goes the way I want, when I come back to Austin, I'll have a new temporary student ID card . . . and a new girlfriend.

CHAPTER NINE

Peaches found herself walking from room to room in her town house Friday morning as she endeavored to ensure she had packed everything she needed for her weekend away. After the third lap, she finally gave up and zipped up her duffel bag. *Well, I packed everything I could think to pack, so hopefully I'm good.*

Once she'd placed her duffel bag and the smaller bag holding her toiletries by the door, she went to the kitchen to fix herself a quick breakfast. After finishing a smoothie and a bowl of oatmeal, she washed up her dishes, then grabbed her keys and headed out the front door with her bags.

She pulled up in front of Jamie's apartment building at about a quarter till eleven. There were no empty spaces available that could accommodate the size of her truck, so she went down to the end of the lane and took up the last two parking spaces there. After turning off the engine, she got out of her truck, walked down the sidewalk, and headed up the stairs until she reached Jamie's door. There she raised her hand and knocked.

Jamie opened the door a few moments later and greeted her with a smile. "Good morning. You're early."

"Yup. Are you ready, or do you need a little bit more time?"

"No, I'm ready. But you didn't have to come all the way up here—you could've just honked your horn."

"Never that. Besides, I wanted to see if maybe you needed help with your bags."

Jamie's smile widened, and Peaches felt her heart flutter inside her chest like a canary in a cage.

"Well, since you're up here, come on in. Just give me a second to wheel my suitcases up here from my bedroom."

Peaches stepped inside the apartment as Jamie headed down the hallway toward the back. Looking around, she took in the sight of Jamie's decidedly feminine decor. A cozy-looking love seat centered the room, flanked by two matching armchairs. A low coffee table, fashioned of some dark, polished wood, sat directly in front of the love seat. The rug beneath the table, as well as all the furniture, were in varying, coordinating shades of soft mauve and pink.

Jamie returned then, dragging two wheeled suitcases behind her. "Okay, here's all my stuff."

"You do know we're just going for a weekend, right?" Peaches joked.

"Yes, I know. And these are all my essentials to get me through from now until when we come back Sunday."

Peaches walked toward her and grabbed the handle of the larger suitcase. "You ready now?"

"Let's go." Jamie wheeled the smaller suitcase toward the front of her apartment, pulled the door open, and slid her luggage out onto the concrete porch.

Peaches followed her out, and after Jamie used her key to lock the door, they both made their way downstairs to her truck.

Jamie was dressed casually today in a yellow velour pantsuit with white trim, along with a pair of all-white sneakers. The outfit wasn't tight by any means, but there was no hiding the slight jiggle of her ass while she walked down the steps in front of Peaches.

At the truck, Peaches opened the rear passenger door and slid both suitcases inside the cab. Luggage loaded, she opened the front passenger door and held out her hand to help Jamie up onto the running board and into the cab.

Climbing into the driver's seat, Peaches asked, "Have you eaten today?"

Jamie nodded. "Yeah, I had a bowl of cereal and a granola bar earlier, so I think I'm good for a little while. We can just go ahead and get on the highway if you want."

"Cool." Peaches slowly backed out of the parking spaces, then drove out of the complex and back onto the main road.

Once they'd left downtown, Peaches said, "I never got to ask you before, but is there a certain kind of music you like, maybe a favorite artist?"

"My taste is pretty eclectic. I like a little bit of everything: R&B, hip-hop, rap, jazz."

"How do you feel about nineties R&B, specifically?"

"It's only the best era of R&B. I mean, you can't go wrong with anything from the decade, really."

"Then I think I know just what to start with for our road-trip playlist." At the next stoplight, she used her truck's in-dash entertainment system to choose what she thought would be the perfect selection. A few moments later the familiar opening strains of Tevin Campbell's 1993 hit "Can We Talk" filled the cabin. And a few moments after that, as they merged onto the highway heading south toward San Antonio, they were both scream-singing along to the familiar lyrics.

For the next forty-five minutes, it was hit after hit from that glorious decade of R&B music, and the two of them spent that entire time singing along to their favorite songs of the era. When the playlist finally ended, Jamie said, "Wow. Your taste in music is just as good as your taste in margaritas."

Peaches laughed. "Thanks a lot. Seems like we have a lot more in common than I initially thought."

"It's like I said before, you can't go wrong with nineties R&B. There's just something magical about it. It's like the feeling you get from a nineties R&B song is what real love is supposed to feel like—you know what I mean?"

"Yes . . . you're making perfect sense." Peaches glanced away before directing her eyes back to the road. "Well, now that we're squarely on our way and you're my captive audience, it's time to pick your brain some more. So, tell me about your first celebrity crush."

Jamie laughed. "We're starting out with the heavy-hitting questions, I see."

"Hey, journalism was my second choice for a major in college before I decided on business."

"Well, it shows. Let's see . . . I must have been about nine or ten when I saw the first *Cheetah Girls* movie. I had a massive embarrassing crush on Raven-Symoné."

"Come on now, it couldn't have been that bad."

"Oh yes, it was. My room was plastered with Cheetah Girls posters, I had Cheetah Girls T-shirts, hoodies, you name it. Whatever I could find with Raven's face on it, I had to have it. My dad really didn't think anything of it—after all, I was the target audience for the movies. I don't think my mom wanted to read too much into it as to why I was so interested in the Cheetah Girls, and particularly in Raven . . . but I think she could tell something was a little off. Isn't it funny how Raven turned out to be one of us? Back then we had no idea she was part of the rainbow coalition."

Peaches chuckled. "Okay, my turn. My celebrity crush was Meagan Good. Lucky for me she was in every single movie ever made about Black people between the late nineties and the late 2010s. I mean, sis was working hard and very much in her bag, because every time you went to the theater or turned on the TV, if it was Black people in the production, you could count on Meagan Good at being among them."

Jamie laughed, hard. "Oh, snap, you're right. I can't think of any movie from the era that she wasn't in."

"That's because there aren't any." Peaches laughed along with her. "No matter what the movie was about—no budget, low budget, million-dollar budget—there was Meagan. I bet she could retire from working anytime she wants."

Peals of laughter erupted from Jamie's lips, and about the time Peaches thought she was over it, she started laughing again too.

After they'd both finally recovered from their amusement, Peaches wiped her eyes. "Okay, now it's your turn—you can ask me something."

"All right, bet. Tell me about your first serious relationship."

"Okay, that would be Tisha, my girlfriend in my junior and senior year of high school. Me and her were thick as thieves—we did everything together. We were both kind of masculine presenting, and I think we bonded over that, and after we were friends for a little while, the connection just sort of became deeper." She still had some fun memories of those days, when unsupervised video game marathons in her parents' basement had morphed into make-out sessions, which had in turn morphed into hormone-fueled sex on the old plaid sofa.

"Have you dated other masculine women?"

Peaches shook her head. "Nah. Tisha and I had a lot of fun, but as time passed, I realized we had way too much in common. You need a little bit of contrast between you and your partner for things to be successful long term, I think."

A few minutes passed in silence between them, and Peaches kept her focus on the road while wondering what Jamie might be thinking about. Finally, curiosity got the better of her, and she spoke up. "I hope you're not offended by this question, but have you ever dated men?"

"I'm not offended. And no, I've never dated men. I knew from a pretty young age that I was a lesbian, even though I didn't know the term. It was pretty clear to me that I liked girls, and couldn't have cared less about boys or whatever the hell they had going on."

"Oh, so you're a gold star just like me, then."

"Is that what that means? I've heard people say it before but had no idea what they were talking about." Jamie shook her head. "I don't think I like that term, now that I know its definition. Seems like it's just a way to stratify and divide people in the LGBT community, and I can't see how that's helpful."

"I agree with you there . . . sorry I said it. It's not a term I use often, but I won't use it anymore."

"Thanks. I guess I should tell you about my first serious relationship, then. It was a girl I dated during my first year of community college—her name was Raquel. I guess you could call her a stud. She was very intense and very masculine in the way she presented. We had some good times coming, but ultimately I couldn't deal with her jealousy. She assumed I was sleeping with any woman I made friends with, and eventually I just got tired of it."

Peaches shifted in her seat. "So you haven't been in any relationship you consider serious since college?"

"No, not really." Jamie leaned forward, riffling around in her purse until she produced a bottle of water. "I guess after that experience, I was kind of soured on relationships for a while. So I just threw myself into work."

I guess I can't blame her for taking some time away from the dating life so she could protect her heart. "All right, enough about that stuff. Tell me a little bit about your family."

Jamie sighed. "I can't say that's any more pleasant than talking about my love life, but here goes. I'm the only girl in my family and the middle child. I have an older brother, Shelby, and a younger brother, Sean. My mom and dad have been married since forever, Shelby's a serial monogamist, and Sean has a wife named Bethany and a baby . . . that's my nephew, Levi—he's almost two."

"That was a very thorough yet succinct description of your family situation," Peaches said with a laugh. "It certainly makes mine seem a lot less complicated. I'm the oldest of two kids. I have a little brother named RJ—that's Rufus Junior—and my dad, Rufus. My mom, Ann-Marie, passed away two years ago. RJ's divorced and has three daughters—my nieces Olivia, Ella, and Reagan—and they are some of my favorite people in the whole world."

"Yeah . . . I remember coming to Ms. Ann-Marie's funeral," Jamie said. "I hope I didn't upset you by bringing that up. I know y'all were close."

She nodded, that familiar twinge of pain squeezing her heart. "Yes, we were. She was actually one of the youngest Black hairdressers ever in the history of Austin to own her own beauty salon. She lived an amazing, inspiring life, and I miss her every single day."

"Well, from what I can tell, your barbershop is thriving. I'm sure she'd be very proud of you; you're creating an amazing legacy for her."

"Thank you, that's very kind of you to say." Peaches could feel some of the fog of sadness lifting off her in the aftermath of Jamie's words. *Gorgeous* and *caring? I definitely made the right decision when I said yes to this road trip.*

"You're welcome. We're getting pretty close to the city now. Let me hold your phone so I can put the hotel address into your GPS."

"You can just grab it out of my hip pocket."

Jamie reached into her pocket and, to Peaches' mind, took an extra-long time to get the phone out. Once she had it in hand, she swiped the screen and opened up the navigation. "You don't have a password on your phone?" she asked, her tone surprised.

"Nope. I already have too many passwords to remember, and I'd most likely end up locking myself out of my own damn phone."

Jamie chuckled as she entered the address into the GPS app. Shortly thereafter, they exited the highway by the off ramp, headed for the hotel.

Jamie checked the time on her phone as Peaches pulled her truck into the parking lot of the hotel. "Oh shoot, we're early. It's only one . . . check-in time isn't until three."

"Okay then," Peaches said. "We passed a burger joint just down the road on the way here—are you hungry? Do you wanna grab something to eat?"

She thought about her light breakfast, which was long since gone. "Yeah, I should probably eat something, so I'll be alert and focused during the tour."

Peaches backed out of the parking space, driving them a short distance down the road to an In-N-Out Burger. Soon, they were sitting at a table in the back with burgers, fries, and shakes. The sun streamed through the window, warming Jamie's skin as she absently swirled her straw around in her strawberry shake.

She looked across the table at Peaches, once again admiring her sense of style. Today she wore a casual outfit consisting of an orange T-shirt with the word "DRIP" printed on it in big white block letters, some baggy medium-blue denim jeans, and a pair of striking orange sneakers. "I've been meaning to ask you—I've never seen sneakers like those before. I really like them. What kind are they?"

"They're actually Skechers brand Uno Night Shade sneakers. They come in this color, but I have a sneaker guy who adds a little razzle-dazzle to my shoes for me. Sometimes he does full custom paint jobs, but for this pair I just had him add a little bit of gold accent to the tongue."

"You have an amazing sense of style," Jamie said. "It's one of the things about you that caught my attention. I always noticed that whenever our group of friends got together, you always look so well dressed and coordinated."

Peaches grinned, apparently pleased with the compliment. "Thanks a lot. I do put a lot of effort into my outfits—it's how my mom raised me. She never let me go out looking unkempt, and I guess that stuck with me."

"Staying true to the way she raised you is a great way to honor her memory." Jamie popped a fry into her mouth and took a moment to look out the window. It'd been sunny when they first sat down, but now clouds were forming overhead, and it looked slightly overcast. *Dang, is it about to rain?* The skin on her forearm began to prickle, and she got the feeling that she was being watched. Turning her attention back to Peaches, she found her staring. "Why are you looking at me like that?"

"I'm just really amazed at the things you've said to me today. This is the first time I've had a chance to really get to know you, and I'm finding out you're really deep and thoughtful."

Jamie drank the last of her milkshake, swallowing the thick, fruity liquid. "It's nice to have someone pay attention to what I have to say rather than dismiss or ignore me outright."

Crumbling the napkin and pushing aside her empty tray, Peaches frowned. "Is that really how it is being a middle child? I've heard that before, but I always thought it was sort of an exaggeration."

"I don't know if all middle children go through it. All I know is that in my household, whatever Shelby does is super important, whatever Sean does is super entertaining, and whatever I do goes completely unnoticed." She waved her hand dismissively, because she knew if they kept talking about her family it was only going to bring her mood down. "That's enough about them, though. They'll be there waiting to stress me out when I get back home. For now, let's talk about something else."

"Like what?"

"Literally anything else."

"Okay, bet." Peaches leaned forward ever so slightly. "Okay, I got a really good question. We talked a little bit earlier about the kind of music you like, so now tell me what's your favorite album for setting the mood. You know, when you feeling sexy and romantic."

Jamie felt her brow arc. "I feel like you're setting me up with this question. But I'm gonna answer it anyway. I have three favorite albums for that particular purpose. The first is 112's self-titled debut album. No skips on that one when it comes to knocking boots. Number two is *A Muse in Her Feelings*, by dvsn. And number three I would say is that enduring classic, *Maxwell's Urban Hang Suite*."

Peaches appeared impressed. "Okay, thanks for answering that question. Those are some pretty good albums you named . . . I don't know if my list can stand up to yours."

"Let me hear it anyway. I'm curious now."

"Okay, check me out. *Ctrl*, by SZA, *Ego Death*, by the Internet, and *Ginuwine . . . the Bachelor*."

"Okay, Peaches, but your list is not too shabby." The albums were different from hers, but the general vibe was the same. Jamie started gathering her trash onto her tray, only to have Peaches slide it away from her, stack it on top of her own tray, and stand, taking them both to the trash can. *She really just gonna keep doing stuff for me, I see. It's not as if she needs to sweeten the pot.*

Returning to the table, Peaches reached into her pocket and took out her phone. "Damn, it's already two thirty. I can't believe we've been sitting here that long."

"I guess the conversation got good, didn't it?"

"Yeah, I guess it did. So what do you want to do now? Do you want to swing back by the hotel and see if they have a room ready?"

"Nah. If we go to the hotel, we'll be heading in the opposite direction from the school."

"True. Plus, once we get there, we gotta park and all that."

"Let's drop off the bags, then head over to campus—there's probably somewhere over there we can hang out until it's time for me to meet
my guide for my campus tour." Jamie pulled out her phone. "I'll do the
check-in on the hotel app right now to speed things along."

"Okay, cool. And just to let you know, when the tour starts, I'm
gonna be quiet and hang back so you can focus on what you came here
to do, okay?"

"Got it." She smiled, enjoying the way Peaches made an effort to be
as unobtrusive as possible. *It's been a while since I've been with someone
confident enough to let me do my own thing without feeling they need to
be involved every second.*

They left the restaurant and made a quick stop at the hotel to drop
their bags, then took the twenty-minute drive to the campus of the
University of Texas at San Antonio. It took some time to find a parking lot with available space that would accommodate Peaches' truck,
but when they did, Peaches slipped into the space and cut the engine.
"Hopefully I got you close to the place where you're supposed to meet
your tour guide."

After unbuckling her seat belt, Jamie partly climbed into the back
seat and dug around in her purse before removing the folder holding
the packet she'd received in the mail from UT San Antonio.

"Hot damn, what a view," Peaches said with a chuckle.

Jamie frowned as she riffled through the papers, searching for the
full-color campus map. "From here? You can't even really see much of
the campus from where we're . . ." Realizing that Peaches was referring
to her upturned ass and not the scenery outside the car, she slowly
turned around and slid back down into a seated position. Her cheeks
hot, she said, "Troublemaker."

"Well, baby, you can't say I didn't warn you."

*She's right. She did warn me last night . . . and ever since then, I've
been doing my best to avoid thinking about all the ways she can make*

me scream. Jamie unfolded the map and hid her smile behind it as she searched for their current location and its relationship to the student union, where she was to meet her tour guide. "It looks like we're pretty close, but I'll check this against my phone GPS just to be sure of how far."

She typed the address into the GPS, set it to "Walk," and let it calculate the distance. "Oh, we're good. It says we're a seven-minute walk away." She looked at the screen again. "Even better . . . there's a coffee shop on the way . . . looks like it's in the same building we're going to." She reached for the door handle.

"Aht, aht! Don't touch that."

Jamie rolled her eyes at Peaches, but she acquiesced and moved her hand.

"Thank you. We'll hang out at the coffee shop until it's time, then." Peaches got out of the truck. After she'd opened her door and helped her out, Jamie walked ahead of Peaches, following the dotted line on her phone screen.

The buildings clustered around 1 UTSA Circle included the student union, the Campus Tech Store, and the Convocation Center. From her reading about the school, she knew the rooftop of the main building containing the student union had been fitted with solar panels to provide greener power and reduce energy consumption.

They stopped off for iced coffee and cookies at the coffee shop, laughing at a silly thread of memes on Twitter, until the time came around for the tour.

Just as Peaches had promised, she kept quiet and trailed behind Jamie and her guide, Karla, at a reasonable distance as they walked around the campus. Jamie asked all the relevant questions she'd jotted down pertaining to campus life, academics, and the university's chemistry department in particular. She stumped Karla for a minute with a question about the percentage of older, nontraditional full-time students on campus, but she was able to get an answer by making a visit to the office of student affairs.

When the tour ended about two hours later, Peaches took her hand to walk her back to the truck. "Well, that was a workout."

"It really was. I feel like I've walked off five pounds. This campus is huge." Jamie swiped a hand over her brow. Turning a wary eye to the sky, she noticed the increasing cloud cover. "It's humid as hell out here, plus, it's getting really gray."

Peaches followed her gaze. "Yeah, this is that weather where my dad starts complaining about his knees aching. It's about to rain."

They headed for the truck, and Peaches drove them to the hotel. As they made it into the parking lot, the bottom fell out. With fat droplets of rain pelting them from every direction, they made a dash for the automatic doors at the hotel's entrance.

"I'm glad we brought the bags earlier," Jamie announced as they walked past the front desk, toward the elevators. "Now I just want to get out of these soggy clothes."

Peaches cleared her throat but said nothing as they stepped into the elevator, the door soon closing behind them.

They exited the car on the fifth floor, and Jamie walked toward their room, toward the western end of the corridor. Waving her phone near the lock, she pushed the lever down and opened the door. After slipping inside, she held the door open so Peaches could enter, then let it click shut.

She flipped a switch, and light flooded the room. The king-sized bed centering the space was dressed in fluffy white linens and pillows, and the room had a desk, a dresser that doubled as a television stand, and two armchairs positioned near the french doors that led out to a small balcony. It was a decent-sized room, but as she glanced between the big bed and Peaches' face, it suddenly felt much smaller.

They'd left their bags just inside the door in their haste, so moving them was the first order of business. After tucking her bags into the closet, Jamie went over to the foot of the bed and sat down. First she kicked off her shoes, then she unzipped her damp jacket, tossing it so that it landed in one of the armchairs.

Peaches deposited her bags in the closet as well, then crossed the room, walking past her to sit in the empty chair.

Jamie eyed her. "What are you doing all the way over there?"

She shrugged. "I'm giving you space, being respectful."

Jamie shifted her body, moving into a side-lying position. Licking her lips, she lowered the timbre of her voice to communicate her mood. "Baby, I want you close to me. And I fully expect things to get very, very disrespectful between us tonight."

CHAPTER TEN

Peaches felt her brow hitch. "So it's like that?"

Jamie nodded slowly. "It absolutely is."

Leaning back in her chair, she stroked her chin. *I've had enthusiastic partners before, but never one who was so comfortable expressing exactly what she wants. I can get into this.* "I gotta say, I love the gusto. It's a real turn-on, baby."

"Good, because turning you on is my intention." Jamie moved again, turning onto her stomach, long waves of dark hair obscuring her face.

Peaches' gaze was drawn to the roundness of her upturned ass, and the perfect way it tapered to her thick thighs. Her heart raced, her mouth felt dry. She cleared her throat. "Come over here, Jamie."

She slipped from the bed, easing onto Peaches' lap. "How's this?"

Reveling in the feel of Jamie's incredibly soft ass pressed against her, she sighed. "Just right." Peaches gently pushed Jamie's hair away from her face and gazed into her sparkling brown eyes. A moment later, as Peaches cupped Jamie's chin, their lips met.

Jamie slipped her arms around Peaches' shoulders while Peaches' arms encircled her waist, and their bodies melted together, the kiss deepening. Lips parted, tongues stroking, the sounds of their heavy breathing began to fill the room.

Peaches could feel her body temperature climbing with each passing moment. The soft weight of Jamie's body in her arms, the lure of her sweetly scented skin . . .

Jamie broke the kiss, leaning back to suck in a deep breath. "If you fuck as well as you kiss, this is going to be an amazing night."

Peaches could feel a smile tugging her lips at that little ego stroke, but the smile faded almost as quickly as it had come. Letting her head drop toward her left shoulder, she asked, "Is that all it's going to be?"

Jamie's expression changed, her brows dipping. "What do you mean?"

"You said it would be an amazing night. As in singular . . . one night."

With a small giggle, Jamie waved her hand. "I didn't mean that. I mean, we're not going back to Austin until Sunday, so we have tomorrow night too."

"And after that?" Peaches let her arms drop from Jamie's waist. "Is the plan just to go back home and pretend nothing happened between us? Because I'm telling you right now, once I make love to you, we're both gonna have a hard time with that."

Now Jamie's face creased into a frown. "Hold on. What are you talking about?"

"I just want a little clarity on what we're doing here, that's all."

"I thought it was obvious. We're fucking."

Peaches cringed. "And that's it? That's the entire balance of what's happening between us?"

"Why are you even asking me these questions right now, when you should be showing me these skills you profess to have?"

Peaches released a low groan. "Listen. I've only known you were interested in me for a week. Seven days. And while you made it clear you want me sexually, that's the only thing you've made clear."

With an exasperated exhale, Jamie slid off her lap and stood. Flopping down on the bed, she said, "I can't believe this. You're really going to do this now? The moment when things start to heat up between us for real, now you wanna talk terms and conditions?" Her tone held frustration that bordered on incredulousness.

"Maybe you're right, my timing sucks. But I can't just ignore what I'm feeling." Peaches stood then. "I'm sorry, Jamie. I . . . can't do this with you right now. I need to clear my head."

Rolling her eyes, Jamie fluffed up the pillows at the head of the bed. Resting against them, she pulled her phone from her pocket. Eyes on the screen, she groused, "Whatever."

Peaches watched Jamie for a moment, seeing the way her body language was effectively shutting her out. *We both need some time to think. I'm just gonna leave, and hope she'll let me back in later.* This little incident definitely revealed a flaw in the whole "using a phone as a room key" techno-wizardry thing the hotel had going on.

She walked past the foot of the bed, went to the door, and let herself out. As it shut behind her, she stood in the quiet, empty corridor for a moment, deciding which way to go. Settling on heading downstairs, she went to the elevator bank and rode a car down to the lobby.

She walked the corridors of the floor for a moment, familiarizing herself with the hotel layout while trying to get her mind right.

I may have screwed up royally just now. But something just felt off to me. We've been enjoying each other's company, but it's been very surface level. Are we moving too fast?

Tired of wandering aimlessly, she returned to the lobby and cut across it to the bar near the hotel's rear entrance. All eight stools were empty, so she slid onto one and waited for someone to appear behind the counter.

After a few minutes, a Black man dressed in all black appeared through a swinging door behind the counter. Seeing her sitting there, he sidled over. "Good evening. What can I get for you?"

"Hey there. For right now, can I just get a ginger ale?"

"No problem."

She watched as he fetched a tall glass from a shelf beneath the bar, then used a metal scooper to fill it with ice. At the tap, he used a small nozzle to fill the glass, then slid it to her along with a paper-wrapped straw.

"Thanks."

"You're welcome." He handed her a beverage napkin. "So, what brings you to San Antonio? Traveling for business?"

She shook her head. "No. More of a leisure trip with a friend."

He nodded. "Yeah, I should have figured. You're a little early to be part of the corporate crowd."

"Is that why it's so quiet down here?"

"Yeah." He raised his wrist, glancing at his watch. "It's not gonna stay that way, though. It's six thirty. By seven o'clock, the bar and the lobby will be crowded with all the suit-and-tie types who just got out of their last meeting of the day."

"Then I came at just the right time." She took a sip of her ginger ale, enjoying the crisp bite of the cold beverage.

"You sure did." He laughed. "So, have you been enjoying the city so far?"

"Honestly, I haven't seen much of it. My friend came for a campus tour of UT San Antonio, so that's really the only place we've been."

"I see." He appeared thoughtful for a moment. "It's a good school; at least that's what I hear from the locals. Personally, I'm more partial to Texas Southern—my parents and my older brother all went there."

She grinned. "What a coincidence. She's got a tour booked there tomorrow."

"Really? She'll love it." He paused. "I'm assuming she's a sistah?"

She laughed and nodded. "Yeah, definitely."

"Oh, then she will love it. I've spent a decent amount of time on campus there, and you can't beat the culture." He gestured to her half-empty glass. "Want me to top you off?"

"Sure." She slid the glass closer and let him refill it, then took it back. "She's a nontraditional student, going back to school after a long break. I really want her to have a good experience."

"That's what's up. You know, she's lucky to have a friend that cares so much about her." Two white men in suits entered the bar, taking seats at the opposite end of the counter. "Here they come. Let me go check on them."

She smiled while she turned the bartender's words over in her mind. *If a total stranger can tell I care about Jamie, can't she see it too? Isn't it obvious to her that I think she deserves more than a one-night stand, or a weekend fuck buddy?*

Her stomach growled, loudly enough to snatch her out of her own thoughts. *Damn. We haven't had dinner yet, and it's almost seven. If I'm hungry, she's probably hungry too.* Raising her hand, she flagged down the bartender.

"Need another refill?"

She shook her head. "No. Actually, I wanna order from the dinner menu for room service."

He cringed. "Sorry, you can't order room service at the bar. But you can order food to go, though."

"Okay, cool. But I'm ordering a decent amount of food."

"Don't worry, I got you." He went through the swinging door again and soon returned with a small wheeled cart. "I'll let you use my cart to take it to your room. When you're done, leave it outside, and the room service attendants will run it back down here."

She smiled as she picked up a menu from the metal stand at the end of the bar. "You're the best."

"You know it. I'll swing back over here in a few minutes to take your order."

Half an hour later, Peaches stepped off the elevator on the fifth floor, pushing the food-laden cart. After navigating it to the end of the corridor, she knocked softly on the door. "Jamie, it's me."

She heard footsteps approaching and then the click as Jamie pushed the lever. The door swung open, and there she stood, clad in flannel pajama pants and a red T-shirt. When she saw the cart, her mouth dropped open. "What's all this?"

"Dinner. While I was out, my stomach reminded me that we hadn't eaten since lunchtime."

Jamie stepped back, holding open the door so Peaches could wheel the cart into the room. Once she was inside and the door was closed, she parked it near the large desk in the corner.

Jamie walked over to the cart. Glancing back and forth between the cart and Peaches' face, she said, "Wow. You didn't have to do this."

Peaches shrugged. "I know. But we both gotta eat, right?"

A soft smile crossed Jamie's face, but there was a lingering sadness in her eyes. "This is really thoughtful, thank you. Now I feel like an asshole for yelling at you the way I did."

Peaches waved her hand, then reached into the pocket of her jeans for the small bottle of hand sanitizer there. She cleaned her own hands before offering Jamie a squirt. "We were both out of sorts. Let's just chalk it up to you being hangry."

Jamie pressed her lips together, her gaze softening as she rubbed the sanitizer onto her hands. "You're really something." Looking over all the foam containers on the cart, she asked, "What did you get?"

Opening containers one by one, Peaches announced each item. "I ordered you a half rack of baby back ribs, fries, and a side salad. I wasn't sure of what sauce or dressing you'd want, so I had them put containers of every barbecue sauce and every dressing they had . . . plus ketchup in case you wanted that. And I got you bottled water and iced tea to drink. I would have gotten dessert, but I didn't know if you'd want it . . ."

Jamie gently but firmly grasped Peaches' face, turned it slightly, and placed a soft, fleeting kiss on her lips. "Thank you. This is really, really sweet."

She winked. "They don't call me Peaches for nothing, shawty."

Soon, Peaches was seated at the desk with her Philly cheesesteak, fries, and bottled water, while Jamie reclined in one of the armchairs with her food on a folding TV tray that had been sitting in the closet. "How are the ribs?"

"Not as good as Stubb's, obviously. But they are pretty good."

"Listen," Peaches began, "about what happened earlier. I hope you know that I want you just as badly as you want me."

Jamie paused her chewing, taking a swig of water. "I'm glad you said that, because I was a little confused by the way you acted."

"There's something else you need to know too. Even though I want you, I've got my self-control and my good sense intact. We need to spend a little more time talking before we go any further. I hope you understand where I'm coming from."

Jamie appeared thoughtful. "I'm not sure I understand all of it, but I respect your position. I don't mind having a deeper conversation with you." She closed her container and patted her belly. "But can we do it in the morning? The itis is hitting, and I wanna go to sleep."

Peaches laughed. "Yeah. I definitely feel it too. We'll reconvene in the morning." She closed her empty box and began cleaning up, and with that done, she pushed the cart out into the hallway, then took a shower.

A short time later, Peaches emerged, feeling refreshed. As she entered the room, she could hear the soft sounds of Jamie's snoring. Smiling, she eased into the bed on the other side, maintaining a bit of distance so as not to awaken her.

Jamie shifted in the dark, turning to face her. "Peaches?"

"Hmm?"

"Can you hold me, please?"

Her heart swelled. "Sure." She opened her arms, and Jamie repositioned herself, laying her head on Peaches' shoulder. A heartbeat later, she was snoring again.

Closing her arms around Jamie's sleeping form, Peaches settled fully into the softness of the bedcovers, and the peace of the moment.

⌐

Jamie awakened early the next morning to find the sunlight streaming in through a gap in the blackout curtains covering the window. Squinting, she started to make the motion to turn over away from the sunlight, but realized she couldn't. Awareness set in and she remembered last night, and that she was not at home alone, but at a hotel in San Antonio, lying in Peaches' arms. Since Peaches had slept in a sports bra and boxer briefs, the warmth of her skin radiated onto Jamie's body.

She wiggled around a little bit, as gently as she could, to extricate herself from Peaches' embrace so she could go to the bathroom. With that done, she returned to the bed to find Peaches still lying in the same position, but with her eyes open. "Good morning."

Peaches yawned. "Good morning to you. I'd ask if you slept well, but the snoring kind of gave you away," she teased.

Coming back around to her side of the bed, Jamie grabbed her pillow and playfully bopped Peaches upside the head with it. "Hush up about my snoring—I can't help that my sinus cavities are narrow."

She laughed. "Don't worry, I promise it'll be our little secret."

Shaking her head, Jamie eased back beneath the covers next to Peaches. "So, are you awake enough to have that talk yet?"

"What time is it?" she asked, the vestiges of sleep still clinging to her voice.

Jamie glanced at the digital clock on the nightstand. "It's six twenty-seven."

"Yikes." Peaches raked her hand over her face. "That's definitely early for me. But since we're both awake, we might as well go ahead and talk."

"Okay." Jamie cozied up next to her. "I'm listening."

"Oh, I get to go first too? Awesome." She raised her arms above her head in a wide stretch. Dropping them, she draped one over Jamie's shoulder, drawing her in closer to her side. "Okay. Last night when you sat on my lap, and I felt that soft ass against me, I nearly lost my mind. Notice that I said 'nearly,' because when you started talking about how tonight was gonna be amazing, and I heard the finality in your tone . . . that brought me right back to reality."

"See, that's what I don't get. Explain to me why hearing me say that was so upsetting for you." Sexual frustration aside, she really did want to know why Peaches had been so bothered by her words.

"Remember yesterday when we were talking about our first serious relationships? And your first serious relationship turned out to also have been your last one?"

"Yeah, I remember that. What about it?"

"Well, we never got around to talking about my last serious relationship."

Jamie could feel just the slightest bit of tension rolling off Peaches, but she had a sense that tension was coming from something she was about to relive through this conversation. "Are you sure you're ready to talk about it?"

"No, I'm not. But I feel like I need to in order for you to understand where I'm coming from." She paused, her eyes closing for a second before reopening again. "So I guess we're officially breaking our squad's 'good vibes only' rule."

Jamie nodded. "I know we all agreed not to talk about heavy things when all of us are together. But it's just the two of us now, and if you want to talk, I'm ready to listen."

"My last serious relationship was with a woman named Denise. She was a regular at the barbershop, though she wasn't my client. We always ended up talking it up while she was getting her trims, because her barber's station was right next to mine."

Wanting to encourage Peaches to continue, Jamie asked, "How long were you together?"

"A little over two years." She scratched the bridge of her nose. "We broke up maybe eight months ago. The thing about my relationship with Denise was that it was unevenly matched."

"How so?"

"I loved her . . . I saw a future with her. But she never truly opened up to me. She would always call or text me, then pull up, when she wanted sex . . . and the sex was amazing. But I never met her family or her friends. We'd go on dates now and then, but always to secluded places. Our conversations were very surface level."

Jamie frowned, reacting to the undercurrent of pain in Peaches' words. "Why did you stay with her so long?"

Peaches shrugged. "The sex was great, but I think the real reason I stayed was because I kept hoping she would change, that she would open up. The day we broke up, we were at a restaurant. I confronted her, telling her that I loved her and that I craved deep connection with her. And do you know what she did? She laughed."

Jamie covered her mouth with a hand. "Oh no."

"Oh yes. Then she proceeded to tell me that she'd only been interested in me sexually, that I should have known that, and that she didn't want to be tied down. I walked out in the middle of her speech, and I sat in my car long enough to block her number and block her on all social sites, email, everything. Then I drove away. I never spoke to her again."

Jamie felt her chest tighten, and she snuggled even closer to Peaches. "That woman is trash, and I'm sorry she treated you that way."

"It took me several weeks to break through the sadness, but I finally did." Peaches looked straight ahead. "I've come to appreciate that experience over time, because it taught me something valuable about myself."

"What's that?"

"I'm not built for this hookup culture. I can't be fuck buddies with someone. I'm just not the type." She shook her head. "Have I had meaningless one-night encounters to scratch an itch? Yes. But that's an occasional thing, not a lifestyle."

Damn. I feel a little called out, even though I haven't hooked up with anyone over the last several weeks.

"And there's something else at play here too. Our friend group is amazing—it's one of the best things in my life. You, Aiko, Claudia, and Taylor are my found family. And let me tell you, I need that, because my family is often less than ideal."

Jamie nodded. "Hard same. My family is kinda trash too."

"So you should understand that what happens between you and I isn't just about us." Peaches grazed her fingertip along the neckline of Jamie's T-shirt. "The last thing I want to do is have the amazing vibe of our found family destroyed because of any strife or conflict between us."

She sucked on her lower lip. "You're right, Peaches. I hadn't considered that."

"At any rate, I'm not getting involved with someone who only wants me for sex." She turned her head, looking directly into her eyes. "Jamie, I'm not going down that road again. If you want to be with me, you need to understand I don't do friends with benefits. I want something real, and frankly, I deserve someone who's gonna give me that."

Jamie nodded. "I understand."

"Good. So if you approach me again, know what you're getting yourself into." Peaches placed a soft kiss on Jamie's forehead before releasing her and slipping from beneath the covers. A moment later, she disappeared into the bathroom.

Sitting alone in bed, Jamie thought about everything Peaches had said. The feelings she'd expressed had been thoughtful and valid, and now, Jamie took a moment to consider how she'd come across in her interactions with Peaches over this last week. *I led with seduction, but maybe my approach is a little too intense. I've really got her thinking that's all I want from her.*

She paused.

Is *that all I want from her?*

In the beginning, her attraction to Peaches had been purely physical. Now, though, she could see a depth to her, a level of maturity and sensitivity that both surprised and delighted her. *As partners go, I could do a hell of a lot worse.*

Peaches returned from the bathroom and opened the closet. "We should probably start getting ready so we can grab breakfast and be out of here before checkout time."

"Peaches?"

"Hmm?" She stuck her head around the closet door.

"Come here right quick." Jamie gestured to her, curling her index finger.

Peaches walked around the bed, eyeing her the whole way. "What is it?"

Jamie knelt on the mattress, bringing their faces level. "Thank you for being honest and open with me."

"You're welcome. I didn't want you to think I wasn't feeling you." She licked her lips. "Because I absolutely am."

Jamie inhaled, filling her nostrils with the delicious scent of whatever fragrance Peaches currently wore. "I want you to know that I heard and understood everything you said. And I would be honored if you'd give me the chance to be the girl on your arm." She pressed her index finger against Peaches' lower lip.

A smile spread over her face. "Really? You not playing with me, are you?"

She shook her head. "I'm serious. You are fine as hell, Peaches. You've been fine the entire time I've known you. And while my hormones are raging for you, I now know how caring and considerate you are. Honestly, that just makes it even better." She spread her fingers apart, slowly caressing Peaches, easing her open palm over her warm skin from the hollow of her throat, down the side of her strong frame until her hand came to rest on her hip. "I know we have somewhere to be. But tonight, after I've done what I came to do on campus . . ." She squeezed her hip. "I'm gonna do what I came to do to you. If you'll let me."

A sound came from Peaches' throat that was part growl, part moan. Slipping her big hands around her head and weaving her fingertips into Jamie's hair, Peaches pulled her in for a kiss.

Jamie heard herself moan as the kiss deepened. Longing coursed through her veins, and she sucked Peaches' tongue between her lips one final time before pulling away. Breathing heavily, she said, "We gotta stop, or we not making it to Houston."

Peaches laughed. "You right, you right." Backing away a couple of steps, she pointed toward the closet. "I'm gonna go ahead and get dressed."

"Me too . . . as soon as I take a quick shower." She scooted off the bed and dashed into the bathroom, laughing when Peaches smacked her ass right before she could close the door.

Once they were both dressed, they took their bags down to the lobby. Jamie walked behind Peaches, appreciating the view of her sure stride, and the way her green polo and khakis showed off her broad shoulders and powerful thighs.

After setting their luggage on the floor next to their table, they sat down and enjoyed the continental breakfast of cereal, pastries, fruit, and coffee. By the time they'd checked out and gotten on the road, it was a little past eight thirty.

"Sorry it took me so long to get ready," Jamie said, looking out the window as the truck rolled eastward down the I-10. "I fell asleep without my bonnet on last night, so my wig was a lil' fucked up. Had to get her right again."

Peaches laughed. "No worries. Besides, it looks good." She signaled for a lane change, moving left to pass around a slow-moving, bus-style RV. "I'm sorta fascinated by lace-front wigs. The way y'all have them laid, it just seems like sorcery to me."

She giggled. "In a way it is. It takes a lot of products and some serious skill to get the right look. Otherwise, you become a tragic example of the wig gone wrong. If you need an example of that, just look at the wigs on any person in a Tyler Perry movie."

Peaches snorted. "Damn. You gonna do my boy Tyler like that?"

"Hell yeah. Madea's lace be laid and slayed. Meanwhile, the other actors' wigs be looking like something they picked up at the local party store. Just crooked and dry . . . struggle wigs."

Between bouts of full, body-shaking laughter, Peaches begged, "Jamie, stop. You killing me. You can't have me rolling like this while I'm driving."

"Okay, okay. I'm gonna try to behave. You know, for safety's sake."

"Whew." Peaches took a deep breath, using one hand to wipe away the tears of mirth rolling down her cheeks. "Thank you."

"You're welcome. But if you ever want a laugh when you're *not* operating a motor vehicle, you should go on Twitter and type 'Tyler Perry wigs' into the search bar. I guarantee, it's gonna have you cracking up."

"I'll take that under advisement."

After a few moments of companionable silence, Jamie said, "I remember you saying your nieces take a dance class. What kind of dance do they take?"

"Ballet and jazz." Peaches paused. "Wait . . . you remember that my nieces take dance?"

She scoffed. "How could I forget? You said you were picking them up from there the night you stood me up for frozen yogurt." She laughed. "You're lucky I'm mature enough that I took it in stride."

Peaches chuckled. "You mean you never had to back out of a date to babysit?"

She shook her head. "No. Levi's not even two yet. Plus, my family barely notices me, so I don't get too many babysitting requests." She paused. "So you're admitting it would have been a date."

With a shrug, Peaches admitted, "That's what I thought from the beginning."

"Well, at any rate, I planned on keeping it PG that night. That's why I invited you for frozen yogurt, instead of drinks."

"So you were gonna behave that night . . . but are you gonna behave today?"

"I haven't decided yet." Jamie winked.

Peaches glanced at the GPS on her phone. "Looks like we've got another two hours and some change before we get into Houston. Can you behave for that long, ma'am?"

She laughed, using the mirror on the sun visor to check her makeup. "I guess we're about to find out."

CHAPTER ELEVEN

Peaches exited the highway in Houston, then pulled up to the stoplight. Glancing at her phone, she said, "It's lunchtime . . . what do you want to eat?"

Jamie shrugged. "I'm not really sure—I haven't been to Houston in years."

She let her eyes move slowly over Jamie's shapely body, clad in black leggings, a sleeveless yellow tunic, and black-and-white Vans sneakers. *No matter how casually she dresses, she's still a knockout.*

A horn honked behind her, shifting her focus back to traffic. The light had changed, so she made a right onto Scott Street. "I have a cousin who lived here for a few years before going back up to Lubbock, and he used to rave about this one chicken place. I'm pretty sure it's still open." Taking in the surrounding scenery, she spotted the yellow sign with the white script lettering. "There it is. French's fried chicken."

"Okay, I'm game."

Peaches pulled off the road into the small parking lot. The building housing the restaurant was a small one-story structure. It was an old-fashioned counter-service eatery, though it did have a covered, fenced-in area in front of it with picnic tables for dining.

Shutting off the engine, Peaches glanced at Jamie, whose eyes were glued to her phone. "What are you doing?"

"Looking at the menu . . . can you get me the three-tenders meal with a sweet tea, the special sauce, and a praline?"

She chuckled. "You're not getting out?"

Jamie shook her head. "Nah. If I stand up now, I'm gonna have to pee, so I'll wait until we get to campus."

Chuckling, Peaches got out of the truck. "I'll be right back."

Entering the fenced area, she got in line behind the three other people already there and waited her turn. At the window, she ordered Jamie what she'd asked for and then got what she wanted. After hanging back at one of the picnic tables until the food was ready, she then ferried the two paper bags and the cardboard carrier with two foam cups back to the truck.

"That smells amazing," Jamie commented as Peaches handed over her bag and drink.

"Have you ever eaten here before?"

Jamie nodded. "Yeah, but it was a long time ago . . . I think I was in high school." She reached into her bag and grabbed the straw. As she unwrapped it and jabbed it into her cup, she asked, "What did you get?"

"A spicy sausage meal. Oh, and I got myself a praline too. I've never eaten here before, but my cousin Greg raves about it."

They ate in friendly silence, and Peaches discovered that the food was just as good as her cousin insisted. *It definitely falls squarely in the comfort-food category . . . no way could I eat like this every day.*

Once they'd finished, Jamie said, "We've still got a little time to kill before I meet Tashaun at the student center. There's an art museum on campus, though, and I'd really like to take a look at that before my tour."

"Sounds interesting. Let's go check it out."

"Cool. We need to go to the West Garage at 3001 Blodgett Street to park, but the actual museum is on Cleburne."

Peaches punched that into her GPS. "Got it."

It took less than five minutes to drive from Frenchy's to the parking deck. Once inside, Peaches circled up to the top level before finding a good spot. After parking, they made their way to the University Museum, located inside the Fairchild Building.

"Apparently, this is the oldest building on campus," Jamie said quietly as they walked down the sidewalk in front of the concrete-block building, with its austere gray facade. They walked hand in hand and entered through the double doors, flanked by block-glass windows.

The main interior gallery space boasted lacquered, highly polished floors fashioned of light-colored wood, along with stark white walls. Artworks of various mediums and artists were displayed, including works created by current and former students.

They took time perusing the collection currently on display, then exited the main building onto the grassy lawn, headed for the Carol Harris Simms Sculpture Garden. According to the pamphlet Peaches had picked up from inside the building, Professor Simms had made quite an impact on the university's art program. An accomplished artist and author who'd traveled the world and brought that expertise back to TSU as a professor, Simms had taught at the university for more than thirty years before his retirement in the eighties. Gazing up at his works in the garden, Peaches could easily see the man's talent.

"Isn't this amazing? From what I read about him, his main influences were artwork from countries in Africa, like Benin." Jamie's awe-filled expression communicated how moved she was by the sculpture.

"Perspective is everything when it comes to art, and I can see how his travel influenced his creativity." Peaches gave Jamie's hand a squeeze. "It's two forty-five, baby."

Tearing her eyes away from the sculpture, Jamie started walking, tugging Peaches along behind her. "We need to get to the Sterling Student Life Center. I'm pretty sure it's this way."

"The way you're dragging me indicates a lot more certainty than your words," Peaches said as they skirted along the sidewalk.

Jamie's instincts turned out to be right, and they arrived in front of the building at five minutes before three. A young woman wearing a maroon-and-gray Tigers tee, along with a pair of black jeans, approached them carrying a clipboard. "Is either one of you Jamie?"

"I am." She grinned. "Hi, Tashaun, nice to meet you."

Tashaun offered an open smile. "It's always nice to meet a potential Tiger in the making. Welcome to TSU." Her gaze shifted to Peaches' face, and she stuck out our hand. "Will you be joining us?"

"Yes." She shook the young woman's hand. "I'm Peaches—"

"My girlfriend," Jamie interjected.

Peaches couldn't hold back her smile. *She might be trolling me, but I like the way that sounds.* "Anyway, Tashaun, don't mind me. I'm just observing while Jamie absorbs all the pertinent information she can about TSU."

Tashaun laughed. "Gotcha. Well, ladies, let's get started, shall we?"

Just as she had at UTSA, Peaches remained a few steps behind Jamie and her guide at all times, content to watch while she indulged every curiosity she had about life as a student at Texas Southern. They traversed the campus on foot, seeing all the important locations that Jamie requested.

The longest time was spent inside the College of Science, Engineering and Technology building, located on Ennis between Eagle and Wheeler Streets, near the university's western gate. While touring the building, Peaches watched as Jamie toured laboratories, lecture halls, and the faculty departmental office.

Peaches listened while Tashaun chatted with Jamie about notable alumni and the department's accreditations and concentrations. As they spoke, she couldn't help noticing the excitement flickering in Jamie's eyes. Peaches smiled. *Looks like UTSA lost out on this one. She's firing on all cylinders—it's way different from how she was acting yesterday.*

After they finished, Tashaun asked, "So, how do you feel about the possibility of becoming a TSU Tiger, Jamie?"

Jamie grinned. "I feel it's a very strong possibility. I'd narrowed it down to my last two schools out of the four that accepted me, and I'm feeling very drawn to this one."

Tashaun clapped her hands together. "That's awesome. Well, our tour is officially over, but I look forward to seeing you around campus next semester."

"Thank you so much for your help," Jamie said, waving as Tashaun walked away, leaving them on the sidewalk in front of the science building.

Peaches reached for Jamie's hand. "I feel like you've already made your decision."

"I think I have." Jamie smiled. "Now I just have to make some arrangements to get down here when the next term starts."

They found their way back to the parking deck and sat in the truck for a few moments, debating where to go for dinner.

"So you don't have a taste for anything in particular?" Peaches asked.

She shook her head. "No. Honestly, I'm beat. Let's just head for the hotel. I always book the same brand, and I know they have room service."

"Bet." Peaches watched as Jamie punched in the address, then mounted her phone on the dash as Peaches circled her way back out of the parking deck.

They reached the hotel and were soon settled in their room. Since it was the same hotel chain as the one they'd stayed at in San Antonio, the room layout was strikingly similar, save for a few changes to the artwork on the walls.

After sliding her suitcase into a corner of the room, Jamie flopped down in one of the armchairs, scrolling through something on her phone. "I'm looking at the room service menu in the hotel app . . . I think I'm just gonna have a salad."

"I'll take a look at it when you get done—I don't have the app." Peaches sat down on the edge of the bed, her knees touching Jamie's.

Jamie passed her the phone. "You can look at it now."

Later, when the food arrived, the two of them sat side by side at the foot of the bed, watching a home-remodeling show on television as they ate.

"Ugh. I can't believe they decided to paint the house that color." Jamie shook her head. "It's way too bright."

"I thought you liked pink."

"For clothing and accessories. Not for houses." She laughed.

Peaches smiled, noting the easy way conversation flowed between them. Finished with her club sandwich and chips, she stood up with her plate and trash. "You done?"

"Yeah." Jamie passed Peaches her refuse.

After setting the stuff outside the door, Peaches closed it and returned to the bed. She eyed Jamie, who appeared relaxed and happy as she giggled at a silly cat-food commercial playing on the screen.

The commercial ended, and as her laughter faded, Jamie's head turned slowly toward Peaches. Frowning, Peaches asked, "What is it?"

"I was just thinking. I'm here because I want to take the next step on my personal career path. With things going so well for you at the barbershop, what do you think your next step will be?"

Peaches felt a smile tug her lips. *Seems like Jamie's genuinely interested in what I've got going on.* "Funny you should ask. I recently asked my accountant to help me determine if I'm fiscally ready to open a second location."

Jamie appeared impressed. "Wow, that's great. And if you do open a second shop, will you keep working at the original location, or switch, or work at both?"

She shrugged. "I don't know . . . I'm still considering it. I'd assume I would need to spend more time at the second location, at least in the beginning. You know, to get the place off to a solid start."

"That makes sense." Jamie stretched, raising her arms above her head and extending her fingers toward the ceiling. "It seems like you're taking a measured approach, and I think odds are good that you'll be successful at it no matter what you decide. I mean, look at what you've already accomplished."

Her smile brightening, Peaches met Jamie's eyes. "Thanks, I appreciate you saying that."

"I mean it. I just hope I'll be able to handle being a full-time student again." Her gaze shifted back toward the television, though she didn't really seem to be watching the images playing out on the screen. "I'm uprooting my whole life to do this, and I can't afford to mess it up."

"None of that negativity, Jamie. You're ready for this, and you know it."

"That's really sweet of you to say."

She shrugged. "It's what I believe."

"I would have taken the risk anyway, you know? Just to get a break from my family. To go out on my own . . . show them that I'm so much more than they give me credit for."

"We could both use a break from our relatives, for different reasons." Peaches shook her head. "Don't worry about them, they can kick rocks. This is about you. And when you walk across that stage with your degree, you'll have accomplished something amazing for yourself."

Peaches' expression changed, morphing into a soft smile. A twinkle danced in her dark eyes, and she rubbed her hands together. "We had a busy day. I was . . . thinking about a long, hot shower." Letting her gaze linger on Jamie's face, she added, "Shower's big enough for two."

Jamie's eyes narrowed slightly, and her tongue darted out, sweeping over her lower lip. "Oh, really?"

"Yeah." She thought back on Jamie's earlier proclamation, and the way her pulse had fluttered when she heard it. "And since you're my girl now, I think it's time for me to show you how I get down." She lowered her head ever so slightly, then swiped the back of her hand over her chin. "Come here, shawty."

Without breaking eye contact, Jamie reached behind her for the remote and flipped off the television. "You don't have to ask me twice." She stood.

Peaches stayed her with a raised finger. "You might wanna put your bonnet on . . . and whatever else you got in that suitcase to keep you from sweating your wig off."

"Oh shit," Jamie murmured. She turned on her heel and went to the corner where she'd left her luggage, then knelt as she searched through the contents.

Peaches leaned against the wall, watching with a mixture of fascination and anticipation as Jamie brushed the ends of the wig, then wrapped and pinned it around her head. Tying a silk scarf over it, she then placed a black satin bonnet over the scarf. Tucking in a stray hair, she stood again and ran toward Peaches.

A moment later, their bodies collided, and Peaches grasped Jamie's hips, turning her so she could press her back against the bare wall between the closet and the bathroom door. Peaches placed soft kisses along her forehead, over her closed eyes, and along her jawline until her lips came to rest at the nexus of Jamie's cleavage, just above the neckline of her top. When Peaches darted her tongue over the sensitive skin between her breasts, Jamie purred like a contented cat.

Peaches remained there for a few moments, licking, kissing, teasing, until she saw Jamie's knees begin to tremble. Placing a steadying hand on her waist, she murmured, "Don't tap out on me yet, shawty. I'm just getting started."

～

Still pressed against the wall, Jamie worked to control her ragged breathing as she watched Peaches undo the clasp of her wristwatch. While holding Jamie's gaze, Peaches set her watch on the dresser, then lifted her polo up and over her head, tossing it aside. Jamie sucked in a breath as Peaches' broad, powerful upper body came into view, and her gaze settled on the full breasts sheltered beneath her black racerback sports bra.

A confident smile spread over Peaches' face as she unbuttoned her khakis, pulled them down, and stepped out of them, revealing boxer briefs that matched her bra. Her motions were slow, deliberate . . . she knew Jamie was watching and seemed to enjoy giving her a private show.

Peaches moved closer, reentering her personal bubble. Dragging her index finger along Jamie's jawline, she whispered, "Strip for me, baby." Trailing her fingertip down until it came to rest between her breasts, she added, "Go slow." She took a single step back, allowing Jamie the space to obey her command.

And obey she did. She grasped the hem of her tunic and dragged it up and off. She tried to maintain eye contact with Peaches but found herself looking away every few moments lest she be singed by the heat smoldering there. Jamie's hands trembled as she peeled off each article of clothing, one by one. First her leggings, then her socks, her fuchsia lace bra, and the matching bikini panties. Peaches watched her the entire time, with an intense stare and a mischievous smile. It only took a few minutes, but with the building anticipation, and the promise of pleasure hanging between them, it felt like hours.

Finally nude, Jamie stood there, leaning against the wall because at this point, she needed the support to stay upright.

Peaches licked her lips. "Good girl."

Jamie sucked in a breath. *Holy shit, praise kink activated.*

A breath later, Peaches grabbed her, the motion rough yet tinged with gentleness, and swept her off her feet. Jamie squealed as she was hoisted up and tossed over Peaches' shoulder as if she weighed next to nothing. Peaches then fireman-carried her into the bathroom, kicking the door open to allow them space to enter.

Dangling over her shoulder, breathless and trembling with wanting, Jamie listened to Peaches' humming as she went about the task of readying the shower. She swung open one door, then the other before walking inside the shower and shutting them in. Turning so that Jamie would be angled away from the stream, Peaches turned on the water and let it run, testing the temperature.

The stall, with its transparent double glass doors and wide travertine tile flooring and surround, had a large rainfall showerhead positioned directly above it. *I always book this hotel brand partly because of their amazing showers . . . and after tonight, I have a feeling I'll love them even more.*

The temperature in the stall quickly rose along with the water temperature, and the air filled with steam.

Positioning Jamie gently on the floor, Peaches grasped her hand and placed her fingertips under the stream. "Is that too hot, baby?"

"No. It's just right." She leaned against the wall again, still in need of support to keep from melting into a puddle at Peaches' feet. "Not that I'm not enjoying the visual of water running down your bra and boxers . . . because it's nice . . . but are you gonna take that shit off?"

Peaches stood back a bit, stroking her chin as if thinking about it. After a moment of silence, she admitted, "I'm . . . not the most comfortable with my shape."

Jamie reached for her, running her open palm over the firm swell of Peaches' belly. "I love your body . . . it's a big part of why I find you so sexy." Putting on her best sexy pout, she eased close to her. "I wanna see all of you." She grasped the edge of her bra. "Can I?"

Peaches stared into her eyes. "Do you promise to be a very good girl?"

"Oh yes, I promise."

"Go ahead."

She lifted the bra, her breath escaping in a woosh as Peaches' ample breasts fell free of their spandex prison. While Peaches raised her arms, she tugged off the soggy garment and tossed it over the shower door. Reveling in the sight of water running down her smooth umber skin, Jamie then knelt to free her of the boxer briefs. Leaving them in the shower floor, she eased a fingertip slowly over the curls crowning Peaches' thighs.

Peaches growled, grasping her shoulders. "Not yet . . ." Drawing her up to a standing position, she drew her into her arms and kissed her.

The kiss deepened as they stood beneath the downpour of steamy water, their limbs entangled and their mouths fused. Jamie's hands roamed the peaks and valleys of Peaches' body as she familiarized herself with every inch within reach.

Peaches eased away from her, and began placing soft, skillful kisses down her body. The tremors set in again, and Jamie fell back against the wall as Peaches' attentions moved lower. She sucked each nipple into her mouth, taking her time and drawing the moans from Jamie's lips before trailing her kisses over the plane of her stomach.

Peaches knelt then and gently captured Jamie's left ankle. Raising it, she leaned forward, nuzzling the lower half of her face into the apex of her V. Her voice deep, she murmured, "Rest your thigh on my shoulder, baby."

Jamie did as she was told, only to feel her right knee buckle a moment later when Peaches' fingertips parted her labia and she stroked the flat of her tongue over her clit. A strangled cry escaped her throat, echoing through the bathroom as Peaches devoured her. Each suck, each measured swirl of her tongue, sent Jamie higher into the stratosphere of ecstasy. She clawed at Peaches' back, her fingertips slipping as she tried to hold on, seeking mooring in the storm. She arched, she purred, tears sliding down her cheeks to mix with the water flowing from the showerhead until finally, the pleasure reached full bloom and she exploded with a tortured, ragged scream.

She would have collapsed if not for the steadying strength of Peaches' arms supporting her. Limp and barely aware of her surroundings, she rested her forehead against the cool tile as Peaches soaped her entire body, then rinsed her. She opened her eyes more fully as the water cooled and watched Peaches scrub her own body clean, enticed by the sight of the frothy white suds running down her form.

Peaches shut off the water, then wrapped Jamie's body in a fluffy white towel before grabbing one for herself. Jamie steadied herself as she stepped out of the bathroom and onto the carpet. At the foot of the bed, the two of them hurriedly dried themselves, pausing a few times to steal kisses.

Peaches caressed her face. "Lay down for me."

Jamie lay atop the comforter while Peaches lowered the lights, leaving a sole lamp lit in the corner across from the bed. The soft glow illuminated her body as she returned and joined Jamie, crawling from the lower end of the mattress until she was on top of her.

Jamie reached up, lacing her hands into the thick depths of Peaches' curls, drawing her closer. "I don't think I've ever been . . . enjoyed like that."

Peaches grinned. "Trust me. I've only just begun to enjoy you." She slipped one hand beneath Jamie's hips to cup her ass, giving it a squeeze.

"Did you bring a strap?"

Peaches shook her head. "Two reasons. A, I don't need it." She kissed her forehead. "B, you're gonna pick the dick when it's time for me to give it to you." She kissed her lips.

Jamie had mixed feelings about that but didn't have much time to experience them. She dissolved into sighs as Peaches began suckling the sensitive skin where her neck met her shoulder. "Mmm."

"Open up for me, sweetheart." Peaches mumbled the words into her shoulder as she traced her finger in lazy circles over her thighs. "Let me touch you."

She parted her thighs and gasped as Peaches brushed her knuckle over her still-swollen clit.

Peaches moaned low in her throat as she eased a finger inside her. "Fuck. So wet . . ."

"Ah . . ." Jamie's entire being came alive, her aura vibrating in response to the rhythmic, skillful movements of Peaches' finger. Blood rushed to her lower regions, and her pulse raced as the sensations rose within. Before long, her hips were moving of their own accord, rocking to meet Peaches' manual magic.

"Yeah. Just like that, shawty." Peaches slipped a second finger inside without missing a beat.

Jamie's moans rose an octave in response to this new, even fuller sensation of pleasure. Her hips bucked, and she squeezed her eyes shut as a second orgasm ripped Peaches' name from her lips.

Panting and shaking, she lay among the rumpled bedding, trying to collect the scattered pieces of her soul. When she opened her eyes, she saw Peaches lying next to her, rather casual as she reclined on her side, propped up on her elbow.

Drawing a deep breath, Jamie sat up, stretching her arms over her head. As she lowered her hands, she placed one against Peaches' chest and pressed, effectively forcing her to lie on her back.

Watching Peaches in the dimly lit room, she felt something unfurl inside. Something soft, yet intense . . . something bordering on dangerous, yet still a haven from the outside world. Something beyond the physical. Sharing her body with Peaches was magical. But all throughout this trip, they'd shared so much more, and Jamie could tell their connection had deepened.

She then straddled Peaches' waist. Looking down at her through passion-hooded eyes, she asked, "How do you feel about being touched?"

"Yes, please," Peaches responded, tucking her hands behind her head.

"Good," she whispered. "Your turn." She circled the pad of her thumb over one of Peaches' nipples, grinning at her sharp intake of breath. A heartbeat later, she captured that same nipple in her mouth.

She sucked and teased each nipple until Peaches' heavy breathing morphed into sultry moans. Then she eased her hand down her belly and between her already parted thighs. "Oh, looks like I'm not the only one wet . . . lemme see if you're as sweet as your name implies."

She used her palms to press Peaches' thighs farther apart, wasting no time before covering her pussy with her open mouth. She nuzzled in and went to work, stroking her tongue over and around Peaches' clit, savoring her as if she were a decadent dessert. Peaches' cries of passion reached her ears, only increasing Jamie's determination to reduce her sexy, solid lover to orgasmic rubble.

She twisted her tongue, then stuck the tip inside Peaches' creamy center, pressing it as deep as it could go.

"Oh fuuuuuuuck!" Peaches shuddered, her thighs trembling as she came. She was flowing now, her insides flexing, and Jamie caught every drop of sweetness she released.

CHAPTER TWELVE

Sunday morning, Peaches awoke with Jamie's warm body tucked next to her in bed. A smile played over her face as she recalled last night's passionate encounter, and if Jamie's loud snoring was any indication, she was still a little worn out from it.

She got up and went to the bathroom. When she returned, she found Jamie still asleep, though she'd shifted onto her stomach. Rather than waking her, she decided to get herself dressed and ready for their trip back home to Austin.

Quietly making her way around the room, she gathered her scattered clothing from the floor and returned it to her duffel. Remembering her soggy bra and boxers, she fetched them, wringing them out in the bathroom sink before tucking them in the mesh outer pocket of her bag. She also picked up Jamie's discarded clothes and piled them up in a chair, not wanting to go into her suitcase without her permission.

She dressed in her last clean outfit, a pair of ripped light-blue denim jeans, a royal-blue T-shirt with the classic winged Aerosmith logo on it, and a pair of blue-and-white Air Force 1s. She was lacing up her sneakers when Jamie rolled over and sat up in bed, rubbing her eyes. In a sleep-heavy voice, she asked, "What time is it?"

Peaches checked her phone. "It's a little after eight." She paused, choosing her next words carefully because she didn't want Jamie to think she was rushing her. "Do you think you'll be ready to get on the road soon? Before I knew I was taking this trip with you, I promised my dad I'd take him grocery shopping today."

Jamie yawned and nodded. "Yeah, just give me a few minutes to get myself together." She got out of bed and made her way to the bathroom, and Peaches couldn't help admiring the sway of her hips and the glow of the sunlight on her gorgeous nudity.

Within the hour, they'd gotten themselves checked out at the hotel. After stopping off to grab iced coffee and bagels, they got on the highway headed toward Austin.

Around a mouthful of cinnamon-raisin bagel, Jamie asked, "What time are you supposed to pick your dad up?"

"Two thirty this afternoon, after he gets out of church. I should get there in plenty of time, even after I drop you off."

Peaches took a sip from her iced coffee before placing it in the cup holder. Keeping her eyes focused on traffic, she let her mind wander to everything she and Jamie had shared last night. That first deep kiss, the initial skin-to-skin contact, had been amazing in ways she couldn't have expected. *And if we hadn't needed to get on the road so that I could fulfill my promise to Dad this afternoon, I would be making love to her again right now.*

Jamie's voice broke into her thoughts. "Damn, in a couple of hours, it'll be back to reality for us."

"True, but after everything that's happened this weekend, reality is just going to be that much sweeter."

Jamie's eyes sparkled, and her smile seemed to brighten the interior of the truck even more than the sunlight. "That's so sweet."

"I mean it," Peaches said. "Now that I've started getting to know you on such a personal, intimate level, I can't wait to find out everything there is to know about you."

Jamie sighed. "Your body is solid, but your heart is soft. I see. What a marvelous combination."

The nearly three-hour ride took them westward on the I-10 toward State Highway 71. Traffic flowed easily, as it often did on Sundays, when people seemed in less of a hurry to get somewhere. The sunlight shimmered on the crystalline particles in the asphalt, the blue sky stretching endlessly above, dotted with only a few puffy clouds.

Peaches put on another nineties playlist about an hour into the ride, and they spent its duration singing along at the top of their lungs. While their singing was at times off key, there were moments when their voices melded together in perfect harmony. Whenever she glanced Jamie's way and saw that radiant smile, Peaches felt a certain lightness claim her spirit. This connection, this relationship between them, was still so new, but whatever it turned out to be in the future, at this moment, it felt right.

The playlist ended a few minutes before they entered Jamie's neighborhood of Highland, and as the music stopped, Jamie grew noticeably silent. Peaches glanced at her, wondering what she might be thinking about. Was it the postvacation doldrums that made her look so sullen and quiet all of a sudden? Or was it something more? Peaches couldn't stop herself from asking, "Are you okay?"

Jamie nodded, but didn't say anything.

Choosing to take her word for it rather than start an argument by pressing her, Peaches turned into Jamie's apartment complex and drove down the lane until she stopped in front of the stairs leading up to her apartment. She was across three parking spaces, but since she wouldn't be here long, she didn't think it would matter. She turned off the engine. "Hold on, I'll come around and help you take your bags upstairs."

She opened the passenger door and extended her hand to help Jamie down, noticing that her facial expression appeared a bit more relaxed than it had a few minutes ago. Reassured by that, she opened the back door to retrieve Jamie's suitcases. As Jamie walked up the stairs, Peaches was right behind her with her luggage in hand.

Jamie stopped at her front door, then took her key out of her purse to unlock it. "Thank you for driving me, Peaches. This was an amazing weekend."

"No problem, thanks for asking me to come along. You're right, it was amazing, and I'm glad I said yes."

Her eyes shimmering, and a soft smile tilting her lips, Jamie leaned in and gave Peaches a lingering kiss on the lips. "Go take care of your dad. I'll give you a call a little later." She opened the door, slid her suitcases inside, and then disappeared into the apartment, closing the door behind her.

Peaches stood on the cement porch for a few moments, enjoying the lingering sensation of Jamie's kiss on her lips. Grinning, she bounded down the stairs and returned to her truck.

Back at home, she placed her duffel on her bed and took a few moments to pull out all the dirty clothes and toss them into the hamper inside her bathroom. After putting the empty bag away in the coat closet, she checked the time on her phone. She had about an hour before she needed to go pick up her dad, so she decided to try to tie up some loose ends around the house in preparation for the upcoming workweek. Even though she had Mondays off, whenever possible she liked to spend them becoming one with her bed.

She'd just finished changing the sheets when she heard her phone ringing. She fished it out of her pocket and glanced at the screen. She smiled when she saw Aiko's name there. "What's up, Aiko?"

"What's up with *you*? Are you back from the road trip yet?"

She chuckled. "Yeah, I'm at home. I just got done making my bed."

"I know you not going to regale me with the boring details of you cleaning up your house when you know I called to see what happened over the weekend." Aiko's tone communicated her impatience. "How did things go with you and Jamie?"

"Calm down, nosy, I was about to tell you." She laughed. "The campus tours went really well, actually. She got a lot of good information at both places, and I think she's already chosen where she wants to go to school."

"That's nice, but you know that's not what the hell I'm talking about."

"I know that, but just like any good storyteller, I'm letting the suspense build up before I give you the good stuff."

"If I could reach through this phone, I swear I'd go upside your head right now, Peaches."

"All right, all right, ease up. I guess I made you suffer long enough. The first night, we kissed and got a little touchy feely, but she said something that threw me off, and things kind of broke down after that."

"What on earth did she say?"

"Yeah, I don't wanna get into it. At any rate, I think we were able to move past it."

"Fair enough. Now, what happened the next night? Because I feel like that's where the story gets juicy."

"You're right, it does." She gave Aiko the play-by-play of her night with Jamie, feeling no need to embellish any of it. It had been amazing, which was just the way she described it to her best friend.

"Damn, homie! Sounds like y'all got it in for real."

"Yeah. I'm telling you, I might develop an addiction." She sighed. "Anyway, now you know the juicy details. I've gotta go. I'm supposed to take Dad to the grocery store at two thirty sharp, and I don't wanna hear him complaining about me being late."

"Okay, I'll let you go. Talk to you later."

"Bye." She disconnected the call and pocketed her phone. After grabbing her keys and wallet, she left and made the drive across town to East Austin.

The old craftsman-style house in a shady corner of the neighborhood remained largely unchanged from when she'd lived in it as a kid, at least from the outside. *The real difference is the vibe inside the house . . . it just hasn't been the same since Mama passed.*

Peaches pulled her truck into the driveway at the same time her father ambled out onto the front porch, with the aid of his carved cherry cane. He wore a white button-down shirt with charcoal-gray pants, held up by a pair of brown leather suspenders. On his feet were his favorite black moccasin-style loafers, and his gray plaid cap was on his head, the brim pulled low over his eyes. Pushing up his silver-rimmed eyeglasses, he stepped down off the porch and shuffled toward the truck.

"Hey, Pops." Peaches got out and walked around to the passenger side to open the door for him. Knowing he'd slap her hand if she tried to help him further, she simply stood nearby as he used his cane to hoist himself up onto the running board before settling into the passenger seat.

"Hey, Peaches." He reached for the safety belt. "Come on and let's get going before the store gets too crowded."

Closing him in, she returned to the driver's seat and carefully backed out of the driveway. "How was service today, Pops?"

"It was all right, I suppose. Pastor was just as long winded as ever. I swear, that man will go off on a tangent at the drop of a hat. We were lucky to get out of there by two. Brother Williams ain't too long ago dropped me off."

She nodded. It was just small talk, but that was usually about as deep as conversations got between the two of them.

At the nearby supermarket, Peaches pushed the cart while her father loaded it down with items, carefully studying his list as he went along. His penchant for once-a-month food shopping made these trips quite the undertaking, but there was no arguing with Rufus Corbin Senior when it came to the right and proper way to do things.

Once he'd finished shopping, Peaches ferried her father back home and helped him carry the groceries inside. As she put away his refrigerated and frozen items, she asked, "Is there anything else you need from me before I go?"

Busy putting boxes of bran cereal into the pantry, he called, "Not right now. But you gonna have to come back over here in a few days and check those mousetraps I set in the crawl space."

Peaches held back a groan. "Wouldn't RJ be better suited for that job?"

"You know all that boy does is work and look after the girls." He chuckled, the sound echoing off the pantry walls. "Besides, you two steps away from being a man."

Peaches cringed. "Pop!"

"You know I don't mean nothing by it. Your brother rarely gets a day off . . . can you just take care of it for me?"

"Okay, Pops. I gotta go. Love you." She rolled her eyes as she headed for the front door.

"Love you too."

Outside, she got in her truck and started it up.

Funny how RJ gets all the consideration, as if I don't have anything important going on in my life. I'm running a business, but I guess that doesn't matter since I'm not raising kids. She loved her father, but his old-fashioned attitudes and his heavy dependence on her to chauffeur him around town and take care of things around her childhood home were starting to wear on her nerves and her patience.

Something's gotta give here.

Sitting in the dining room of Stubb's Bar-B-Q, Jamie leaned back in her chair, peering at the menu. "I don't even know why I'm looking at this! I order the ribs every single time."

"Yeah, you do." Taylor laughed. "Maybe you can switch it up by getting different sides this time, girl."

She squinted, looking at the sides section of the menu. "You know what? I'm gonna be adventurous and try the sweet potato fries."

"Instead of the regular ones?" Taylor scoffed. "You're a real thrill seeker, ain't you."

"Oh, hush." She set the menu down with a shake of her head. "I still can't believe you came pounding on my door, like before I could even get in the house good."

"Whatever." Taylor waved her off. "I heard Peaches' loud-ass truck pull up, and then I heard it again when she pulled off. After that, I waited five full minutes before I came upstairs and knocked on your door."

She snorted. "Oh my God, Taylor. You are such a mess."

"Don't judge me, Jamie. I needed the tea, and I waited as long as I could to get it."

The waiter came by then to drop off their drinks and take their orders. Jamie asked for her usual pork spare ribs and coleslaw, but she mixed it up by ordering sweet potato fries. After Taylor ordered the Angus beef brisket with mac and cheese and fried okra, the waiter left with their menus.

"I'm really glad you had a good time with Peaches," Taylor said, sipping from their glass of iced tea. "It's been a while since you got down . . . it was about time to get those cobwebs knocked out."

Jamie dropped her head in her hands. "Taylor! This is why I can't take you nowhere!"

"You know I'm right."

"You are, but can you be right a little more quietly?" She fought to control the laughter bubbling up inside. "Anyways . . . what did you do this weekend?"

"Work, what else? You know how busy Fridays and Saturdays are at the barbershop."

"Yeah, about as busy as they are at the nail salon."

"Right. I did hang with Claudia after work last night, and . . ." Taylor paused, lips pursed. "Um, about that. You might wanna brace for impact with her."

She frowned. "What are you talking about?"

"I mentioned you being out of town . . . with Peaches . . . and she seemed kinda mad."

Jamie cringed. "Oh shit. You told her?"

Taylor gawked at her, wide eyed. "Bitch, how come *you* didn't tell her? I mean, she said you went by her house the day before you left. You were there for over an hour and it never came up?"

She swallowed. "No. We were talking about school . . . she gave me all this really useful stuff for when I start my classes . . ." She sighed. "I really wasn't thinking about it then, because I was so overwhelmed with all the things she gave me."

"I know I'm your bestie, but since literally everybody else in the squad knew, I can see why Claudia feels left out." Taylor swirled their straw in their glass.

"There's only two other people in the squad."

Taylor's pursed lips said what their silence didn't.

"All right, noted." She fell back against her chair, blowing out a breath. "I guess I'll have to talk to her about it at some point."

"Oh, you will. She's gonna catch up with you, just wait and see."

Jamie wasn't looking forward to the conversation. If their friend squad could be divided into two groups, it would be Peaches and Aiko, and her, Taylor, and Claudia. And while she hadn't left one friend out intentionally, she knew she'd still have to make it right.

The waiter returned with plates laden with food. Jamie inhaled deeply, taking in the savory aroma of perfectly barbecued meat, and her stomach rumbled in anticipation. When she took the first bite of tender, fall-off-the-bone meat, she groaned. "Ugh. Nobody can make something this good except my granny, may she rest in peace."

Taylor nodded while chewing a mouthful of food. "Girl, the mac and cheese here is legit. Best in town, as far as I'm concerned."

For a few minutes, the only sounds at the table were of silverware striking plates and ice clinking in their glasses.

"I got a question," Taylor asked, breaking the verbal silence.

"Hmm?" Jamie raised her glass to take a sip.

"When you going back to test out the strap game?"

Jamie coughed, nearly choking on her orange soda. Clutching her chest, she struggled a moment before getting her breath. "Taylor!"

"What? Inquiring minds wanna know." Eyelashes fluttering, Taylor feigned innocence.

Jamie burst out laughing. When she finally got herself together, she admitted, "ASAP. Because if the strap is as good as the head, I definitely need to get it in my life, stat."

"Now who's acting up in public?" Taylor's face folded into a mock frown.

"Anyway, we had a great time. But the real news is that I'm definitely going to TSU. The whole vibe on campus was so much more welcoming. It's hard to explain."

"I feel you. And one of the big selling points is that the Houston Hottie herself, Megan Thee Stallion, can now be counted among the notable graduates."

She chuckled. "It definitely doesn't hurt. I focused more on some of the great chemists who've graduated from there, and gone on to make really impactful contributions to science. That's what I want to do, and I think it's something I *can* do, even in the nail industry."

"Yes, girl." Taylor nodded in agreement. "People love to pretend like the entire beauty and grooming industry is all about frivolity and vanity, but it's so much more than that. It impacts people's everyday lives."

"'Frivolity'? That's a five-dollar word for sure. You wanna go back to school with me? We can be roommates."

"Girl, hush. I got vocabulary for days, but I'm not tryna go back to school. Anyways, like I was about to say, I've seen the impact a simple haircut and shave can have on somebody. I've seen folks come into the shop, not just looking shaggy but downright downtrodden. But when they leave with that fresh lineup and that beard looking right, or with that fly shape-up, they're like a whole new person."

"Right. I can say the same for the folks coming in to get their manis and pedis and full sets." Jamie popped the last sweet potato fry into her mouth and pushed aside the empty plate. "These people, mostly women and femmes, spend so much time taking care of folks, either at their jobs or their homes or both. Being in the nail salon may be the only time they get to just take care of themselves. It's so valuable."

They sat and chatted for a little while longer, lingering after the waiter had cleared the table and they'd paid the bill. Finally, Taylor rose. "Let's go home before I get too sleepy to drive."

"Yeah, let's." Jamie got up, and the two of them left the restaurant, headed for Taylor's coupe, parked out front. Taylor's devil-may-care driving got them back to the apartment complex in under ten minutes. As Jamie climbed the stairs to her place, she waved at her friend, headed to the level below. "Bye, T. I'll call you tomorrow."

"If you have more tea to spill, you better call me before that," Taylor called out as their door shut behind them.

With a laugh, Jamie entered her own apartment. She kicked off her shoes for the second time today and headed for her bedroom, all the while thinking back on her conversation with Taylor. Talking with her friend about the weekend had effectively kept everything that had occurred between her and Peaches at the forefront of her mind. And now that she was alone with her thoughts, she realized she was craving the comfort of Peaches' energy.

She sucked her lower lip into her mouth, eyeing her phone, which she'd tossed on the bed. After a few moments of internal debate, she grabbed it and dialed Peaches' number.

She answered on the second ring. "Hey, Jamie. What's up?"

"Are you busy? I mean, did you get your dad squared away and all that?"

"Yeah, he's good. I'm just at the house watching TV." She paused. "What is it? You need something?"

"Actually, I do. And I'm gonna need to stop by and get it."

"Did you leave something in my truck?"

"No, but . . ." She giggled. "I'm about to pull up on you."

"Ohhh." Peaches' voice changed as recognition entered. "So you tryna come see me? You miss me already?"

"Yeah, I guess you could say that." She kept her tone low and sultry. "Do you smoke?"

"I'm guessing you mean weed. Yeah, I spark up every now and then."

"Good. Then I'll be there in like twenty minutes." She paused. "I'll bring the bud. You . . . get the strap."

"I'll have the collection ready for your review," Peaches promised. "I got a few still in the packaging."

"See you soon, sexy." Grinning, Jamie ended the call and went to the wooden box where she kept her stash. After she'd packed an overnight bag and changed her clothes, she left her apartment.

As promised, she pulled into the driveway in front of Peaches' town house in Crestview in seventeen minutes. The street was dark, illuminated by the glow of the streetlamps and by the muted lights shining in the windows of neighboring residences.

I haven't been over here in a minute . . . not since the last time she hosted game night. Well . . . we 'bout to play tonight. She knocked on the front door with the bag slung over her shoulder. Peaches opened it, and her mouth immediately dropped. "Gaht damn, shawty!"

"You like it?" She twirled around, letting Peaches see the skintight, orange tube minidress from all angles.

"You look very edible." Peaches stepped back to allow her inside. "Are you wearing anything under that?"

With a sly shake of her head, Jamie slipped past Peaches into the living room.

Soon, Jamie found herself in Peaches' bedroom reviewing the collection of silicone dicks, which they both agreed she should do before they smoked. After she'd chosen a still-sealed, sparkly seven-incher, she freed it from its packaging. "That way we ain't fumbling with it when we're both high as fuck." She used the suction base to stick it to the wall, just above Peaches' low-profile headboard.

"Good looking out." Peaches climbed into the bed and produced a small wireless speaker, which she set on the nightstand. A few moments later, the familiar notes of dvsn's "No Good" filled the room. Resting against the wealth of pillows, Peaches touched the empty spot on the comforter next to her. "Come here."

Jamie joined her, with her kit in hand. While Peaches watched, Jamie packed and rolled. Peaches passed the time by placing occasional kisses along the side of Jamie's throat. Later, as the room filled with haze, they laughed together while passing it back and forth between them. Jamie felt the relaxation flowing through her, bringing a slight heaviness to her limbs. Sinking into the soft bedding, she sighed. Peaches pressed the cardboard tip into the tray, extinguishing the tiny remnant of embers. "That's some good shit."

"Yeah." She laughed, crawling into Peaches' lap. "Now gimme some of your good shit."

Peaches growled, snatching down the top of the dress so Jamie's breasts fell free. Jamie's head fell back, and she moaned, enjoying Peaches' skillful sucking.

Jamie gave herself over to the pleasure, intensified by her elevated state of mind. She let Peaches peel the dress off her body and watched with heavy-lidded eyes as Peaches snatched off her own clothes, tossing them on the floor.

Lying naked across Peaches' lap, Jamie leaned into the passionate kisses they shared. The feel of Peaches' body beneath her was amazing . . . both soft and solid, a glorious combination of well-trained muscles wrapped in delicious, juicy packaging, and smooth skin that smelled of cedar and earth. Peaches pulled away from the kiss, her gaze intense. "Baby, you ready to let me in?"

"I been ready." She dragged the tip of her tongue over Peaches' parted lips, then moved aside so she could get up.

Peaches moved quickly to the dresser, and Jamie saw her step into a black leather harness with brass fittings. Snatching the dick off the wall, Peaches stared at Jamie as she deftly fitted it into the O-ring, one handed. She then grabbed a small bottle from the nightstand and dripped a clear liquid onto the tip before using her other hand to spread it over the entire surface.

Jamie sucked her bottom lip.

Peaches returned to the bed then and gently nudged Jamie onto her back.

Jamie put up no resistance, parting her thighs as wide as she could manage. The next sensation she felt was Peaches' fingers, delving between her pussy lips.

Peaches' tone was low and sultry as she spoke. "I see it's wet for me." She flicked her finger over Jamie's clit and, a moment later, slipped the member inside.

"Shit." The delicious feeling of fullness made Jamie's hips rise to meet it, her back arching. Then Peaches began to move, teasing her with a series of slow, deep strokes that set her insides ablaze. The sensation built and Jamie gave herself over to it, not bothering to hold back the moans escaping her throat.

Peaches leaned down, her hips still rocking as she placed kisses along Jamie's jawline, trailing them down to her collarbone, her lips searing every inch of skin they touched. Then she dragged the tip of her tongue over the shell of Jamie's ear.

Jamie whimpered.

"Open wider for me, baby." Peaches lingered near her ear. "Put them legs up." Her large hands cupped the backs of Jamie's thighs, assisting her in raising her legs until they were high enough for her liking. "Just like that. Hold them there."

By now, the weed and the pleasure were conspiring to push Jamie to the brink of her sanity, but she grasped her ankles anyway, eagerly complying with her lover's command.

Peaches rewarded her obedience by circling her hips in a skillful, rhythmic fashion, ensuring the veined surface of the dick touched every nook and cranny of Jamie's pussy.

"Yesss," Jamie hissed, amazed that Peaches had found a way to take her even higher into the stratosphere of pleasure. Her breath came in urgent bursts, like punctuation sprinkled between moans and cries of passion.

Peaches growled and picked up her pace, her powerful thrusts rocking both the bed beneath them and Jamie's entire existence.

Jamie's head fell back, cradled against the soft pillows. Her eyes closed as she dissolved into brilliance and bliss, her pussy quivering and a strangled scream escaping her throat. When she opened her eyes, she saw Peaches watching her.

A self-satisfied grin crossed Peaches' face. "Had enough, baby?"

Licking her lips, Jamie crooned, "You're amazing."

"Thank you." With a chuckle, Peaches rolled to the side, coming to rest on her back next to Jamie.

Easing into a sitting position, Jamie drew a deep breath. "Sit up, Peaches. Rest your back against the pillows."

"What you about to do?" Peaches asked as she dutifully moved into the prescribed position.

Wordlessly, Jamie positioned herself in front of Peaches. Grasping her ankles, she bent her legs at the knee and pressed them open. As she lay down between them, she wrapped her hand around the dick, still damp with her juices.

Peaches cursed under her breath as Jamie eased the dick and the harness to the side.

A moment later, Jamie slipped her fingers beneath the harness, teasing the damp flesh. "Count to one hundred, Daddy."

Before Peaches could reach the number three, Jamie leaned in and traced her tongue over her swollen clit. And just as she'd suspected, Peaches soon forgot how to count.

CHAPTER THIRTEEN

Peaches stood at her stove Monday morning, dressed in a clean sports bra and a pair of black running shorts. With a green-and-white-striped kitchen towel tossed over one shoulder, she used a spatula to flip the six strips of bacon sizzling in the skillet.

As she cooked, memories of last night's lovemaking replayed in her mind, the images and sounds forming an erotic movie. She licked her lips, recalling the way Jamie had responded to her strokes . . . the soft, feminine moans . . . the sting of her long acrylic fingernails digging into her back . . .

Making love to her the first time was amazing. But being able to give her the full experience, while we were both lifted . . . perfection.

With a smile, she reached up to grab a few paper towels from the mounted dispenser, then lined a plate with them to drain the bacon. The digital display on the built-in microwave showed 9:17 a.m., and as she opened the fridge to retrieve the carton of eggs, she thought of Jamie, whose snores still radiated from the bedroom.

I never asked her how she likes her eggs. After setting the carton on the counter, she slipped into the room and approached the bed. Jamie had burrowed herself into the bedding so deeply that the only visible part of her was her left foot, which dangled off the side of the bed.

Stifling a laugh, Peaches reached out and touched the lump of fabric. Leaning in, she asked, "How do you like your eggs, baby?"

Jamie bolted up, her face coming into view as she peeked from beneath the comforter. "Oh shit. What time is it?"

"It's like nine twenty."

"Shit!" Tossing the covers aside, Jamie scrambled out of bed. "I'm supposed to be at work in ten minutes."

"Damn." Peaches stepped back to give her more space to move around. "I didn't know you had to work today."

"Yeah, I told my boss I'd come in early to help get the shop together for a corporate visit. The lady that owns this shop, and four others in Texas, is coming to visit tomorrow." She darted around the room as she spoke, picking up clothes and throwing them into her bag. "I brought my work clothes . . . I'm gonna take a quick shower, okay?"

"Yeah, sure." She watched as Jamie disappeared into the bathroom. Moments later, she heard the water running.

A strong, acrid scent reached her nose then, and a loud beeping sound began to fill the hallway. Peaches dashed into the hallway. "Oh shit, the bacon!"

By the time she'd grabbed the pan off the stove and set it on the ceramic trivet on her counter, the blackened stuff in the pan barely resembled bacon. With a sigh, she scraped the crumbly mess into the trash can and went to the sink to scrub the pan.

She was just returning the clean pan to the stove when Jamie power walked into the kitchen. Dressed in black cotton scrub pants and a yellow top, she'd wound the ends of her hair into a low bun. Gesturing toward the eggs on the counter, she said, "Aww. I'll have to take a rain check on the breakfast, sexy."

"It's just as well—my bacon was several stages past edible." Peaches moved close to Jamie, wrapping her arms around her waist.

Jamie leaned in and gave her a juicy kiss on the lips, lingering for just a moment. Then she extricated herself from the embrace. "I gotta go. I'll reach out later, okay?"

"Okay. Have a good day." Peaches could barely get the words out before Jamie disappeared through the front door. Alone with her thoughts and her rumbling stomach, she fetched the package of bacon and restarted the process of making breakfast, this time for one.

While she cooked, a sense of unease that she couldn't quite place took over, dampening her previously sunny mood.

After she'd had her bacon, scrambled eggs, and orange juice, she threw on a pair of gray sweatpants and a black tee. *I'm restless. Need to burn off some of this energy.* Grabbing her essentials, she headed for the gym down the road.

She entered the double doors, then headed for the women-only area, without so much as a pause in the main gym. She rarely worked out around men, who seemed to have all kinds of weird-ass reactions to her presence. *They can't decide if they wanna date me or compete with me. It's exhausting.*

The women-only workout area, however, provided a refreshingly different experience. Her interactions on that side were much more pleasant on the whole. Women came to work out, and most of them were content to do just that, minding their own business. Those who were more socially inclined were polite, and even when they were flirtatious, they did it in a noncreepy way.

Once she'd crossed the line of demarcation, she passed through the locker room, where she deposited her bag before going past the sauna and hot tub area, and into a large room filled with cardio and weight lifting equipment. There weren't many people in the gym this time of day on a Monday, when a lot of folks were already trapped at their desks, so she knew she'd have her pick of machines.

She chose her old nemesis, the stair-climber, knowing the exertion would be the most efficient way to burn through her excess energy and settle her mood. After programming the machine to the interval setting, she got her feet into position. As she climbed, the fire building in her quads and glutes, she did her best to focus on something, anything, other than Jamie.

That mission quickly failed as the image of Jamie, standing on the front porch in that tiny orange dress, scorched itself into Peaches' brain.

Then she remembered Jamie leaving this morning, the abrupt parting that left her questioning the encounter.

She left in such a hurry . . . and it made me feel some type of way. I just don't know why. Almost on cue, the intensity level rose, and she leaned forward slightly to keep her balance, the muscles in her legs searing.

Sweat began running down the sides of her face, and without pausing her steps, she grabbed her towel to swipe it away. Something popped into her brain then, as if it had somehow been knocked loose by the exertion.

Denise.

That's why I didn't like the way Jamie left this morning.

She pushed that thought away, setting the clarity aside until she'd completed her full workout. After thirty minutes of stair-climbing, she headed for the lateral pulldown. She put in her wireless earbuds and started a dancehall playlist on her phone to accompany her strength training. The music started, and she bopped her head while making the necessary adjustments to the equipment. She took a seat on the bench and reached up to grab the handlebar.

Her phone rang then, and her earbuds automatically paused her music as the electronic voice announced the incoming call. "What is it, RJ?"

"Good morning to you too, sis. Are you busy?"

"I'm lifting weights right now, so, yes."

He scoffed. "Why do you work out so much? Planning on trying out for the Olympic team?"

She rolled her eyes, exhaling as she finished her first set of reps. "I could if I wanted, smart-ass. I train to stay strong and healthy, not to lose weight and not to be an athlete." She flexed her fingers before grabbing the bar again for her second set. "If ever I get hemmed up, and hands need to be thrown, I got 'em."

"Well, while you're training for this hypothetical street brawl, you mind telling me where you were this weekend?"

She frowned. "I was out of town. What's the problem?"

"With a woman?"

She balked. "I know you're not asking me about my personal business, dude."

"I'm just going by what the girls said. Olivia claims she gave you advice."

Shaking her head, Peaches asked, "Did you actually want something? I mean, other than to stick your nose in my affairs?"

"No. I just wanted to confirm what I heard from my daughters." He laughed. "But don't take any more weekend trips on the fly, though. There's a lot going on at work, and I may need you to babysit."

Not even bothering to dignify that with a response, she hit the button on her phone to disconnect the call. Once her music restarted, she returned her focus to lifting weights.

When she'd finished moving between the various weight lifting machines and the free-weight station, she did a quick stretch before heading for the shower. Beneath the stream of hot water, she couldn't help but be reminded of that hotel shower in Houston, where she'd had Jamie's thigh tossed over her shoulder like the end of a scarf.

She cringed, splashing handfuls of water over her face. *I can't do this to myself again. I can't let her do something that makes me uncomfortable, and not tell her about it.*

Once she was clean and freshly dressed, she fought the urge to pull up to Jamie's job. As much as she wanted to, she didn't think Jamie would appreciate that. Based on what she'd described on her way out, she'd likely be too busy to engage with her on the subject in any meaningful way.

Back at home, she kept herself occupied watching television until the lunch hour, when she received a text message from Jamie. The message was only one character, a lipstick kiss. Peaches found herself smiling at the phone, and a moment later, she dialed Jamie's number.

"Hey, Peaches. What's up?"

"Hey, baby. How's it going at work?"

She sighed. "I'm tired already, but we've still got so much left to do."

"I'm sure y'all will get it done." She paused, looking for a good segue from small talk to what she actually needed to say. "Listen. Um, when you left this morning, my feelings were a little hurt."

"Why? I know I should've told you I had to work today, but I forgot. I mean, we were both pretty high."

"Yeah, we were. And like DJ Luke Nasty said, 'High sex is the best sex.' But that's beside the point." She took a deep breath. "For a little while, I couldn't figure out why I was so upset after you left. But while I was working out at the gym, it became clear."

"I'm listening, Peaches."

"It's because of my ex. The one I told you about, Denise. She had a habit of pulling up on me, then bouncing when she got done with me. Hell, sometimes she'd be gone when I woke up."

"Why are you telling me this?"

She shrugged, even though she knew Jamie couldn't see the motion. "I just wanted to be honest with you about how I felt. I think we've got something good going on, and I don't want it to go badly the way things did between Denise and I."

"Well, damn." Jamie was silent for a moment. "I didn't realize."

"I mean, it's no way you could have known how she treated me . . . not to this level, anyway."

When Jamie spoke again, her tone held an edge of annoyance. "No, that's not what I meant. I meant, I didn't realize you were gonna start comparing me to your ex, and putting the blame on me for your hang-ups."

Peaches twisted her head to the right, taking several slow blinks. "Excuse me?"

"I think I was clear the first time. Listen, I don't have a lot of time to talk, since there's so much going on here. I'll talk to you later." The call disconnected.

For a moment, Peaches stared at her phone in disbelief. *I choose to take the mature approach, and be real with her about how I'm feeling, and this is how she reacts? What the fuck?*

She tossed her phone on the sofa cushion next to her with a shake of her head. How had they gone from this deep connection and passionate sex, to Jamie disregarding her like this, in a matter of days?

I was skeptical from the beginning. I don't know why she'd give me confirmation of all the doubts I had from the start.

꩜

Jamie pocketed her phone, trying to push away any thoughts of Peaches and that rather random, accusatory phone call. Still, her annoyance lingered like an unwelcome houseguest.

Why would she call me with that mess, when she knows I'm at work? How am I supposed to focus on what I'm doing and babysit her ego at the same time?

She'd spent a lot of time pining for Peaches, fantasizing about her, imagining what it would be like to feel her touch. Honestly, the reality of their sexual connection had far surpassed her fantasies. But that didn't mean she wanted to take on someone else's emotional baggage.

This thing is so new, but holy fuck is it intense. I don't know if I like how serious she's making it . . . I mean, we're just getting started. Why is she already looking for problems?

She switched her attention back to the floors, and after giving the area around the pedicure chairs a final scrubbing, she leaned the mop against the wall and flopped down in an empty chair.

Barbara Watts, her boss, walked over with a clipboard in hand. A petite Black woman in her early fifties, she wore black scrubs, and a matching headband held her shoulder-length, salt-and-pepper bob back from her face. "We're about wrapped up with the cleaning, Jamie. Your first client is coming in at one fifteen, so you've got about twenty minutes to get your station set up."

"Thanks for the heads-up, Barb." She grabbed the handle of the mop she'd been using, placed it back inside its bucket, and wheeled it to the supply closet in the back.

When she returned to her station, she was surprised to find her boss still hovering nearby. "What's up, Barb? Is there something else you need?"

She rested her hip against the table as Jamie sat behind it, and a wistful expression came over her face. "I just can't believe you're leaving us in a few weeks. You're one of the best nail techs I have."

"Thanks, Barb. That's really sweet of you to say." She smiled as she reached to the hook beneath her table and grabbed the sanitizer bottle. Careful to avoid spraying Barb's shirttail, she spritzed the table's surface.

"I mean it . . . you know I'm not one for empty praise." Barb straightened, giving Jamie room to do a thorough wipe-down. "Five years has gone by so quickly."

"Yeah, it has." She chuckled. "Remember the first day I came in, when I glued Margot's middle finger to my tabletop by mistake?"

"How could I forget that?" Barb laughed. "Thank goodness she took it in stride."

"And became one of my regulars too." Jamie shook her head, recalling how mortified she'd been, and how calmly Margot had reacted. "I've really had some great experiences working here."

"Part of me wants to try to convince you to stay," Barb admitted. "But I'm not going to, because for one, I know you've made up your mind. I also have a lot of respect for what you're doing."

"Really? According to my mother, it's 'ill advised' to make such drastic life changes at my age." She rolled her eyes as she heard her mother's snide remarks replaying in her head.

"With all due respect, I disagree with your mom." Barb tapped her finger against her chin. "It's true, it's not gonna be easy to make a career pivot. But you're still relatively young, resourceful, and smart. I think you'll do well as a student, and as a scientist after you graduate."

She felt her smile broadening. "Thank you so much. I really appreciate that little ego boost."

"Enough to put off school for a bit and stay through the summer?" Barb pressed her palms together in playful supplication.

She laughed. "Now, you know I'm trying to get ahead by taking classes in the summer terms."

"I know, I know." Barb turned and headed for the back of the salon, calling out, "But I knew it wouldn't hurt to ask."

With a shake of her head, Jamie went back to tidying her station in preparation for her first client.

She'd just laid a clean layer of paper towels down when the doorbell chimed. She looked up from the task . . . and froze when she saw Claudia breeze into the shop. She'd leaned into her tomboy side today and was wearing a pair of khaki cargo shorts with a white polo, white sneakers, and an upside-down visor, turned backward over her silken strands.

Oh shit.

As if she heard Jamie's panicked thoughts, Claudia narrowed her eyes and made a beeline for her station. "Hey, Jamie . . . what's new, homegirl?"

She cringed. "So I'm gonna guess you're my one fifteen appointment?"

"And your two thirty," she said as she hung her purse on the metal hook attached to the table.

She eyed her friend. "You booked two appointments? Really?"

"Hell yeah, I did. For two reasons. I need a fill-in and a pedicure, and I need ALL the details on your weekend." She placed her hands, with fingertips spread, on the table. "Let's start with why you ain't tell me you and Peaches were going away *together*?"

This was it . . . the moment she'd been dreading ever since Taylor's warning. "I'm sorry. Honestly, when I came over to your house Thursday, I was so overwhelmed by all that useful stuff you gave me, I really wasn't thinking about it."

Claudia's eyes narrowed again.

"No, seriously. That's the truth, I promise." She opened her top drawer and took out her nail drill. Choosing the proper sanding bit, she reached for her friend's right hand.

Claudia sighed but offered her hand. "I want to believe you. But I feel like there's more to it than you're letting on."

The low buzz of the drill filled the silence that fell between them as Jamie removed the old polish and smoothed the surface of the existing acrylic to prepare it for the fill. She could hear the hurt in Claudia's voice, and it felt pretty bad to know she'd caused it. Finally, as she began to work on Claudia's left hand, she said, "I . . . was worried you wouldn't approve."

"Oh, you're right. I don't approve." She delivered the statement in a matter-of-fact tone. "That doesn't mean I wanted to be left out of yet another important happening in your life, though."

Jamie frowned. "What do you mean by that?"

"Let's be honest, Jamie." Claudia used her free hand to gesture toward herself. "When it comes to our squad, I'm the fifth wheel."

"What? No."

Claudia offered a bitter chuckle. "Yes, I am. Think about it. I'm the most recent addition to a group of people that have known each other for years. I'm the only one in the group who came out as queer well into adulthood. I'm the only one who likes nerdy shit like arthouse films and early-modern literature." She blew out a breath. "You and Taylor, and

Peaches and Aiko, have been besties since Lord knows when. Y'all were already paired off when I came into the picture."

Jamie set her drill aside and grabbed her buffer. Pausing with the tool hovering over Claudia's hands, she took a deep breath. "I never really thought about it, but you're not wrong."

"Of course I'm not." She flexed her fingertips, then straightened them again. "Remember Peaches' birthday party last year?"

She snort-laughed. "How could I forget it? It's still one of the most epic parties I've ever been to. Well, at least the part of it I can actually remember. I was pretty plastered that night." As she recalled, the next morning she'd come to in the hall closet, surrounded by all of Peaches' cold-weather gear.

"Right, we all were . . . except for Taylor. But I'm really asking you to remember who planned the party, handed out all those sweet gift bags, with free dicks for all, and hired those gorgeous, yet very expensive dancers to come entertain us."

"Damn." Jamie processed what Claudia had just said, really turning it over in her mind for the first time. "I thought it was very generous of you to go to all that effort for Peaches. But until now, I never stopped to think too deeply about why you did it."

Claudia's eyes closed. "I don't want to say I was trying to win favor with the group, but I was. And up until last week, when I was left out of this whole incident, I thought it had worked."

Jamie kept silent as she started to buff. *What can I say? She's making some valid points.*

"I need you to understand where I'm coming from, Jamie. And it's not just that I think friends becoming lovers ends badly most of the time." She met Jamie's eyes. "It's that I know that if things go badly in this instance, the friend group will fracture. It's already stratified—you and Taylor are tight, and Peaches and Aiko are thick as thieves. And even though I feel like I'm on the outside sometimes, I still don't want the squad to crash and burn."

Jamie swallowed, unable to respond.

Claudia looked away, and wetness gathered in her eyes. "Everybody in the group knew about y'all going away together. Everybody except me, and that really hurts."

"I mean, that's really only two other people besides Peaches and I, and . . ." Jamie stopped talking when she realized how she sounded.

Claudia shook her head. "I just want to feel like I fully belong. Why do you think I gave you all that stuff for your classes? I was showing you just how good of a friend I can be. For the last year and a half, I've been trying to show you all."

Jamie set the buffer down and grabbed both of her friend's hands. "I'm sorry, Claudia. I should have told you, and there's no excuse for leaving you out."

She nodded, tugging one hand from Jamie's grasp so she could swipe at the tear sliding down her cheek. "I'll accept your apology in the form of interpretive dance . . . or free pedicures until you leave the shop."

Jamie giggled. "I'll take the second option. Trust me, you don't wanna see me break out my remorseful dance . . . it might start raining."

Rolling her eyes, Claudia laughed. "All right, all right. Now get cracking. I don't want to hold you up from your other appointments."

She obliged and picked up the buffer to continue smoothing Claudia's nails. After layering on and smoothing out a new layer of acrylic, she gestured to the built-in shelves running along the back wall. "You forgot to pick out a color."

Claudia got up and headed for the shelf, while Jamie used a fluffy brush to dust the surface of her table. Switching out the paper towels for a clean layer, she watched her friend peruse the dozens of colors displayed on the shelf.

She's gonna want to know everything that happened this weekend, and I'm gonna tell her . . . at least as much as I can tell her in this setting.

But there's no way I can tell her about my doubts. She's already doom-saying as it is, and even if she's right, I don't want to add fuel to that fire.

Claudia returned to the table then, brandishing a bottle of hot-pink polish along with a bottle of silver glitter. "You know what I'm thinking, right?"

She nodded. "Yep. Accent nail."

CHAPTER FOURTEEN

When Peaches walked into the barbershop Tuesday morning, just after ten, she was laughing at a silly video on social media. As the door swung shut behind her, she slowly began to realize that her laughter was the only sound inside the shop. Closing the app, she raised her eyes from the screen of her phone . . . and found three sets of eyes staring at her. "Yo . . ."

Alonzo, Kev, and Evan all stood by their respective stations, studying her in silence. There were no clients in the shop, making Peaches feel like the unwilling center of attention. The one person in the room who appeared to be going about their business was Taylor, who was looking at something on the company laptop.

Peaches swallowed. "Damn. I know y'all wanna hear about my weekend, but this is starting to freak me out a lil' bit."

"I told them not to make it weird," Taylor announced. "I see they didn't listen."

"And I'm assuming you're not acting like them because you already heard it all from Jamie?" Peaches asked pointedly.

A grinning Taylor nodded. "Yep."

Shaking her head, Peaches strolled to her station and sat down in her barber chair. "Let's make a deal, folks. I'll tell the story if y'all look busy while I talk. I mean, the least you can do is pretend to be working."

On cue, a flurry of activity began around her. Alonzo began spraying his mirror with cleaner, Kev dashed to the back room and returned with a broom, and Evan opened the drawer beneath her station counter and took out her shears kit. Sitting in her barber chair, she used the included cloth to polish each individual item in the kit.

Chuckling, Peaches recounted the events of her weekend adventure through Texas with Jamie at her side. Her barbers managed to keep up the appearance of work the entire time by continuing to use their hands, even as all their eyes remained locked on Peaches' face.

"Wow." Kev grinned. "Seems like y'all hit it off."

"I really think we did." Peaches knew that things were less than perfect between her and Jamie right now, but she was on a roll with the story, and she saw no need to kill the low buzz of excitement moving through the shop right now.

"And that's not even all," Taylor called, without turning around on the stool at the desk. "Tell them about how Jamie pulled up on you *again* on Sunday night."

Peaches rolled her eyes. "I was getting to that, but thanks for the subtle nudge, T."

Taylor threw out a thumbs-up.

Alonzo whistled. "Damn, boss lady. You got this lady shook for real."

"Hush, Al." Evan waved her hand in between implements, then shifted her gaze back to Peaches. "Tell us about Sunday."

Shaking her head, Peaches said, "I'm not about to give y'all too much . . . a customer could walk in at any minute. Let's just say my strap game remains undefeated, and leave it at that."

Kev snorted a laugh.

"Taylor, can you confirm that statement?" Alonzo asked.

"I sure can." Taylor offered another thumbs-up. "Jamie gon' be singing her praises from here to eternity."

Peaches couldn't hold back the yelp that escaped her throat. "Well, I guess that's settled, then."

She thought about their conversation yesterday, and how short Jamie had been with her, and how she hadn't heard from her since then. *The sex was amazing, but everything isn't perfect between us right now.* Shaking off those thoughts, she stood and began preparing her station for any potential clients she might have today. Her appointment book was empty, but there was still a decent possibility of walk-ins.

Within a half hour, all the chairs were occupied and Peaches got her first client of the day. He wanted a lineup, a fresh fade, and a beard trim. Peaches worked on the man's requests with slow, deliberate precision. As she evened out the lines of his beard, she could feel her mind drifting to thoughts of Jamie.

What is she doing today? Is she still upset that I called her at work? Why hasn't she texted? Even with all the lingering awkwardness from their last conversation, Peaches couldn't seem to get Jamie out of her mind.

"Hey, ease up," her client groused.

Snapped back to reality, Peaches turned off her beard trimmer. "It's still not like I want it, Vic." She looked at her client's face, and she could see where she'd trimmed his right sideburns about an eighth of an inch thinner than his left ones. "Shit. Let me clean up the edges a little bit more."

"Cool, cool." Vic laid his head back against the top of the barber chair.

Giving her full focus to the task at hand, Peaches spent the next twenty minutes perfecting Vic's sideburn and beard, until they were as neat and tidy as the client had requested.

After Vic left, Peaches seated Jason, a freshman from UT Austin. "You know that's my alma mater. What's your major?"

"Business."

Peaches nodded as she switched combs on her clippers. "Oh, word? That was my major too."

They chatted for a few minutes while she worked on tapering Jason's sides, but then the young man started to get wrapped up in something happening on the screen of his phone. As conversation waned between them, Peaches found her mind wandering yet again to Jamie.

I want this thing between us to work . . . she's so sexy. But if I can't be honest with her about my feelings, is there really anything deeper there? I mean, she was so dismissive earlier.

Her grip loosened, and the clipper blades skirted just above Jason's left ear as the trimmer fell from her hand. It bounced against the arm of the barber chair, and she caught it before it hit the floor. "Damn."

"Damn is right!" Jason swiveled his chair, looking at his reflection in the mirror. His face folded into a frown. "This ain't good, P."

She pressed her knuckle to her mouth as she looked at the jagged line the blades had left just above the young man's ear. Narrowing her eyes, she put her creative mind to work. "My bad. Listen, I'll give you a custom design with a series of parts on this side to fix the mistake. And no charge for your cut, of course."

He relaxed a bit, his shoulders dropping and his expression leaning more toward a smile. "That'll work."

Taking a deep breath, Peaches switched to the smaller precision trimmers she mostly used for mustaches and got to work correcting her error. By the time she'd finished and turned the chair so Jason could see the result, a bright grin crossed over the young man's face. "Wow. This actually looks really dope."

Peaches nodded, admiring the series of lightning bolts she'd fashioned along the side of his head. "I'm glad you like it." Removing the cape, she dusted his shoulders off. "See you in a couple of weeks?"

He nodded, shaking her hand. "Yeah. Now that I know you can turn a mistake into artwork, then I'll definitely be back."

After he left, Peaches noticed Alonzo watching her. "What?"

He shook his head. "I haven't seen you screw up a haircut since you were with that girl . . ."

"Aht, aht." Peaches held up her hand, cutting him off. "Don't even say her name."

Evan cringed. "That bad, huh?"

"Worse." Peaches glanced at her watch. "But I know Alonzo can't resist rehashing my past. So I'm gonna go sit in my office and wait for Spencer." Based on the time, she knew she could expect her accountant within the next ten minutes.

Alonzo had the decency to wait until she'd shut herself into her office before he started talking again, and odds were he was airing out all the tea about her ex. As Peaches sat in the black leather executive chair behind her black lacquer desk, she blessed the foresight she'd had to soundproof this room. What had originally been done so she could escape the buzz of the clippers and a half dozen conversations now offered protection from something she'd rather not relive. Taking out her phone, she sought out a bit of distraction to pass the time.

A knock sounded against the office door, and she called, "Come on in."

The door swung open, and Spencer Hart, CPA, strutted in. Wearing stylish brown loafers and a bright-blue suit with a crisp white shirt beneath, he carried a brown leather briefcase. Pushing the tortoiseshell frames of his round glasses up his nose, he said, "Hey, honey. How've you been?"

"What, have they stopped analyzing my personal life out on the haircutting floor?"

Spencer laughed. "Of course not. But I thought I'd get the dirt straight from the shovel, if you know what I'm saying."

Peaches laid her phone down on her desk and gestured to the guest chair across from her. "Nice suit, by the way. Lemme guess . . . skyline blue?"

He popped the lapels of his jacket as he slid into the chair. "Close . . . cerulean."

She snapped her fingers. "Dang. Almost had it."

"It's about the closest you've ever gotten." He laughed as he set the briefcase across his lap and opened the latches. "At any rate, let's talk money, Peaches."

She waited while he took out a black notebook with her name printed on it in gold calligraphy, and opened the cover. "So, what's my financial picture?"

"It actually looks pretty good for you, Peaches." He turned a few pages and paused on one that had a printed spreadsheet stapled to it. "I ran the numbers just like you asked me to. Analyzed all your assets and debts, account balances, the whole nine. And honestly, you're very much in the black."

Peaches grinned, leaning forward. "How good is it?"

"You're right on target with your contributions to your retirement account, and to the college fund you have for your lil' nieces . . . How are they doing, by the way?"

"They're doing good, thanks for asking." She paused. "So I'm good on that front, but what about profits from this place?"

"Oh, there's even better news there, my friend." Spencer smiled. "You're actually ahead of your projected profits for the first quarter."

Peaches' brow cocked. "By how much, exactly?"

"How about thirty-three percent." He snapped his fingers. "You've got a solid customer base here, honey."

"And more people coming in every day, thanks to some really great online reviews, and word of mouth, of course."

"Absolutely. That positive-whisper-campaign magic is the bread and butter of any successful business marketing effort."

Peaches stroked her chin. "Wow. This is amazing to hear. I've worked so hard to get this place on solid footing—it's nice to see it pay off."

He nodded. "I know. And with your profits moving like they are, I think it's time you gave serious consideration to opening another location."

"I have been thinking about it, honestly. But hearing all this has made those thoughts seem a lot more concrete and attainable."

"Definitely." He pulled out a small stack of stapled pages and handed them across the desk. "Here's all your paperwork for quarter one. I've included a projection for possible costs in opening another location, and I think you should take a look at it."

"I will." Accepting the papers, she looked them over. "What information do you have for me?"

He leaned back in his chair as he shut his briefcase. "Honestly, Austin is full. If you want to get commercial real estate at a reasonable price, you've gotta look outside the city proper. You can try Round Rock, Cedar Park, Brushy Creek, places like that. But you had the right idea—your best bet is to look beyond Travis County too."

She placed the papers in the top drawer of her desk. "Thanks for the heads-up on that."

"No problem . . . that's just the kind of sound advice you pay me for." He leaned to his right, resting his bent elbow on the armrest. "Do you have any other items you want to discuss with me while I'm here?"

She shook her head. "We're good. But I do have something for you, though." Rising from her seat, she went to the safe behind the desk and punched in her combination. She handed two envelopes over to Spencer. "Here are my retirement and college fund contributions for this month." Putting aside something for her own retirement was a given, but being able to put money toward her nieces' futures was a blessing.

He accepted them and added them into his briefcase. "I'll drop these off on my way back to my office."

"Thanks, Spence."

A few moments later, he left with a tip of his imaginary hat.

Alone in her office, Peaches contemplated what she'd just heard.

Financially, I'm all set for that second location.

But mentally? That's a different story. And I don't think it's a good idea to let Jamie, or anyone else, distract me from this.

⁓

Jamie pulled up to Sean and Bethany's ranch-style home in Parker Lane around 4:00 p.m. on Wednesday. After parking her car near the balloon-festooned mailbox, she turned off the engine and popped the trunk. She walked around the car to retrieve the huge gift bag she'd brought for her nephew, then shut the trunk and strolled up the sidewalk to the front door.

She entered the open door and immediately picked up the sound of some festive kids' music being blared from an unseen speaker. Parents and guardians nodded and waved in greeting, and she responded in kind as she moved along. Wading carefully through the living room to avoid the strewn toys and crumpled napkins, as well as the tiny toes of the pint-sized party guests who'd come to celebrate Levi's second birthday, she made her way to the kitchen, near the middle of the house.

There, she found Bethany standing at the center island, pressing a small wax number two into the top of Levi's red-and-white Elmo-themed birthday cake. Wearing a red tunic and black leggings, she'd piled her dark hair into a messy bun on top of her head. "Hey, Jamie. Glad you could make it." She spun around long enough to open a drawer.

"Hey, Bethany." She held up the heavy bag for a second. "Where should I put this? And where's Levi?"

"He's in the dining room with Sean. You can put the gift on the buffet under the window in there." She gestured in the direction of the dining room with a pastry spatula. "I'm sure he'll be happy to see his aunt Jamie."

"I doubt he'll notice me with all the commotion going on in here." She tugged the bag along as she rounded the island and went through the archway into the dining room. After parking it on the floor next to the buffet, she headed for the end of the rectangular table, where Sean sat with Levi on his lap. Sean wore a red tracksuit with a white stripe, as well as a white tee and sneakers.

The toddler, dressed in a red tee, denim shorts, and red-and-white sneakers, had a conical Elmo-themed party hat placed haphazardly atop his head, his brown curls peeking out from beneath it.

Glancing down at her own dark denim skinny jeans, purple tank, and black cardigan, Jamie realized she'd missed the whole Elmo-themed red-attire memo.

Miraculously, Levi did notice her, and the grinning little one held up his arms to be picked up.

Her heart melted. "Hey, Levi!" Jamie reached for him and settled his little body against her hip. "How's my little birthday boy?"

"Auntie J!" Levi grabbed her face with both hands, giving her a slobbery kiss on the cheek.

Feeling the stickiness against her face, she chuckled. "Somebody's had sweets, I see." She reached out and gave her brother a playful punch in the shoulder. "Hey, Sean."

"Hey, Jamie." He stood. "I can't believe you're the only one from my side who came to Levi's party."

"You know I'm the last one to make excuses for them," she said, switching her wriggling nephew onto her other hip, "but Mom and Dad are out of town at that church marriage-retreat thing."

He rolled his eyes. "True enough. Their excuse is better than Shelby's."

"What was his?"

"He doesn't 'do' kids' parties." Sean frowned. "Basically, my child's uncle thinks he's too cool to spend an afternoon with him, even if it is his birthday."

Jamie felt her lips purse. "Don't worry about it, Levi. Auntie Jamie is here, and I'm easily the most fun one from our household."

Sean looked as if he took offense. "Really?"

She ignored him, instead turning and carrying her nephew to the gift table. Setting him down on the floor, she said, "You should open mine first. It's pretty epic."

"Not yet!" Bethany swept into the room then and scooped her son up. "We have to sing the song and let him blow out his candles first; then he can open gifts."

She shrugged. "He's two, so I don't think he really cares about the proper order of ceremony, but whatevs."

After Bethany and the other parents had wrangled their little ones into the dining room, Levi was secured into his high chair at one end of the table. Two party guests set the cake in front of Levi, and with his parents flanking him, everyone sang to him while he clapped and giggled. As she warbled along with the others, Jamie had to admit that the whole thing, while a bit corny, represented the pinnacle of cuteness.

The song ended, and Sean lifted Levi from the seat, hoisting him to the top tier of the two-tiered cake. Between father and son, they managed to get the candles blown out after a few tries, and the room erupted into boisterous cheers.

Jamie watched as Levi devoured a slice of cake with his bare hands. After Bethany had scrubbed his face and hands with baby wipes, he was released to open gifts. She grinned as he tore the huge bag away from the tiny barbecue grill she'd gotten him, complete with all the utensils and play food he could want.

Bethany sidled up next to her. "That was the perfect gift for Levi . . . he loves those little segments where Elmo cooks. Thank you."

"No problem. It's wooden, so it's sustainable and it should last him awhile." She pointed to the box. "There's a chef's hat and a little apron in there too."

Bethany squealed. "I'll make sure they get put away before we toss the box." She headed for the gift table and joined Sean, who was busy stuffing paper into a large black trash bag.

Drifting away from the epicenter of the gathering, Jamie left the dining room, using the french doors to go outside onto the patio. Despite the nice weather, very few people were outside, save two parents who stood in the corner of the fenced backyard, talking. Looking at their expressions and gestures, Jamie could only guess they'd needed a respite from the full-tilt kid-o-rama going on inside the house, and she couldn't say she blamed them.

Flopping down on the cushion of the white wicker love seat near the door, she sighed. The air was thick with the scent of magnolias in bloom, and the sun shone down from a cloudless blue sky. Letting her head fall back, she stared up, watching a small flock of birds as it passed overhead, their dark wings spread wide.

As she began to sink into the solitude of the moment, thoughts of Peaches entered her mind. She frowned. *I don't want to think about her right now. We haven't spoken since she called me at work, and I'm already bracing for seeing her at game night tomorrow. No need to dwell on her now.*

It's the physical connection . . . the amazing sex. That has to be it.

The immaculate strap, the way Peaches seemed to know just when, where, and how to touch her body to make her entire being shudder. That had to be why Jamie couldn't stop thinking about her, even though she'd much rather be focused on something else.

She felt a presence near her, and the awareness brought her back to the present moment. Looking to her right, she watched Bethany fall into the armchair there. Bethany looked exhausted as she blew a lock of dark-brown hair out of her face.

"It's been a long day, I'm guessing." Jamie shifted her body to face her sister-in-law.

She nodded. "Extremely. I've been up since six o'clock this morning getting ready. And I know I'll probably be up late tonight, cleaning up all the carnage."

Jamie crossed her legs at the ankle, sensing a venting session coming on. "Let me guess . . . my brother isn't much help, is he?"

Bethany shook her head. "No, he's not. That trash bag he brought in, to clean up the gift wrap? He just announced that he's happy he could help, and that he's gonna spend the evening working on his latest app."

Shaking her head, Jamie said, "He really hasn't changed much since we were kids. When he was a little boy, he always had creative excuses to get out of doing any actual work. And because he was Mom and Dad's 'precious baby boy,' they let him get away with it."

"Great. Now I'm stuck with that, I guess." Bethany slouched back in her chair. "I love Levi so much. But raising a kid is so draining. Sean does okay with helping, but you know how it is. Child rearing, housework, all that . . . it's 'women's work.'"

"Levi is an awesome little dude." Jamie smiled. "But motherhood looks exhausting on a level I can't handle. I think just being his aunt will be enough for me."

"I'm good with that, so long as you don't expect me to have any more."

Jamie chuckled. "Nah. With my brother as your mate? I'm sure one child will be sufficient."

Bethany appeared thoughtful. "Do you think if I tattle on Sean to your parents, they'll come over and whip him into shape when they get back from their trip?"

Jamie snorted. "Nope. He's already their precious baby. And now that he's the first of their kids to give them a grandchild, he's basically untouchable." Deep down, she wondered if her brother had cracked that particular code. Had he gotten Bethany pregnant so he could ascend to astronomical levels of favor with their parents?

"You're probably right. Even when Mother Bernadette looks after Levi, she has to have everything 'just so' for her grandbaby." Bethany sighed. "Oh well. I guess I'll just have to make Sean sleep on the couch until he's acting right."

Jamie cringed. "Ew. He's my little brother. As far as I'm concerned, he always sleeps on the couch, and Levi was dropped off two years ago today by the stork."

They both laughed.

Stretching her arms above her head, Bethany commented, "It's so nice outside. Maybe the kids should come out here and burn off some of that sugar they've been eating all day."

"Good idea." Jamie stood. "I'm gonna head home, though. I think I've had my fill of small children for the day."

"I get it. Thanks for coming, though." Bethany got up, and the two of them reentered the house. No sooner had they shut the doors behind them than Sean came running up to his wife.

"Beth, I've been looking for you. Some kid threw up in the hallway, and I don't know where the foaming carpet stuff is."

Bethany rolled her eyes. "I'll get it." Turning toward Jamie, she gave her a nudge. "Get out while you still can, J. Thanks again for the gift."

"Yeah. Bye, you two." She gave her brother a playful bop against his forehead. "Kiss Levi for me, and tell him Aunt Jamie loves him."

As they ran off to deal with the rather gross results of too much excitement and too many sweets, Jamie slipped out the patio door. After going down the steps, through the back gate, and around the side of the house, she finally made it back to her car. As she got into the car and slung her purse into the passenger seat, she took her phone out of her pocket, checking it for the first time in the last few hours.

There was a text from Peaches, sent about an hour prior.

Are you still coming to game night?

Annoyed, she fired off a quick response.

Yeah, why wouldn't I?

CHAPTER FIFTEEN

Peaches walked from Aiko's kitchen to her dining room table Thursday night and set down the huge plastic bowl filled with tortilla chips. "Dang, Aiko. Did you get enough chips?"

Aiko laughed. "Summer did that. It's like two whole bags in there, I think."

"Three bags," Summer called from the middle bedroom, which the couple used as an office. "And a half gallon of homemade salsa, thank you very much."

After returning to the kitchen for the salsa, Peaches carried the large ceramic bowl and placed it on the dining room table, careful not to splash any on her clothes. While she'd never tried to get a salsa stain out of a white polo shirt, it wasn't an experience she wanted to have.

"Is this all the food?"

Aiko shook her head. "Of course not. You know Summer made a whole lot of stuff for us to snack on. I'll get the rest of it out of the fridge, though." She got up from her seat at the table and moved across the open-concept dining room back into the galley-style kitchen. She took a large crudité platter out of the fridge and placed it next to the chips and salsa. A fruit and yogurt platter followed that, along with a large pitcher of lemonade.

"Damn," Peaches said. "I guess I could have skipped dinner before I came over here."

Aiko chuckled. "If there's one thing my baby is gonna do, she's gonna make sure I eat good. Y'all are just reaping the benefits of being my friends."

As if summoned, Summer entered the room then and strolled over to Aiko, cuddling close to her side. Aiko leaned down, giving her wife a peck on the cheek. "How's lesson planning going, baby?"

Summer sighed. "Slowly but surely, I suppose. I might come out here and sit with y'all—I'm getting a little restless."

"Why don't you sit over there on the sectional? That way you can spread out all your papers, and we won't be in your way."

"Good idea, I'll do that." Giving Aiko a quick kiss on the lips, Summer slipped back into the office to grab her supplies.

Watching the two of them together made Peaches' stomach do flips. They were so sweet and so happy together, and while she loved it for her friend, it only reminded her of all the things she was missing out on in her own life.

She helped Aiko fetch the board games and card decks from a cabinet in the kitchen and then arranged them on the table around the bounty of food. Per the established rules of their friend-group game night, Aiko had provided two options for board games, Scrabble and Monopoly, and two options for card games, Uno and spades.

"Are we going to coin-flip again to decide which games to play?" Peaches asked.

"Probably." Aiko sat down at the head of the table. "Folks should start pulling up any minute. Go ahead and pick your seat, homie."

Peaches chose the chair directly to Aiko's right and eased into it. After taking an empty cup from the stack from the table, she poured herself some lemonade. As she sipped, she considered what the mood might be once Jamie arrived. *Whatever the case, I'm not going to talk about what's going on between us. Tonight, it's good vibes only.*

Claudia arrived soon after that, wearing a pair of loose-fitting jeans, a black tee, and a backward baseball cap that matched her shirt. Sitting down to Aiko's left, across from Peaches, she asked, "What are we playing first?"

Aiko shrugged. "We won't know until we do the coin flip, and we won't do that until everybody gets here." She fished a quarter out of her pants pocket and laid it on the table.

Peaches made eye contact with Claudia briefly, noting the way Claudia looked down almost immediately. *What's going on with her?*

Taylor breezed in, and Jamie wasn't far behind them. Taylor's ensemble of black-and-white vertical-striped leggings with a matching button-down shirt was very much in contrast with Jamie's muted beige scrubs.

Looks like she came straight from work. Peaches watched as the last two members of the group took seats at the table, with Taylor next to Peaches and Jamie to Claudia's left.

"What's up, Jamie?" Aiko then nodded toward Taylor. "How you doing, Beetlejuice?"

Taylor laughed. "Say it two more times and I'm going upside your head, Aiko."

Summer chuckled as she walked by, carrying a large canvas bag to the sofa. "Y'all are a mess. This is about to be the most entertaining background noise ever."

"Coin-flip time," Aiko announced. "Jamie, call the board games."

She looked at the boxes on the table and said, "Heads, Monopoly. Tails, Scrabble."

"Got it." Aiko tossed the coin in the air. "Looks like we're playing Scrabble."

Claudia grinned and cracked her knuckles. "Hell yeah. Finally another use for all that studying."

Peaches handed out the wooden trays and made sure each person started with an equal number of letter tiles. With the board in the center of the table, the game began, and Taylor placed the first word.

The five of them took turns building out the board with words both long and short while nibbling on Summer's buffet of snacks. Peaches thought about trying to pass off the name "Steve" as a word but, when she imagined Aiko chewing her out about it, decided to pull a few more letter tiles from the vinyl bag instead. Luckily, she found two useful letters among the ones she grabbed, allowing her to place the word "invest" on the grid.

Aiko placed the word "Shoto" by building on Peaches' letter I, and after a short but spirited debate about the validity of a word that only existed in the Star Wars universe, the word was deemed playable. Claudia played her word; then came Jamie's turn.

Holding eye contact with Peaches for a long moment, Jamie then placed an E and an X tile below the S in Peaches' last word to spell "sex."

Peaches swallowed, heat gathering beneath the neckline of her polo. She gave the collar a quick tug, hoping to release some of the steam.

Jamie smirked. "Your turn, Taylor."

The rest of the game went by without much drama, to Peaches' relief. Claudia won by over a hundred points, as she'd predicted . . . her double-letter, triple-word-scoring sorcery proved too powerful for the others at the table.

Aiko's second coin flip determined Uno as the card game, and Peaches released a slow exhale. If there was any one game guaranteed to get spicy among a group of Black people, it was spades. And while they avoided that game, Uno was definitely a close second in the "games that might start a fistfight" category.

Taylor dealt the cards and the game got underway. Intensity rose as they moved around the table, slapping down cards in succession, each person trying to get rid of their own cards while simultaneously increasing the number of cards in other players' possession.

Aiko held up her single remaining card, declaring, "Uno." She was the first to win.

Peaches felt like she'd already stress-eaten her weight in tortilla chips, though she still had five cards in her hand. Her gaze shifted to Claudia, whose turn was next.

"Draw Four." Claudia slapped down the card.

"Nope." Jamie slapped down another Draw Four.

"Ha!" Taylor added another to the pile. "As if. Color is green."

Peaches closed her eyes for a brief moment. When she reopened them, she still had only blue and yellow cards in her possession. Plucking twelve more cards from the draw pile, she settled back in her seat and awaited her impending defeat.

Jamie was next to win, followed by Taylor.

Jamie stood, her gaze on Peaches. "We gotta go, early day at the nail salon tomorrow. Thanks for hosting, Aiko . . . bye, Summer."

"Bye, y'all." Summer waved from her spot on the sofa.

Peaches watched the two of them leave, unable to draw her eyes away from the tempting sway of Jamie's hips.

Claudia snapped her fingers. "Yo, Peaches. You still in this?"

"I guess." *Even though it looks basically hopeless for me at this point.* She glanced at the thick fan of cards in her hand, shaking her head. Her friends triumphed within the next ten minutes; when the game ended, Peaches still had six cards.

Summer stood, stretching and yawning. "I'm done with my lessons. Are y'all finished with the food?"

"Yeah, baby." Aiko gestured to the mostly empty trays, where nothing more than a few loose carrots, chip crumbs, and a small amount of salsa remained. "Let me help you clean up."

The newlyweds whisked away the dishes from the table and moved into the kitchen. The sound of running water soon filled the space, accompanied by Summer's giggles as Aiko playfully patted her behind.

"Gotta love open concept," Claudia quipped. "Now we don't just get to hear them canoodling—we gotta see it too."

Peaches laughed. "They've only been married a few weeks. Maybe it'll cool off as time passes?"

Claudia shook her head. "I doubt it. And, annoying as they are, I hope they stay just as goofy and in love as they are now. Always."

"Me too," Peaches admitted. She glanced over at the two of them and saw Summer sitting on the counter, with Aiko standing between her parted legs. The passion rolling off them felt as thick and impermeable as molasses.

"Listen, I wanna talk to you," Claudia announced, leaning in.

"Better make it quick. Looks like the lovebirds are about to rock the nest."

With a laugh, Claudia said, "You're probably right. Anyway, things seemed a little . . . awkward between you and Jamie tonight."

"A little? They were very awkward." Peaches shrugged. "If you're asking me why, I really don't know what to tell you."

Her eyes narrowed. "Seriously? You know I'm aware of y'all's little secret rendezvous, right?"

"I assumed you knew. Yes, we went away together, and we had amazing sex while we were gone. But ever since we've been back in Austin . . . I really don't know where Jamie's head is at."

Claudia shook her head slowly. "This is precisely why I think friends shouldn't try to change their relationship into something romantic. It's bound to get weird, and I don't know if there's any good way to stop that from happening."

"I don't either." Peaches rubbed her chin. "Honestly, my thoughts on this kind of thing are similar to yours. The only reason I agreed to this trip, and to doing anything remotely like a relationship with Jamie, is because she insisted. She came on so strong, I had to say yes."

"You always have your free will, Peaches."

"I know that. My attraction to her may have overridden my cautious nature . . . and possibly my good sense, but it is what it is. We've started something together, and now we're gonna have to figure it out the same way."

Claudia sighed. "I just don't want to see either of you get hurt. And I also don't want this friend group to fracture. Outside of my academia peeps, y'all are my only close friends."

Peaches looked at Claudia, seeing the sincerity in her eyes. She could also see the fear there, and it reflected her own initial fear of causing irreparable damage to what she considered her found family. "I can't make any promises, because I can't speak for Jamie. But I'll do my best to make things right, and to maintain our little squad on good terms."

"That's all I ask." Claudia got up from her chair, stifling a yawn. "Man, she gave us all the good snacks. I gotta get my ass home before the itis hits and I fall into a food coma."

"Same." Peaches stood and stretched. "I'm gonna head out in the next few minutes myself. See you later, Claudia."

After Claudia left, Peaches went to the threshold of the kitchen and loudly cleared her throat. "I'm leaving, y'all."

Separating her lips from Summer's, Aiko grinned. "Thanks for coming, P."

"Go easy on your wife, Aiko. You're about to devour her whole face."

"The rest of her isn't safe from me either." Aiko winked as she snaked her arm around Summer's waist, pulling her closer.

"Lemme get out of here before I get a free show." Shaking her head, Peaches left. The last sound she heard as the door shut behind her was Summer's high-pitched giggling.

~

From the moment Jamie arrived at Stellar Nails on Friday morning, she served back-to-back clients. It seemed everyone in Austin had gotten together and collectively decided they all needed their nails or feet done, on the same day. Luckily the salon was fully staffed, with eight nail techs and two aestheticians working the waxing rooms in the back.

Even Barbara, who was rarely seen working on the floor, dusted off her implements and took on a few clients.

Around one o'clock, foot traffic in the shop finally slowed down, allowing Jamie and the other techs a much-needed breather. After finishing up a set of gel nails, she dashed off to use the bathroom. When she returned, she sat behind her table and pulled out her phone.

Barbara's voice interrupted her scrolling. "Hey, Jamie. You can go ahead and take a thirty for lunch."

"Cool." Tucking her phone away, she grabbed her purse and headed out into the late-April sunshine.

She went into Morelli's, the small deli that occupied the storefront four doors up from the nail salon. After ordering a club on wheat, a small container of potato salad, and an orange soda, she went to one of the picnic tables outside in the breezeway next to the restaurant and sat down to eat.

The day was beautiful, if slightly overcast, and a breeze blew through the area, carrying with it the scent of pollen, blooming flowers, and coming rain.

While she ate, she watched the activity happening in the shopping center around her. Cars entered and exited the lot, and people moved up and down the covered sidewalk to shop, dine, or otherwise patronize the various businesses there.

She thought back on game night. *This is the first time there's ever been any weird feelings around the game table. We're always competitive, but still friendly.*

Last night felt different, and I didn't like it. I know I was a bit snarky and standoffish with Peaches, but I couldn't seem to stop myself. It definitely wasn't her finest hour; she'd failed at self-regulation, big-time. She also recalled that Claudia had lingered after Peaches and Taylor left, and she wondered if Claudia and Peaches had talked about the situation. Taylor had actually pointed out that the vibe seemed a little off, having noticed it as well. Thinking that they might have discussed her in her absence made her somewhat upset.

Pull it together, girl.

A piece of tomato fell out of her sandwich and landed on her lap. "Dang." She grabbed a napkin, collected the fallen slice, and then used a clean one to dab at the juice staining her soft-gray pants. "I would get clumsy on the day I'm wearing light-colored pants," she groused to herself.

"You're always clumsy, actually," a deep, familiar voice teased.

She glanced up from her pant leg and into the smiling face of her older brother. "Shelby? What are you doing here?"

Wearing a black suit, black leather wingtips, a crisp white shirt, and a red paisley tie, Shelby helped himself to the seat across from her. Sitting down, he answered, "I went to the nail salon looking for you. One of your coworkers said you were on lunch, and saw you walking this way."

"That explains why you're here, at Morelli's. Care to explain why you came looking for me in the first place?"

He released a breath. "I'll get to that. Meanwhile, how was Levi's party?"

"You mean the one you were too cool to attend?" She rolled her eyes.

He frowned. "Come on. Don't give me that judgy look. Besides, I stopped by on the way to my office this morning to leave the kid a gift."

"Oh yeah? What did you get him?"

Folding his arms over his chest, Shelby announced, "One of those little fake tool benches, with a little toy saw on it. It spins and makes a sound and everything."

"Whatever. He'll probably enjoy playing with the pretend grill I got him even more than your crummy tool bench." She winked, letting her brother know she was teasing him.

He shook his head. "Was it a good party or what?"

"It was a real wild one—Levi and his friends party hard."

"Don't give me that look, by the way. I just can't do kids' parties."

"Yeah, we all know that." She finished up the last spoonful of potato salad. "I just hope you get over it by his next birthday. He isn't gonna stay small and precious forever, Uncle Shelby."

Appearing appropriately contrite, he sighed. "Listen, I didn't drive all the way over here from the firm to have you lecture me about being a bad uncle. I wanted to tell you . . . I met someone."

Her brow crinkled, and she perked up at the chance of having someone else's love life distract from her own. "Really? Tell me all about . . . them."

His smile brightened. "It's a guy. His name is Matthew—everybody calls him Matt. I met him at a bar a couple of weeks ago."

Resting her chin on her hand, she said, "Go on. I'm listening."

"We both ordered the same drink . . . a brandy Alexander."

She laughed. "Congrats, bro. You linked up with the one other guy under the age of sixty who drinks brandy Alexanders." She paused. "Wait. He is under sixty, right?"

Shelby rolled his eyes. "Oh, hush, Jamie. I don't need your cocktail judgment ruining the story. For your information, Matt is thirty-nine."

"You check his license to verify that?"

He glared.

She folded. "Sorry, sorry. Go on with the story."

"Anyway, we struck up a conversation and ended up staying out past ten, just chatting. He asked me out, and we've been on two dates since then."

She smiled. "This is great news, Shelby. You're finally coming out of your dating drought. For a while there, you were less bi-sexual and more . . ."

"By myself." He finished the line with deadpan delivery. "If you tell that tired joke one more time, I'm gonna snatch that wig right off your scalp."

Placing her hand on her chest, she leaned back in feigned offense. "Well, I never. Good thing I used my favorite extra-hold glue on this unit." She shook her head. "Anyway, you really drove here in the middle of the workday just to tell me about Matt?" She and her brother had a good relationship, but not one that would create the expectation of such a visit.

He nodded. "Yeah. I think we might be getting serious, you know? I feel like maybe . . . he could be my boyfriend. Potentially."

She pursed her lips, watching him. "Shelby, I only have a thirty-minute lunch break, and twenty-two minutes of that is already gone. So whatever bush you're beating around, I suggest you just say what you came to say."

He drew a deep breath. "I . . . was thinking about coming out to Mom and Dad. You know, when they get back in town."

She cringed, shaking her head. "Bro, I don't know if that's the best idea."

"Why not? I really like Matt, and I feel like I can't tell our parents about him just because he's a man. You know how desperate Mom is for more grandchildren—she's always asking me if I've met someone nice. For the last two weeks, I've been lying and saying I haven't."

After taking a long sip of orange soda from the foam cup, Jamie set it back down. "Shelby, I'd advise you to hold off for two reasons. Number one, you haven't known Matt long enough for whatever you share to warrant this kind of cataclysmic revelation."

"'Cataclysmic'? Don't you think that's a little dramatic?"

She stared at him. "No. Have you met Mom and Dad? They'll make a capital case out of anything that doesn't fit into their carefully curated plans."

He paused, appearing to consider her words. "Point taken. What's the other reason?"

"Think about where Mom and Dad have been for the past few days. A church marriage retreat." She drummed her fingers on the tabletop.

"Do you see what I'm getting at here? They've spent seventy-two hours talking about what Jesus said about marriage, with people who think exactly the same as they do. On a scale of one to ten, their Christianity will be turned up to approximately . . . one hundred. Do you really think that's a good headspace for them to be in when you tell them you're falling in love with a man?"

"Yikes." His eyes widened. "I hate it when you're right, but you've made two really cogent arguments."

"Hey, just because you went to law school, that doesn't make you the only intelligent Hunt sibling."

He laughed, the same squeaky vibrato sound he'd been making since they were kids. "Touché, sis." Resting his forearms on the tabletop, he laced his fingers together. "I'm probably going to sit on this for a little while longer, I think."

"I think that's best." She reached out and touched his hand. "Don't get me wrong: I want you to come out when you feel ready. I just don't want you to set yourself up for a hard time when you do."

He nodded. "I can understand that. I mean, you've already been through this with Mom and Dad . . . that's why I feel comfortable talking to you about it."

"I know." She'd still been pretty young when she admitted to her parents that she was different: that boys made her feel apathetic, while girls made the butterflies flip in her stomach. "They were as accepting as they knew how to be . . . which wasn't much. Lucky for me, as the middle child, they'd never hung their hopes on me anyway. So it was easy for them to go back to babying Sean and cheering you on, and just leave me to my own devices."

He blinked. "Wow. I . . . never knew that's how it went."

"Yeah," she scoffed. "No biggie. It's water under the bridge and fodder for therapy now." She stood, gathering her trash. "I'd love to stay and talk, but I've got to get back to the shop. If the afternoon looks anything like the morning did, they're gonna need me at my table."

"Yeah, I'm gonna have to get back across town myself. We have to be in court at three thirty . . . right now I'm officially on a coffee break."

"Hey, you just made partner. What are they gonna do, spank you?"

Shelby chuckled. "No . . . but I'm hoping I can convince Matt to . . ."

She threw a crumpled napkin at him. "Don't you even think about finishing that sentence."

He picked up the napkin and tossed it into the nearby trash can. "Love you too, Jamie. I'll see you later."

"Bye, Shelby."

Moments later, he headed out into the parking lot while she made her way back to the nail salon. She slipped into her chair just as her coworker passed by her, headed out on her own break.

She looked at her phone. Something about Shelby's visit, the excitement sparkling in his eyes when he spoke about his new potential boyfriend, had her wanting to see Peaches. Dialing her number, she turned her chair around.

"Hello?"

"Hey, Peaches. Listen, I'm at work and I can't talk for long. But I really want to see you this weekend."

She sounded surprised. "Really? You were a little . . . Well, you know how you acted last night."

She grimaced. "I know. But still, I really want to see you. Can I come over?"

"I'm pretty booked this weekend. I'm working four hours at the barbershop and running errands with Dad tomorrow, then doing inventory and spring cleaning at the shop Sunday and Monday."

She wanted to pout, but she refrained since she was in public. "I'll swing by this evening . . . if it's okay with you."

"I'm cool with it if you wanna come over."

"Yeah, I do."

"All right. See you around seven."

"Okay. Later." She disconnected the call and spun her chair back around just as her next client approached. "How are you doing, Mrs. Russell?"

"Chile, I can't complain," the elderly woman said as she slipped into the chair. "I think I'm gonna do the french nails this time, with some of those tips added on."

"No problem." Jamie opened her drawer and began placing the necessary supplies on her table.

CHAPTER SIXTEEN

As seven o'clock approached, Peaches carried a plastic tray filled with cut strawberries, melon, and grapes into the living room and placed it on the coffee table. After grabbing a bottle of prosecco from the fridge, she set it and two glasses down near the fruit.

I wonder why she wanted to come over. The vibes were certainly off at game night, and I really don't know what to expect. She hoped her little contingency plan would keep things chill between them.

She changed out of her work clothes, throwing on something casual. As she ran a wide-tooth comb through her curls, she heard the doorbell chime.

At the door, she checked the peephole. A moment later, she opened the door and stepped back, allowing Jamie to enter the house.

Jamie wore a blue cap-sleeved maxi dress, printed with a white floral pattern. Her hair was in a low ponytail at the base of her neck. She crossed the threshold and entered the living room. "Hey, Peaches. Thanks for letting me come over."

"Hey." She reached out and gave Jamie's shoulder a squeeze, her way of testing the waters. Relieved that she didn't pull away, she gestured toward the sofa. "Sit down, make yourself comfortable."

Obliging, Jamie sat, tossing one long leg over the other. "So, what are we doing tonight?"

"Oh, I get to choose?" Peaches grinned.

Jamie rolled her eyes. "It's your house, goofball."

Strolling over, she took a seat next to Jamie. "I'm just messing with you. Anyway, I got my lil' spread here, in case you wanna nibble on something . . ."

"I'm sensing some innuendo there."

"I will neither confirm nor deny that." Peaches laughed. "Tonight, I've arranged for us to screen some fine cinema." She tossed her right arm over the back of the sofa.

Jamie leaned in, resting her head against Peaches' shoulder. "All right, let's see this movie."

Peaches grabbed the remote and aimed it at the big-screen TV mounted over the fireplace. A few button presses later, the opening sequence began.

Jamie giggled. "*Clue*? Really?"

"You said it's your favorite comfort watch. I was listening." Placing her hand on Jamie's shoulder, she gently tugged her body a little closer.

While they watched the campy movie, Peaches enjoyed the feeling of Jamie's soft curves pressed against her, the sound of her laughter, and the sweetness of the wedges of fruit Jamie occasionally fed her. Even better were the stolen kisses and the way Jamie kept her hand on Peaches' thigh, gripping it just enough so she could feel the tips of her long nails through her pants. *This is turning out to be a really nice evening.*

Right at the moment that Cook's lifeless body fell from the pantry, the sound of the other characters' screams was punctuated by someone pounding at the door.

Peaches frowned, pausing the movie. "Who in the world is at my door?" Releasing her hold on Jamie, she went to the door and flipped on the porchlight. A glance through the peephole showed her brother standing on the porch. Her nieces were there as well, as indicated by their familiar chatter. "Oh, for fuck's sake."

"Who is it?" Jamie leaned forward in her seat.

"My brother," she groused. Swinging the door open, Peaches said, "What the hell, RJ? You can't call first?"

His expression was equal parts exhaustion and remorse. "I'm sorry, P. There's an emergency at work. There's been a massive software failure on the new system. It's already got seventeen percent of the power grid on the blink . . . including Dad's neighborhood."

"Okay, yikes." Peaches stepped aside to let them in. "Still, you could have called me on the drive over. I have company."

RJ swiveled his head, seeming to notice Jamie for the first time. Offering a wave, he said, "Good evening, ma'am."

Jamie waved back, offering a tight smile.

Turning back to his sister, he said, "The whole team is on emergency work call until we get this resolved. I may not be done with this until morning, and I didn't want to ask you to come to my house."

"I wouldn't have. I can't sleep in your bed—your room is way too tacky."

He pursed his lips. "I'm gonna let that pass because I'm in a bind. Can you look after them just for the night? They've already eaten dinner."

She looked from her brother's face to the faces of her tiny girl bosses. "Yeah, RJ. But I'm dropping them off at nine in the morning, and your narrow ass better be at home."

"You're a lifesaver, sis." He leaned in and gave her one of those hurried half hugs he was famous for. Leaning down to peck each girl's forehead, he said, "Good night, girls. Be good for your aunt." A few moments later, he was gone.

Left standing in her living room with three tiny humans and a rather perturbed-looking companion, Peaches cleared her throat. "Jamie, I want you to meet my nieces. This is Olivia, Ella, and Reagan."

"Hi, girls. Nice to meet you. I'm Jamie."

Olivia and Ella each offered a wave, while Reagan hid behind Peaches.

"Reagan is kinda shy," Ella announced.

"Yeah." Peaches tousled Reagan's unruly curls. "It can take some time for the littlest Corbin to warm up to people."

"So what did you girls have for dinner?" Jamie asked.

Peaches glanced between them. *She's making conversation with them . . . that's probably a good sign.*

"Dad made us fish and chips," Olivia volunteered. "They were okay but not as good as Auntie's."

"Yep. Auntie Peaches' famous fish and chips." Peaches rubbed her hands together. "Often imitated, never duplicated."

"It's our favorite thing that she makes," Ella said.

"Second favorite, after breakfast for dinner," Olivia corrected.

"Yeah, but y'all can't have that every time. If I made breakfast for dinner, what would you have for actual breakfast?"

"Ice cream!" Reagan shouted, her tiny voice echoing through the house.

Jamie laughed. "So she does speak."

"Yeah, when she's passionate about something." Peaches chuckled at her niece's boisterous words. "As I recall, her first words were 'Ben' and 'Jerry.'"

"You're kidding." Jamie giggled.

"Of course. But Reagan's obsession with ice cream is very real."

Shaking her head, Jamie said, "I'll have to have you make me dinner one day. Seems like Auntie Peaches' cooking is not to be missed." Standing, she walked over to where they stood and gave Peaches a peck on the cheek.

"Ooooh." Ella tugged her aunt's hand. "Auntie, I thought you said you had company, like a visitor. Do all your visitors give you smooches?"

"Ella, hush before I make you eat vegetables."

Ella's expression changed, and she pressed her lips together.

Jamie laughed. "Wow. Is this what I have to look forward to when Levi gets older?"

She shook her head. "Nah. He's a boy, so just prepare to have your house wrecked. Maybe pay up your insurance."

"Noted." Jamie returned to her seat on the couch.

Peaches joined her, and while the older girls sat on the floor in front of the table, Reagan tucked her small body between the sofa's armrest and Peaches' left side.

Well, this is less than ideal. At least this movie's kid friendly. Everything had been going so well, and now her brother had thrown the most intrusive wrench possible in her quiet, romantic evening.

As the end credits rolled, Peaches announced, "All right, girls, time to start the bedtime routine." She rolled her eyes at the groans her older nieces released. "Come on now. It's nine o'clock, and you know the rule."

Ella stood, grousing. "Yeah. We gotta be in bed by ten."

Peaches nodded. "Right. So you and Olivia get your little booties up the stairs and take your showers. You know where to find your supplies in the bathroom." She stifled a yawn. "When y'all get done, I'll bring Reagan up and help her out."

The two older girls trudged up the stairs, leaving Peaches alone with Jamie and Reagan, who was still sitting to her aunt's left on the sofa. Reagan's eyes were already heavy, and Peaches knew she wouldn't be awake much longer.

Next to her, Jamie sighed. "Damn. I thought you'd be tucking me into bed tonight."

Peaches licked her lips. "Trust me, this wasn't how I planned for things to go tonight."

"I know. It's cool, I'll be here when you finish up."

"I'm gonna guess you don't really babysit your nephew, huh?"

She shook her head. "I don't really get asked that much. I watched him twice during his baby days, and that was pretty intense. I love Levi, really. He's super cute. I go by my brother's house and hang out with him, but only when at least one of his actual parents is present."

"I love my nieces, but beyond that, I actually enjoy their company." She listened, letting the sound of running water upstairs confirm that one of her nieces was indeed in the shower.

Jamie shrugged. "Maybe it's because Levi is so young and he hasn't really developed a personality yet. Hopefully as he gets older, I can take him to do some fun stuff."

Considering that statement, Peaches couldn't help wondering if Jamie was more upset about the girls' presence than she was letting on.

"I don't hate kids or anything," Jamie volunteered, as if reading her mind. "I think they're awesome . . . in small doses, and under someone else's jurisdiction."

"I get it. Not all of us are meant to be caregivers or mothers." The water stopped running then, and she directed her gaze upward. "Let me check on them—it's too quiet up there." She stood. "I'll be back once they're all settled in bed."

"Okay."

She scooped Reagan up into her arms. Balancing her youngest niece on her hip, she walked up the stairs. Olivia was in the hall, wrapped in a white towel and wearing a blue shower cap. "You're done with your shower?"

She nodded. "Yep. It's Ella's turn next."

"You could have just left it running for her."

Olivia shook her head. "No, Auntie. My science teacher said we should conserve water and energy whenever we can."

She couldn't suppress her chuckle. "Your teacher's right: tell her that me and my water bill said thanks."

As Olivia disappeared into the spare bedroom, Ella exited. She wore a pink cotton bathrobe, and her dark curls peeked from beneath a matching shower cap. "I'm 'bout to take my shower, Auntie."

"Well, get a move on. Your sister's fading." Reagan yawned, rubbing her eyes before resting her head against Peaches' shoulder.

Peaches walked into the spare bedroom and sat at the foot of the queen-sized bed. Olivia, already in her nightgown, pulled back the navy-blue comforter and slipped into bed.

After Ella had showered, Peaches helped Reagan, who was still learning the finer points of bathing, to get clean. Soon, all three girls were tucked into bed together, and she sat in the armchair she'd moved from the corner of the room with a storybook in hand.

By the time the tale had ended, Reagan was fast asleep, while Ella was looking sleepy. Olivia grabbed her small e-reader from the nightstand. With the soft glow illuminating her face, she whispered, "Good night, Auntie."

She kissed each of their foreheads. "Good night, y'all." Quietly, she slipped from the room.

After descending the stairs, Peaches found the room almost pitch black, save for the digital display on her microwave and the dim light over the stove. Jamie sat with her back turned, leaning over the arm of the sofa, her eyes glued to her phone screen. The device's backlight allowed Peaches a shadowy view of Jamie's position in an otherwise dimly lit space.

"Did you turn off all the lights for a particular reason?" Peaches moved into the space between the sofa and the coffee table.

As if noticing her presence for the first time, Jamie looked up from her phone. She returned to a sitting position and patted the cushion next to her. "Come here."

⌁

Jamie watched as Peaches sat down next to her on the sofa. After setting her phone on the coffee table, Jamie moved closer to Peaches, cuddling up to her side. "So, the kids are squared away, then?"

She nodded. "Olivia's still awake, but the other two are asleep."

Jamie frowned. "The oldest one's still up?"

"Yeah. She's got an e-reader . . . she'll pass out once her eyes get tired."

She felt annoyance rising within. *I know I'm being a Petty Patty . . . but I want Peaches' full attention.* Brushing those thoughts aside, she ran her fingertips up Peaches' bare arm. "I don't think I said it out loud, but I like this look on you."

Peaches glanced down at her clothes. "A tank top and khaki shorts? This is just my usual comfortable outfit for hanging around the house."

"I like that it shows your arms, and how strong they are."

Peaches chuckled. "Well, in that case, thanks." She closed her right fist and did a little bicep curl. "How's that?"

"Amazing." Jamie dragged her fingertips up to cup Peaches' chin. Turning her face, she leaned in and kissed her.

Jamie felt Peaches' arms go around her waist as the kiss bloomed and deepened, their tongues mating and playing. Jamie's hands roamed, her caresses mapping the sturdy planes of Peaches' body. Jamie eased her hands between them, loosening the button of Peaches' shorts. She felt the anticipation building within . . . until Peaches suddenly broke the contact.

"What's wrong?" Jamie stared into Peaches' eyes in the shadows, trying to gauge her feelings.

"Why did you unbutton my shorts?"

Jamie smiled. "You know why."

Peaches' eyes narrowed. "Humor me."

"I wanna fool around." She leaned forward and pecked her on the lips.

"My nieces are right upstairs."

"Didn't you just say the younger ones are asleep?"

Peaches balked, her voice a harsh whisper. "Yeah, I did. I also said Olivia is still awake. Or did you not hear that part?"

Jamie could feel her lips turning into a pout. "So you're telling me we can't have adult time? Even though the kids are in bed?"

"Is that why you came over here tonight? To get laid?" Peaches shook her head. "That would explain why you looked so bored while we were watching TV earlier, but damn."

Jamie blew out a breath. "I asked to come over here to hang out with you, plain and simple. I can't help the way you affect me."

"I'm flattered. And I don't mind us making out on the couch."

"If we keep doing that, I'm gonna want more," she replied truthfully.

"I can't give you the red-light special while the girls are here." Peaches moved away from Jamie, scooting her hips over the cushion. "Let's face it, you're a screamer."

"Wow." Jamie eyed Peaches, seriously thrown off by her change in body language. "And what if I did come here because I wanted sex? What's so wrong with that? Are we not both consenting, open-minded adults?"

"See? You're already getting loud, and I don't want my nieces to hear us." Peaches stood, gesturing toward the rear of the house. "Let's take this to the back porch."

I know I should be handling this better. But I'm tired of always being passed over for something or someone more important. Rolling her eyes, Jamie got up and followed her through the kitchen, the dining room, and out to the screened-in porch.

Peaches then lowered herself into one of the bright-orange adirondack chairs, gesturing to the other. "Have a seat."

Sliding into the depths of the hard plastic seat, Jamie said, "Now that we're out here, you wanna explain to me why you're being so uptight?"

Peaches stared. "That's how you see me right now? You think I'm being uptight just because I don't wanna fuck you while there are literal children in the house?"

She shook her head. "No, Peaches. That's not the issue here. There always seems to be something holding you back from me."

A bitter, humorless laugh escaped Peaches' lips. "That's rich. So, we're just gonna ignore the way you've been acting over the past week?"

"What are you talking about?"

"When I called you Monday, I was doing the mature thing. I opened up to you about my feelings, trudged through the mud of my own trauma, so that I could be honest with you. And what did you do?" Peaches shook her head. "You dismissed me, made it seem like I was wasting your time."

Jamie swallowed, knowing her reaction that day had been less than ideal. "I was at work! I'd been busting my ass all morning, I was exhausted, and I didn't have time to babysit your emotions and . . ."

Peaches held up her hand. "I'm not finished. Last night at Aiko's house, you had a funky attitude the whole night, and barely spoke to me. You fucking trolled me during a game of Scrabble, which has got to be a new level of childishness."

Jamie seethed, irritation turning to anger. "Don't hate because I got a triple-letter score on the X, Peaches."

"This ain't about the game, and you know that."

"Whatever."

"You haven't reached out all week until today, when you asked me to come over here."

"The phone works both ways, Peaches. You could have called me."

"Why would I, after the way you spoke to me?"

"Peaches, come on. I was tired and I shouldn't have snapped at you. But why are you bringing that up now?"

"Because it's pertinent to the conversation. I know the girls weren't part of the plan—"

"No, they weren't. I'm disappointed, because I wanted you to myself, but I tried to make the best of it." *Ugh, I hate these chairs. It's like sitting on the toilet with the seat up.*

"You know I couldn't say no after my brother showed up here the way he did."

"I understand that he put you on the spot—"

"Well, you're not acting like it."

Lifting her hips toward the edge of the chair, Jamie leaned forward. "And how am I acting, Peaches? Since you know everything and are so much more mature then me, why don't you tell me about myself." *Why is it that no one in my life ever takes the time to consider that I have feelings, or that they might be valid?*

Peaches merely shook her head. "If you can't see how your behavior is out of line, even after I've painted a picture for you, I'm not going to keep explaining it."

Jamie's heart squeezed in her chest. *Once again, I'm being dismissed: set aside for something that matters more.* "Oh, you're not? Let me tell you what I'm not about to do. I'm not about to sit here and be lectured like a child by you. Like I said before, we're both adults."

"Are we? I wasn't sure when you started pouting. I've seen Reagan react better to a change of plans than you did tonight."

Jamie jumped to her feet. "Uh-uh, Peaches. Don't play in my face. You were the one who didn't even believe I had real feelings for you to start with. The one who had to be 'convinced' that I wanted something more than friendship between us. And now I'm the problem?" She could hear her tone becoming loud and high pitched as her emotions began to bubble over.

With a dry chuckle, Peaches said, "You know, Claudia said it would turn out this way. She said this would lead to disaster."

Tears welled in Jamie's eyes. "You . . . talked to Claudia about us?"

"For a minute, after you left game night."

"I can't believe you're agreeing with her . . . that you really think our connection isn't more meaningful than that."

Peaches blinked. Her expression reflected that she'd lost interest in the conversation. Elbows on her lap, she laced her fingers together. "Are you done, Jamie?"

There it was, that laid-back stance that Jamie usually found so attractive. Now, at a moment when she needed Peaches to actually give a damn, that aloof shit threatened to make her head explode. Narrowing her eyes, she yelled, "Abso-fucking-lutely! I'm done with this stupid conversation. But beyond that, I'm done with you." She snatched open the back door.

She glanced back once she reached the kitchen. Peaches hadn't followed her.

When she reentered the living room, she grabbed her phone and keys from the coffee table. Moments later she was out the door and inside her car.

I feel like I'm a reasonable person. But something about her . . . she just sets me off in so many ways, good and bad. I don't know how to handle this.

Tears clouded her vision as she started the engine, backed out of the driveway, and drove off down the darkened street.

CHAPTER SEVENTEEN

As soon as Peaches detected sunlight hitting her eyelids Saturday morning, she grabbed a pillow and used it to cover her face. Resisting the urge to scream into its fluffy depths, she finally set it aside and turned away from her bedroom window before opening her eyes.

She'd slept maybe three hours, having spent most of the night rolling around the bed, looking for a comfortable enough position to remain in. No matter how much repositioning, pillow pounding, and blanket rearranging she'd done, restful sleep had proven as elusive as a pair of designer sneakers on release day.

After a brief sojourn to her bathroom, she emerged showered and groomed. She pulled on a plain white tee and a pair of denim shorts over her racerback bra and boxers. She put on a pair of white socks and all-white sneakers before making her way to the spare bedroom upstairs.

All three girls were awake but had dutifully remained in the bedroom as Peaches had requested. She mustered a smile for her tiny entourage. "Morning, y'all."

"Morning, Auntie." Ella, sitting up at the foot of the bed, eyed her. "You okay?"

"I'm fine. I didn't sleep the best, but I'll be all right." That was as much of the truth as she thought appropriate to share with them.

Olivia, still beneath the covers with Reagan on her lap, looked up from her e-reader screen. "What's for breakfast? I'm hungry."

Reagan grinned. "Ice cream, please?"

Shaking her head, Peaches tweaked Reagan's cheek. "Nah, you know ice cream isn't a good breakfast. I don't feel much like cooking, though, so how about cereal, toast, and fruit?"

"Do you have the fruity cereal?" Ella scooted off the bed.

"What do I look like, an amateur? Of course I have the fruity cereal. Two different kinds, for your information." Peaches laughed. "Y'all can get dressed and come on downstairs."

Back in the kitchen, Peaches took down the two cereal boxes, glancing at the clock as she set them on the counter. *It's eight twenty-eight. I told RJ to expect me around nine . . . not that he'll be upset if I'm late bringing the kids back home.* RJ was famously not a morning person; they'd be lucky if he was fully awake by the time they arrived.

The girls came running down the stairs, dressed and ready to devour a bowl of fruit-flavored carbs. Olivia sidled up next to Peaches. "I'll do the toast, Auntie. Make yourself some coffee."

She smiled. "Thanks, Olivia." Following her niece's sage advice, she went to her single-cup brewer. She grabbed a mug from the wooden tree next to it, set it on the platform, popped in a coffee pod, and pressed the button. Peaches then joined her nieces at the table, eating cereal and toast, even though she was mainly interested in the coffee. Once they'd eaten and tucked their dishes into the dishwasher, she asked, "Did one of you remember to bring your bags downstairs?"

After a long silence, Ella said, "I'll get them." She dashed back up the stairs, returning soon after with the two bright-pink duffel bags they'd brought with them.

They left the town house in Peaches' pickup, and she drove them home to RJ's house in Franklin Park. After knocking on the door, she was greeted by her groggy, robe-clad little brother. "Hey, Peaches." He yawned. "Is it nine already?"

"Try ten, RJ." Stepping aside, she let her nieces file into the house, one by one. "I already gave them breakfast, so you're off the hook until lunch, sleepyhead."

He yawned again, then scratched his scruffy chin. "Thanks, sis. You're a lifesaver."

"I know." She looked him up and down. "Disheveled" seemed too kind a word to describe his current state. "Meanwhile, what did you even do last night?"

"It was absolute chaos at work. I didn't get home until a little after five this morning, and I was asleep until I heard you knock on the door." He blinked a few times. "I'm still exhausted."

It's oddly comforting to know that neither of us slept last night. "All right. I'll see you later. I've gotta get to the barbershop. I told Alonzo I'd be there for a half shift today."

"Dad's expecting you this afternoon," he reminded her.

"Yeah, I know. I'll be there." She waved, and as he closed the door, she returned to her truck.

She entered the barbershop to find it just as jam packed as she'd expect for a Saturday morning. Every single barber station except hers was occupied, and there were butts in every chair, including the five chairs in the front waiting area. Clippers buzzed, laughter and conversation flowed, and baseball commentary blared from the wall-mounted TV.

Walking past the desk, she nodded to Taylor.

"Hey, Peaches. You haven't spoken to Jamie today, have you?"

She shook her head. "Nope. She was at my place last night, but . . . I don't think she'd want to talk to me."

Taylor's face twisted into a pout. "Something happened, didn't it?"

"Yeah. You'll have to get the messy details from her, though. I don't wanna talk about it."

"Gotcha." Taylor appeared accepting, but not particularly happy.

Peaches worked her way through the shop floor to her station in the rear, speaking to her employees along the way. She then gestured for Taylor to send her the next client, intending to help clear out some of the people waiting for their cut or style.

Once she'd served all five of the waiting clients, she sat down in her chair for a quick break. She pulled out her phone, and while part of her hoped to see a text or missed call from Jamie, she wasn't surprised there weren't any.

"What's going on with you, boss lady?" The question came from Alonzo, who was busy working on an undercut at his station across from her.

"What makes you think something is wrong?"

"You're not yourself today." Alonzo squinted as he trimmed behind his client's ear. "You haven't said a word to us since you came in . . . just head down, barbering."

She shrugged. "I was being efficient. We needed to clear out the queue up front, so I did."

Alonzo met her gaze with narrowed eyes. "I don't believe that for a second. I'm just gonna assume that whatever is on your mind, you don't wanna talk about it."

I already told Taylor as much. Knowing Alonzo probably hadn't heard their exchange over all the other ambient noise in the barbershop, she simply nodded and said, "Thanks for that."

Her break ended as quickly as it had begun, and she stood, pocketing her phone. As a second wave of clients came in, she was soon faced with another steady stream of people sitting in her chair. She put her full focus into the fades, the lineups, the beard trims, and the shaves until the alarm on her phone went off, indicating the end of her four-hour shift.

As she wiped down her station, Stax asked, "How many clients did you service today, Peaches?" Tall and lanky, he wore chinos with his black T-shirt. His big, fluffy black afro was gray around the roots, giving him an air of distinguished wisdom.

"Eleven." She polished her countertop to a nice shine, then tossed the rag into the hamper in the corner. "Quite a morning."

"I've done ten, I think." Stax ran a hand over his curls. "When it's busy like this, it reminds me of why I only do this two days a week."

"I'm glad I came in today, to take the pressure off," she teased. "Plus, I haven't seen you in like a month. How's Millie?"

Stax grinned, as he always did when someone mentioned his wife of thirty years. "She's right as rain. Meanwhile, if you came in on the weekends more often, you could treat yourself to this handsome face."

Clyde Bagaduce, her other weekend barber, who was fresh out of barber school and the only non-Black member of her staff, scoffed. He'd been hired only a month before Kev and loved to hold that perceived "seniority" over the other barber's head. Running a hand through his wavy, black chin-length locks, he said, "I'm sure she misses me just as much."

Look at these two goofballs. "Now, boys. Don't fight." Peaches chuckled in spite of her mood. "Seeing you both has lifted my spirits immensely."

She left the barbershop around two thirty and headed for her dad's house. She had no idea what kind of errands he had planned for the day. All she knew was he'd told her to clear her afternoon, and she'd done as he requested.

He was waiting on the porch today, just as he had for their last outing. This time, he wore a white short-sleeved button-down shirt with tan stripes, a pair of tan slacks held up by brown leather suspenders, and a pair of weathered brown loafers. A straw fedora-style hat with a wide brim, accented by a brown fabric strip and a white feather, covered his balding gray head.

Seeing him all decked out made a smile tilt her lips. *He may be getting forgetful, but he's still got his sense of style, and he can coordinate with the best of them.*

When she helped him up into the passenger seat, she commented, "Nice outfit, Pops."

"Just something I threw together." He reached for his cane, and when she handed it over, he propped it on the seat next to him.

Back in the driver's seat, she asked, "Where to?"

"The home improvement warehouse place. I wanna put me in a little vegetable patch. You know, a little patch in the backyard."

She pulled out of the driveway and headed for the nearest home warehouse store. "What kind of veggies are you gonna plant?"

"Nothing major. Few tomatoes, some lettuce, cucumber. Maybe some carrots or spring onion . . . might put in a few herbs, just for good measure."

"Sounds like quite an undertaking."

He shrugged. "We'll see, I suppose. Been a while since I had a garden, but with produce prices being what they are, and me being retired and all, seems like a good idea from where I'm sitting."

She took a deep breath but said nothing more. *Once he's decided to do something, there's nothing I can do to change his mind. Let me just go with the flow.*

At the warehouse store, he ambled around with the aid of his cane while Peaches pushed the shopping cart. They circled around the store's interior, stopping once when all the traipsing across cement floors had started to get to him. When he was ready to resume, they hit up the greenhouse, and as he pointed out the items he wanted, she loaded them into the cart. By the time they left, she was testy, to say the least. She'd been trying her hardest to stop thinking about Jamie, and to even out her mood. Two hours of pushing a cart, lifting heavy bags, and listening to her father soliloquize about his past gardening mishaps hadn't helped.

They returned to the house, where he unlocked the gate so Peaches could carry everything to the backyard.

While she pinned down landscaping fabric in the spot he'd designated, beneath the shade of one of his old willows, he sat in a folding chair nearby. "You don't have to pound the stakes quite so hard, child. You're gonna tear the fabric."

Looking at her hand, she could see the whiteness on her knuckle where she was holding the handle of the rubber mallet she wielded. Loosening her grip a bit, she tapped the last stake into place, then turned to fetch the boards for the raised bed.

"I ain't never seen you pounding anything so hard, least not as I can recall." He frowned. "Whatever's troubling you, get yourself together, Patricia."

She cringed at the sound of her government name. "Come on, Pops. You know I hate that name."

"Well, it was my mama's name, so I love it. At any rate, you'll need to adjust your attitude. And don't bother telling me about your youthful problems—it don't make me any difference. Just straighten up and fly right, you hear?"

"Yes, sir." Training her expression into a neutral one, she began placing the slats for the raised bed.

I don't know whether I'm more offended that he doesn't care what my problem is, or more relieved that I don't have to explain it to him.

⁓

Jamie awakened to the sound of rather insistent pounding against her front door. Cursing under her breath, she rubbed her bleary eyes and grabbed her phone to check the time. *Five? In the evening?*

While scrambling out of bed, she knocked over her stash box and cursed again. *Why did I leave this on the bed? I must have passed out.*

Once she'd put everything back into the box and set it on the dresser, she looked in the mirror. Seeing her wig askew and her waves standing in all different directions, she righted it as best she could while the pounding continued to assault her ears. Tugging the hem of her nightshirt so it would cover her bare ass, she ran through the apartment toward the front door.

She checked the peephole and rolled her eyes. Opening the door, she said, "Taylor, we talked about this."

"Talked about what?" Taylor's arms were crossed over their chest.

"About how you can't pound on my door like this, because it makes me anxious."

Head dropped to their right shoulder, Taylor said, "Oh, really? Well, if you answered the damn phone any of the six times I called you today, or at least texted me, we wouldn't be in this predicament."

"But, Taylor, I . . ."

"Don't you 'but, Taylor,' me, Miss Ma'am. Me knocking on your door like this makes you anxious, huh? Wanna know what makes me anxious? Worrying about your ass, that's what!"

Jamie offered a sheepish grin. "My bad, T. I got so fucking high last night . . . at some point I passed out, and I'm just now waking up from it."

"So you were in a weed coma." Pushing their way into the apartment, Taylor wagged a finger at her. "Girl, listen. I don't know what the hell you got going on, but this"—she gestured to her—"ain't it. First, I can't get you on the phone, and when I do come up here, I find you like this, looking all confused and bedraggled."

Jamie sighed. "Taylor, can you lecture me a little more quietly, please? I'm sure the entire complex can hear you yelling."

Taking a deep breath, Taylor pushed the door closed. "Fine. I'll lower my tone, but I won't lower my standards. Now, get yourself in the shower and get dressed. And for the sake of all that's right and holy, please do something with that wig."

Feeling thoroughly chastised, Jamie returned to her bedroom to get herself together. In the adjoining bathroom, she took a hot shower, getting some semblance of relief from the steamy stream of water and the jasmine-scented lather of her favorite bodywash.

After her shower, she threw on a pair of straight-leg blue jeans, a yellow V-neck, a short-sleeved tunic, and a pair of tan sandals. *Ugh, I don't feel like fucking with lace glue right now.* Peeling off the wig, she wrapped her cornrows in a yellow scarf. She returned to the living room then, where she found Taylor reclining on the sofa, looking rather comfortable as they scrolled through a phone. As she sat down next to her friend, she realized who it belonged to. "T, why are you nosing through my phone?"

"I'm looking for evidence of whatever happened last night between you and Peaches." Taylor sighed, handing the phone back. "Other than a phone call between y'all yesterday, I'm not really seeing anything."

"How do you even know I was with Peaches?"

"Duh. I asked her this morning and she told me." Taylor laughed. "That was all I could get out of my boss: she pleaded the Fifth and said I'd have to get the tea from you."

Jamie sighed deeply. "And what makes you think I want to talk about it any more than she does?"

"It's cool if you don't wanna tell me now." Taylor regarded their nails. "We got time. Because I'm breaking you out of this house, Miss Sad Sack."

She shook her head. "I don't feel like going anywhere."

Taylor fake pouted. "Aw. Po' lil' Tink Tink. Guess what? This outing is mandatory. Time to get some fresh air in your lungs and some food in your belly, girl."

Jamie yawned. *I don't have the energy or the strength to fight Taylor on this.* "Fine. But can we at least get coffee first?"

Taylor nodded. "I'll allow it." Giving Jamie a playful jab in the side, they added, "Okay. Up and at 'em."

They were in Taylor's car and halfway to the coffee shop before the tears started flowing. Jamie did her best to hold them back, but by then, she'd lost the battle.

"Oh no, baby." Taylor placed their hand on Jamie's thigh. "Please don't cry. I know I probably scared you out of your sleep, but I was just concerned about you, and I . . ."

"It's . . . not that," Jamie managed between sobs. Taking a few deep breaths to gather herself, she said, "It's this thing with Peaches. Claudia was worried things would go sideways between us, and they sure as hell did last night."

Eyes still on the road, Taylor's mouth drooped into a sympathetic frown. "I'm sorry I teased you earlier, Jamie. It looks like you really going through it."

She sniffled, nodding. "Yeah. I got baked last night because I knew it was the only way I'd get any sleep. Two blunts later . . ." She shrugged. "I must have passed out. I don't even remember falling asleep, and my stash box was still on my bed when I woke up just now."

"Good thing your blunt wasn't still lit when you fell out."

"Right."

"Damn. Just tell me what happened."

Between sniffles, Jamie recounted what had happened the night before, ending with her argument with Peaches and her subsequent mad dash for the door. "I was so pissed. I couldn't get out of there fast enough."

Pulling into the parking lot at the coffee spot, Taylor cut the engine. "We'll hit up the drive-through when you're ready." Squeezing Jamie's hands, they added, "I'm here for you, girl."

"Thanks. So, does this mean you're not gonna lecture me about how this was a bad idea, doomed from the start?"

"What good would that do, when you obviously already feel like shit? Besides, I'm friends-to-lovers agnostic. I believe the outcome is determined in real time by the two parties involved." Taylor took a breath. "The real question is, What are you gonna do now?"

"I honestly don't know. I ended things between us, and even though I think I did the right thing, I . . . regret it. I'm already feeling like I miss her."

"Listen. Right now, your feelings are too raw for you to be making any big decisions. I think the best thing is for you to just focus on putting yourself in the proper position for school."

Taylor's making good sense. I don't really know what's going to happen going forward with Peaches, if anything. But I do know I want my degree.

"Yeah. Maybe I'll just focus on that." She blew out a breath. "After I get some coffee, that is."

"Bet." Taylor started the car and pulled into the drive-through.

CHAPTER EIGHTEEN

Peaches absently perused the menu at the Winner's Circle sports bar in Austin's Rosedale neighborhood. It was just past noon on Sunday, and the interior of the establishment echoed with its usual soundscape of laughter, various conversations, and the sporting events being broadcast on no fewer than twelve wall-mounted televisions and projection screens.

Considering that they'd come to watch a tennis match for their alma mater's Lady Longhorns, competing against the Horned Frogs of Texas Christian University, she'd worn an orange UT Austin tee that had the word "Longhorns" printed diagonally across it in white script lettering, with a pair of blue jeans and her favorite custom-painted orange sneakers.

"What are you gonna get, P?" The question came from Aiko, who sat across from her inside the brown leather booth. She wore the same orange UT Austin Longhorns tee, paired with white jeans and sneakers. Her long, loose curls were piled on top of her head, styled in the messy bun she favored in nonprofessional settings.

Peaches shrugged. "I can't decide . . . I've narrowed it down to two things, though."

"Just get a sampler," Aiko suggested. "The match has already started, and I'd like to eat sometime soon."

Peaches glanced at the big screen above the bar. Sure enough, the first match was underway, and the competitors had a pretty good rally going on. "Yeah. I'll just do that." After two days spent overthinking what had gone wrong between her and Jamie, she saw no need to spiral into endless self-debate about lunch.

When the waiter came by, Peaches ordered an appetizer sampler with pretzel bites, nachos, and boneless wings, while Aiko chose lemon-pepper wings and fries. After he replaced their large plastic-coated menus with two glasses of ice water, he left to ferry their food order to the kitchen.

Aiko looked across the table, studying her face. After a brief moment of scrutiny, she said, "I'm going to go out on a limb here . . . albeit a very safe one . . . and say that something happened between you and Jamie."

Peaches rested her forearms on the table. "I see your psychic powers are on ten today."

"Nah." Aiko shook her head. "But my powers of observation are always turned up. I noticed the way the two of you were acting at my house the other night. That's got to be the most intense game night we've ever had, at least since we all agreed to stop playing spades."

The memories of that night made her shake her head. "Yeah, the vibe was super weird. It's hard to describe it. I just know things were . . . off."

"Same. I mean, I know y'all just started hanging out, so I wasn't expecting y'all to be booed up and hanging all over each other, not necessarily." Aiko took a sip of her water. "But I wasn't expecting y'all to act like you did either."

"Listen, I was chilling. I promise she brought most of the weird vibes with her the moment she stepped in the room." Peaches remembered that she'd been feeling miffed about their conversation earlier in the week. "It's true, I called her Monday and let her know that she did something that basically triggered me, and made me feel some type of way, and she wasn't trying to hear me. Still, I wasn't about to come to our game night and air any of that out, or even address it. I just didn't think it was the right time or place."

Their food arrived, and Aiko grabbed a fry from her basket. "I guess Jamie had a different idea."

Peaches shook her head as she munched on a cheese-laden nacho chip. "I wish I could say that was the worst of it. But she came over to my place Friday night."

Aiko's expression changed into a confused half frown. "You had her over, even though she hurt you and disregarded your feelings?"

"I did. I wasn't even gonna bring up any of that. And everything was actually going along fine . . . until RJ showed up with the girls." Taking a drink from her glass, Peaches set aside eating long enough to fill her friend in on what had occurred that night. "She was stomping when she left, and I heard just a brief pause in her steps. I think she thought I was gonna chase after her, and it probably pissed her off that I didn't." She dug back into her food.

Aiko appeared to be mulling over what she'd said while eating. When she was done chewing, she said, "I've known you long enough that I don't have to ask why you didn't follow her. She was being petty, and you didn't want to buy into it."

"Nope. We're adults and we should act as such. I don't have time for childish games and temper tantrums."

"Well, I'm glad you stuck to your beliefs." Aiko dipped a wing into her small cup of ranch. "But I'm sorry things turned out the way they did, homie."

Peaches waved her off. "I guess it's for the best."

They settled into friendly silence then as the current tennis match heated up. For a while, Peaches was able to turn off the part of her brain that had been analyzing her situation with Jamie, and just focus on enjoying the company of her closest friend and the athleticism being displayed on-screen.

About an hour later, they were still sitting in the booth, though the remnants of their meals had been cleared away.

Aiko spoke for the first time in a while. "Hey, P. You said you think it's for the best that you and Jamie aren't an item anymore. What makes you think that?"

Her brow hitched. "Are you advocating for us to try to patch things up?"

"No, that's not what I'm getting at." Aiko rubbed her hands down with a lemon-scented, premoistened wipe. "I'm just trying to make sense of your point of view on this."

She took a deep breath. "Well, I think the main thing is that Jamie doesn't understand or appreciate the relationship I have with my family. I mean, she told me herself she's a middle child, and often feels left out or ignored by her family. Things aren't like that for me, and I don't think she can relate."

"Your people could never ignore you, honestly . . . they call on you constantly, for everything." Aiko emptied a piece of ice from her glass into her mouth and began crunching.

Peaches bristled. "I feel like that was some shade."

"No shade, just my observation skills again." Aiko shook her glass and drained the last of the water from it. "I've known you approximately forever. And in the years we've been friends, I've seen you drop everything to deal with your family's issues or needs more times than I can count."

Peaches stared. "I mean, that's what family is all about, right? Having each other's backs?"

She nodded. "That's true. But you gotta remember, that relationship is supposed to be reciprocal."

She blinked, but she couldn't conjure a rebuttal to that.

"Think about it. Our friend group is like found family. We all do for each other, step in when we can to take the burden off, whatever." She leaned forward. "I see you doing that all the time for your dad, your brother, your nieces. But when is the last time they did something for you?"

Well, that didn't last long. Peaches drew a deep breath. Her friend had started up the analysis portion of her brain again, and she was decidedly displeased with its findings. Knowing she had to say something, lest Aiko keep watching her with that self-satisfied expression, she said, "Okay, you made your point. But I'm the oldest, and obviously the most responsible . . . they need me. Especially since Mama passed."

Aiko nodded slowly. "They probably think they need you. Even when Ms. Ann-Marie was still with us, you did a lot. I don't think a family could ask for a more dedicated, loving eldest child than you." She paused. "At some point, though, one of two things has to happen. Either you get some of that love and dedication back, or you burn out. At that point you're no good to anyone, P."

She swallowed and, feeling the growing heaviness in her throat and chest, reached for her own water glass.

"Please know I'm saying this from a place of love for you. You're my closest friend, and I want to see you win, always." Aiko pinched her nose, then released it, keeping her voice gentle as she spoke. "You gotta look back at Ms. Ann-Marie, and the circumstances that led up to her passing. It was heart disease . . . you can draw a straight line between stress levels and heart disease. Remember how much RJ depended on her for childcare, and doing the girls' hair?" She held eye contact. "I'm saying this because I want you to acknowledge that connection, and take the steps to keep from going down that path. Trust and believe, you get on my last nerve sometimes." She chuckled. "But I don't want to lose you, P."

Grabbing a napkin from the table dispenser, Peaches dabbed at the tears forming in her eyes. It wasn't just the memory of her beloved mother that had her emotional. It was hearing the love and the genuine worry radiating through Aiko's words. "Thank you for being real with me, Aiko. And you're right, I really need to make some changes when it comes to Pops and RJ, especially."

"You know I'm just looking out for you. Same as always."

"It's hard to explain. But ever since I was a kid, I've felt this insistent, consuming pressure to be the best big sister and the best daughter on earth. I was always Mama's helper: I looked after RJ, helped her do the ironing and lunch prep for Pops." She paused. "And when we lost her, something inside me just broke. I doubled down on my efforts to take care of everybody then, and I haven't been able to break the pattern."

"Admitting that it's a pattern at all has to be a step in the right direction." Aiko smiled. "Now that you're looking at it through logic instead of emotions, maybe it will be a little easier to fix."

Peaches nodded, wiping away another tear. "I gotta get in with my therapist. I've got one, but I've really been slacking on appointments for the last two months."

"Then you know what you gotta do, P." Reaching across the table, Aiko offered her closed fist. "And you know I got your back, right?"

Peaches bumped her fist against Aiko's. "Yeah, I know." She chuckled. "This is so funny. Earlier, I expected you to give me advice, but about Jamie, not this."

"The way I see it, you gotta fix this first. Whatever's meant to happen with Jamie, it'll work itself out."

"Damn, Aiko. You making a little too much sense today."

Aiko laughed. "What can I say? Claudia may be the brainiest academically in our group, but I'm probably the most emotionally intelligent." She held up her forefinger. "And don't worry, I won't let it go to my head."

Peaches laughed—a real, humor-fueled laugh—for the first time in the last forty-eight hours. "Bad news . . . I think it already has."

Jamie pulled her car up to the curb in front of her parents' house around six Sunday evening. There was no room in the driveway—her parents' crossover, as well as the midsize sedan and convertible driven by Sean and Shelby, respectively, were taking up all the available space there.

Seeing the full driveway solidified the rightness of what she was about to do. It was the dinner hour, and though she'd already eaten, she knew it was the best time to visit. With Sunday service long since ended, she could catch all her family members together, to avoid repeating herself later.

She stood on the front porch for a moment, taking a deep breath of warm, spring air. Then she knocked on the door.

Sean opened it a few moments later. "Hey, sis. Come on in."

She entered, closing the door behind her before she could be chastised for "air-conditioning the whole neighborhood." Once inside, she followed her brother through the front portion of the house.

The living room, like most of the home, had changed very little since she was a kid. The red-and-black-plaid sofa and love seat were the same furniture she and her brothers had clambered over as kids during their games of hide-and-seek. She passed over the solid-red throw rug and walked into the dining room.

The rest of the family, save for her mother, was still seated around the table, though their empty plates and leftover food had been cleared away. She could hear the sounds of running water and clinking dishes coming from the kitchen.

"Hey, Jamie." Shelby waved from his seat at the far end of the table, opposite their father.

Clarence looked up from the newspaper he'd been reading. Noticing his daughter's presence for the first time, he pushed his glasses up his nose. "Hello, dear. How are you?" He was dressed in the black-and-white tracksuit ensemble he often changed into after getting out of his church finery.

"I'm fine, Dad. How's the team?" Anyone who knew her father well asked this question over the standard "How are you?" Clarence Hunt had been coaching rugby at Austin Technical Academy for more than thirty years; at this point, he knew the state of the team better than he knew himself.

"Season's over . . . but we're gearing up a pretty good squad for next year." Clarence turned the page in his paper. "Meantime, I'm helping out with the boys' softball team."

She nodded. "Sounds good. I'm sure they'll do great." This was how she and her father related to each other. Their conversation rarely went deeper than sports. "So, Sean, where are Bethany and Levi?"

"She took him home to Las Cruces to see her family." Sean leaned back in his chair, his eyes glued to his phone. "They'll be back Saturday."

"Dang. Sorry I missed my lil' guy." She sat down in the empty chair between Sean and Shelby, to her father's right.

Bernadette Martin-Hunt emerged from the kitchen then, looking every bit like the homemaker she'd been for the last thirty-seven years. Still wearing the pale-pink skirt and white blouse she'd likely worn to service, she had her favorite strawberry-print apron tied around her neck and waist. Her shoulder-length waves were styled into an elegant updo, with a few wispy strands framing her beautiful yet tightly set face. "Hello, Jamie. I didn't know you were coming over today."

"Hi, Mom. It was sort of a spur-of-the-moment decision."

Her pink lips pursed, as if she disapproved of such a lack of planning. "I see. Have you eaten?"

"Yes, ma'am, I have."

"Lovely. Then I won't need to take out all the leftovers I've just put away and reheat them." She eased into the chair to Clarence's left. "What brings you by, unannounced no less?"

Jamie cleared her throat. "I wanted to share some news with you all. Out of the five schools I was applying to, I was accepted at four. I had it narrowed down to two, and I've decided to attend Texas Southern."

Clarence folded his newspaper and looked at her, his eyes narrowed in confusion. "You're going where?"

"TSU. You know, the HBCU in Houston."

"And . . . you're going there to do what, exactly?" Clarence still looked as if he didn't follow.

"I'm enrolling to complete my bachelor's degree in chemistry, remember? I'm gonna study chemistry . . . I have some ideas on how to improve the products used in the beauty business, specifically the nail industry."

Bernadette blinked several times. "Jamie, I don't remember you saying anything about doing this."

She sighed as her mother's passive-aggressive selective memory reared its ugly head. "I told you when I got my first acceptance. I actually told everybody, at a Sunday dinner several months ago. Remember the last time I was here on a Sunday?"

"I remember," Sean announced, even glancing up briefly as he spoke. "Congrats, sis."

"Thank you, Sean."

"I remember too." Shelby held up his hand and gave her a high five. "I know you'll do great."

"Well, I'm just confused," Bernadette said. "Not only do I not recall any talk about you going back to school, Jamie, but I can't reconcile for the life of me *why* you'd do such a thing."

She turned her attention back to her mother. "What's unclear, Mom?"

"I mean, don't you already have a job? You seem pretty well settled into what you do now. Why on earth would you want to start over in a whole new career, at your age?"

She balked. "At my age? Are you serious?" *What am I, ninety? I'm still in my thirties, and she makes it sound as if I have one foot in the grave.*

"You're not so old," Clarence chimed in. "But it's gonna take a lot of time and money to get a degree . . . is that really the best use of your resources right now?"

She closed her eyes against her parents' sour faces and took a deep, cleansing breath. "I hear your concern, but I've given this a lot of thought. I'm not satisfied with where I am professionally, because I know I could be doing so much more. I know it won't be easy navigating campus life among a bunch of twentysomethings, but I'm prepared for the challenge. This is something I really want to do. We need more Black women in STEM, and within the next few years, I intend to be one of them."

Bernadette shook her head. "I mean, it's up to you. You're grown. I can't stop you if you want to do this crazy thing."

Eyes narrowed, she asked, "Mom, would you say that if Shelby decided to go back to school? I mean, he's older than me, which by your estimation must make him geriatric, and you and Daddy, well, y'all must be dust."

"Oh, Lord." Clarence opened his paper again, effectively hiding his face behind the pages. "Here we go."

"Watch your tone, missy," Bernadette snapped. "You're talking nonsense. What degree is your brother gonna get beyond a JD? He's already got the terminal degree for his field."

"That's not the point. The point is, if one of your perfect sons sets out to do something, you shower them with praise and congratulations." She stood, knowing she wouldn't be there much longer. "But when I do something, the only two reactions you're capable of are disregard and dismissal."

"Jamie!" Bernadette slapped her palm on the table. "Enough of this!"

"You're right, Mom. I have had enough. I'm done looking for your acknowledgment or approval, because I have a whole squad of real ones who look out for me, love me, and always have my back. It's time for me to live my life on my terms. If and when you decide you want to be a part of that, you know how to reach me." She started toward the door, then paused. "Shelby, Sean, I'll text you my class start date, and my new address, once I have it."

Shelby nodded. "Okay, sis."

"Let us know if you need help with the move," Sean offered.

With her mother shouting behind her, she turned and strode across the living room. She yanked the front door open and left her childhood home, only barely able to resist slamming the door behind her.

She drove back to her apartment, rerunning the conversation in her mind. While her brothers had shown at least slight interest in her plans, her parents still seemed so far out of reach. *Seems like Mom and Dad just are who they are. There's no changing them. Fortunately, I don't have to change them. I only have to change myself.*

It occurred to her that there were people in her life who'd known about her plans from the beginning and had displayed genuine excitement and support. Claudia, who'd given so generously to help her succeed. Aiko, who'd helped set up her tour at TSU through a coworker at her job. Taylor, who'd cheered her on the entire way, and who'd wiped her tears when she'd felt too depressed and defeated to even think about her dream.

Then there was Peaches.

Peaches, who'd been one of the last to learn of her plans, yet who'd supported her just as enthusiastically as the rest of her found family had.

Peaches, who'd driven her around as she crisscrossed the state chasing her own personal star, putting hundreds of miles on her truck and refusing to even accept gas money in return.

Peaches, who'd left behind her business, her weekend errands, and an extremely needy extended family to be there for her, and to give her a chance to explore the feelings that still burned within her soul like an eternal flame.

Peaches, who'd shown a rather impressive emotional maturity and a refreshing willingness to communicate in an open and honest way, only to have her shit on it.

Fuck. I've made a terrible, terrible mistake.

Alone in her car, she sat in the parking lot of her apartment complex and racked her brain, trying to figure out a way to get Peaches back.

She's really special. My heart has always known that, even when my head was too dense to see it. After everything it took for me to even approach her, to get her to see that my feelings were real, I can't just walk away now and leave things like this.

I can't let her go.

CHAPTER NINETEEN

At around ten minutes to eight on Wednesday morning, a groggy Peaches sat down at her dining room table and opened her laptop. She was barely awake but hoped to be within the next ten minutes for her therapy session. The large cup of coffee next to her would go a long way toward increasing her alertness.

I'm not a morning person, but this was the only time she could see me. If I hadn't taken this appointment, I wouldn't have been able to get in with Dr. Jones for another two weeks. According to Aiko, my problems can't wait that long.

She went to her browser and navigated to her therapist's virtual waiting room. Taking a long sip from her mug, she waited for the good doctor.

Soon a musical chime sounded, and the face of Dr. Lenita Jones appeared on the screen. "Good morning, Peaches. It's good to see you again." Dr. Jones was in her late forties and had long black locks accented by blond tips. Right now, her locks were braided around her head in a sort of halo style that beautifully framed her copper-brown face. Wearing a white shirt beneath a yellow cardigan, she appeared to have been awake for much longer than Peaches.

"Morning, doc." Peaches raised her mug in salute. "I'm just glad I was able to snag your last available appointment until May."

"Me too. It's been a while since we've had an appointment." Resting her elbows on the edge of her desk, Dr. Jones tented her fingers. "So, what is it you'd like to talk about today? Catch me up on what's been going on in your life since we last spoke."

Taking a deep breath, Peaches gave her a rundown of the highlight reel of things that had happened since mid-February. She paused as she finished describing her talk with Aiko at the sports bar on Sunday. "So as you can see, a lot has happened, but my best friend really got me thinking about one particular issue, and that's my relationship with my family. She says it's unhealthy, but I really want to know what you think."

Dr. Jones appeared thoughtful for a few moments. "Sometimes the people around us can see things better than we can. Let's try this. I'll ask you a series of questions, and you answer honestly. That will help me determine the nature of your relationship with your family."

"Okay, I think I can handle that."

"Let's begin. I know you have an aging parent. When he has any type of emergent need, who does he call?"

Oh, this is an easy one. "Me."

"Does he only call you, or does he sometimes call your brother?"

She shook her head. "No, he only calls me."

"What about your brother? Are there times when he needs something, either for himself or his daughters, that he might call on your father? I know he's not physically able to do much, but he can probably still offer brief periods of babysitting, and definitely advice, given his age and life experience."

"No. When RJ needs something, or my nieces need something, RJ calls me."

"Hmm. Okay, interesting. So when you need something, who do you call?"

Peaches felt the gears in her mind grind to a halt. She blinked. "When I need something? That doesn't happen very often, but I usually call on Aiko, or somebody else in my friend group."

"Okay, I think I see what your friend is getting at. Based on everything you just told me, your family knows they can turn to you when they need something. No matter the time or place, they call on you, and they know you'll be there. But it doesn't seem like you can say the same is true for them. Your nieces are still children, so they don't factor here. But you can't call on your father or your brother when you're in need . . . that means the relationship is definitely unhealthy and unbalanced."

Yikes. Peaches rested her forehead on her palm. *I super hate it when Aiko is right about something . . . makes her insufferable for at least a couple of days.* "So what am I supposed to do to fix this?"

"Your best bet is to give yourself some space from them. Stop being their hero—take off your cape and let them handle their own lives . . . even if that means they may struggle, or fail."

She cringed. "I don't know if I can do that. Honestly, I feel guilty just thinking about it."

Dr. Jones smiled. "I know you do. You wouldn't believe how common this is. I have so many female patients who complain about the same type of relationship with their families. And candidly speaking, most of them are Black. I call it 'eldest sister syndrome.' I've been theorizing on it for years now, and I think it's part societal, part cultural. Whatever the cause, women like us sacrifice themselves on the altar of their family's needs, leaving no time, energy, or resources for their own needs."

Double yikes. "It has a name?"

"Not officially, just the one I gave it after hearing about it a million times."

"Well, at least I'm not alone in this mess."

Dr. Jones chuckled. "No, Peaches, you're not alone. And you don't have to remain in the mess either. It's going to take some work, and it isn't going to be easy, but I think I can help you resolve these issues."

"That's a relief." Peaches felt some of the pressure in her chest releasing. *Maybe there is a way out of this after all.*

When her session ended around nine a.m., Peaches went into the kitchen to make herself a bowl of oatmeal. She planned to go into the barbershop around ten as usual, but right now, her rumbling stomach took precedence over putting on pants. Knowing her therapist could only see her upper body and face on screen, she'd thrown on a black T-shirt over her sports bra and boxers but hadn't bothered with pants yet. *I'll put on some jeans once I finish eating.*

She was spooning up the last bit of warm oats, raisins, and maple syrup when she heard a commotion coming from her front yard. She frowned. *This is normally a pretty quiet neighborhood. What in the world is going on out there? Why do I hear music?*

She cut back through the kitchen, placing her bowl in the sink before she headed toward the front window. She pulled back her curtains, separated two slats of her blinds, and peered out.

What she saw made her eyes widen. "Oh. My. GAWD."

Jamie stood in the grass in the center of the yard. She was dressed in an orange-and-white ensemble that included a custom UT Austin Longhorns jersey bearing the number eight, a pair of white denim shorts with fringe that grazed her at midthigh, and orange sandals. She was holding a wide black object high above her head. It took Peaches a few moments to realize what the object was . . . a wireless speaker, the source of the sound she'd heard.

And she stared at the scene. Peaches took a moment to listen to the notes of the music blaring from the speaker. She snorted a laugh as recognition hit . . . it was the old Barry White classic "You're the First, the Last, My Everything."

Wow. Look at this. Say Anything, *but make it lesbian . . . and Black.*

She went to the front door and opened it. Mindful of the fact that she still wasn't wearing bottoms, she didn't go outside, but instead waved to Jamie, calling out, "This is incredibly cute, but you gotta turn that off before my neighbors flip their wigs."

Jamie grinned, cupping her hand to her ear. "What? I can't hear you over the music."

Peaches made the motion of turning an invisible dial and shouted, "Turn that off!"

Switching off the music, Jamie said, "Well, you're speaking to me, so that's a good sign. I've got one more thing to show you."

"I can't imagine what that might be," Peaches quipped.

Jamie turned around then, lifting her long hair and revealing the back of her jersey. The words "PEACHES' GIRL" were printed across her shoulder blades in large block lettering.

Peaches felt her heart flutter in her chest. "This is too precious. Now put away the speaker and get your fine ass in this house."

~

As soon as Jamie entered the house, Peaches shut the door behind her and asked, "Where did you get this crazy idea?"

"I came up with it mostly on my own . . . with a little assist from Taylor." Jamie grinned. "I know it's weird, but I'm just glad it worked."

"It's hands down the most creative apology I've ever gotten," Peaches admitted.

"That was more of a gesture." Jamie began walking toward the sofa, gently tugging Peaches along by the hand. "Here's my actual apology. I'm sorry, Peaches. I'm sorry that I hurt you, that I was dismissive of your feelings, and that I acted like a spoiled brat." She sighed, the embarrassment rising inside her as they sat next to each other. "You're just as amazing as I imagined you to be when I first started crushing on you—hell, even more so. It's when I started to let pettiness get in the way that I lost sight of how special you are. That, and my own unrealistic fantasies of what being with you would be like." She stroked her palm along Peaches' jawline. "Can you please forgive me?"

Grasping her wrist, Peaches kissed her palm. "Yes. I forgive you . . . I kind of have to, since I've missed you so much these past several days."

"I'm glad to know I wasn't alone in my suffering." She paused. "Can we talk for a minute? I want to explain to you why I behaved the way I did."

"I'm listening. I definitely want to hear this."

Taking a deep breath, Jamie began: "I wasn't in the right headspace to articulate it to you the other night, but my problem wasn't with your nieces coming over—they're adorable, by the way—or with you not wanting to make love. My real issue was the feeling that I wasn't important to you."

Peaches frowned. "What gave you that impression?"

"I mean, you dismissed me when I first approached you. Like, I shot my shot and it was a brick. Then you stood me up when I asked you out." She sighed. "Every step of the way, it seemed like you were looking for reasons not to trust me or my intentions. Then, when the girls showed up the other night, it felt like just another time that I was getting pushed to the side for something more worthy of your time."

Appearing thoughtful, Peaches offered a slow nod. "Damn. I hadn't really thought about that, but considering all you've told me about being ignored by your own relatives . . . I guess I could have been a little more considerate." She reached out, grabbing Jamie's hand. "The same way I opened up and told you my triggers, and wanted you to acknowledge them, I should have done that for you."

Jamie blew out a breath. "Listen, you're way better at breaking your baggage down than I am. But yeah, you're right. If we trade in mutual respect, I think we can have something really special."

Peaches squeezed her hand. "I agree."

Jamie laid her head against Peaches' shoulder. "Can we try this thing again? You know, just start over?"

"Yeah, I'm cool with that." Peaches' tone sounded light, relaxed. "I need you to know something first."

"What's that?"

"If you're gonna be my girl, you're never gonna be put on the back burner of my life. I'm taking care of myself in ways I never have before, which means I'm always gonna keep my own well filled first. But as long as you're with me, you'll never have to wonder how I feel about you. I'm gonna love you right, treat you the way you deserve." She cupped Jamie's chin, tilting her head at the perfect angle. For a long, silent moment, Peaches stared into Jamie's eyes. "Can you handle that?"

"Hell yes." Jamie felt herself melting like ice on a hot sidewalk.

A breath later, Peaches kissed her.

Jamie leaned into the contact, relishing the joy of feeling Peaches' touch again. Her large hands moved over Jamie's skin like a whisper, caressing every bared inch. She groaned, greedy for the experience, for the sensation only her much-desired lover could give.

Peaches broke the seal of their lips. Staring at Jamie with unbridled intensity in her eyes, she said a single word: "Strip."

Jamie kicked off her shoes and was on her feet in a second. Hurriedly, she snatched off the shorts, the expensive custom-made jersey, and the black bra and thong panties beneath.

Peaches smiled, a wicked gleam lighting her brown eyes. "Good girl." She patted her lap. "Now take a seat."

Jamie did as she was told, and a moment later the kissing began again. Peaches kissed her while slowly circling the pads of her thumbs over Jamie's hard nipples, the glorious sensation growing and blooming until Jamie feared she might implode.

Peaches stared into Jamie's eyes as she dragged her fingertips down Jamie's belly until she moved low enough to ease her thighs apart. Holding Jamie's gaze, Peaches gently stroked the dampened bud of Jamie's clit.

"Shit." Jamie's head dropped back. And when Peaches eased a thick finger inside her, Jamie shuddered. The moment was so filled with magic she could barely breathe. Peaches placed lazy kisses all over Jamie's face as her finger stroked, touched, and played, setting Jamie's pussy on fire.

Letting her finger slip from Jamie's wetness, Peaches whispered, "Here. Sit up on the back of the sofa for me, baby."

Nearly limp, Jamie was able to sit on top of the sofa's generously padded backrest, with Peaches' assistance. Once there, she gripped the fabric as Peaches shifted in her seat, bringing her mouth level with Jamie's parted thighs. Before she could take another breath, she trembled at the first long, deep stroke of Peaches' tongue against her pussy.

Peaches growled, tossing Jamie's thighs over her shoulders and gripping them with her hands. Jamie's eyes rolled back in her head, moans pouring from her throat in response to Peaches' impassioned attentions. Before long, she became aware of the warm liquid oozing down her inner thighs, a product of Peaches' unmatched oral skill.

The building pressure became too much, the glow brightening until it became a flare, encompassing Jamie's entire being. Her hips bucking against Peaches' steadying grasp, she screamed into the silent house: "Fuck!"

Peaches loosened her grip slightly, allowing Jamie to slide down onto the sofa cushions. As she lay there in a satisfied heap, she registered faint awareness of Peaches moving around the room. Still under the haze of bliss, she murmured, "Come back."

Peaches appeared over her then, naked. Jamie licked her lips at the sight of her strong, solid frame. Raising herself to a sitting position, she found herself eye to eye with the dark curls crowning Peaches' mound.

Jamie grabbed Peaches' thigh, bringing her foot to rest on the sofa. "Remember that first night, in the shower?"

"Yeah," Peaches admitted, sounding somewhat nervous.

"Payback time." She leaned in, her mouth open, and thrilled at the initial taste of Peaches' own brand of sweetness.

Peaches wove her fingertips into Jamie's hair. "Aw shit." Her broad hips began to rock as she held on to Jamie's head.

Jamie could feel herself smiling against the slick heat of Peaches' pussy, but she didn't dare stop licking and sucking her. The warmth flowing from her was like a heavenly nectar, and Jamie hungered for every single drop.

Peaches groaned as she continued bucking her hips, riding Jamie's face. Suddenly, she stopped moving, her legs stiffening, and a high-pitched shriek left her lips. Releasing her grip on Jamie's head, she stumbled before setting her foot back on the floor to rebalance herself. "Damn."

Jamie licked her lips.

"C'mon, baby. We 'bout to finish this right now." Peaches grabbed Jamie's hand and nearly dragged her to the bedroom.

After a bit of maneuvering and preparation, Jamie smiled as she straddled Peaches' harness-encased hips. Lying on her back atop the soft comforter, Peaches grabbed a handful of both of Jamie's ass cheeks. Lifting her hips, Jamie eased herself down on the sparkly dick.

She rode as if she were a cowgirl skirting across the open plains, her hips rocking and rotating. "Yes," she breathed, enjoying the way every corner of her pussy was touched by the veined silicone.

Beneath her, Peaches watched with passion-heavy eyes. "Damn, shawty . . ." With a grunt, she flipped Jamie onto her back and took over control of the strokes.

Jamie sank into the bedding, letting it cushion the impact of Peaches' long, deep strokes. "Shit . . ." She clung to Peaches, her hands sliding as she tried to grip her sweat-slickened hips.

The strokes became harder, faster, and the entire bed shook with the force of their passion. Jamie watched Peaches' breasts bouncing in time with her movements and felt the familiar heat blooming inside. Squeezing her eyes shut, she moaned, long and loud, as her entire world collapsed like a dying star.

They lay together, the morning sun streaming between the slats of the closed blinds to illuminate their sweaty bodies. Peaches turned, slowly rolling off Jamie, and chuckled as she landed on her back. "Fuck. I was supposed to go to work today."

Jamie laughed. "Good thing you own the place. My boss may not be too pleased with me, though."

Snaking her arm around Jamie's neck, Peaches said, "Be honest, though. Was it worth it?"

"Hell yeah," Jamie replied emphatically. "Of all the ways I could get in trouble with my job, this is hands down my favorite."

CHAPTER TWENTY

One Month Later

Peaches left the barbershop around four on Thursday afternoon and headed to her brother's house. Several weeks had passed since her appointment with Dr. Jones, and her next one was less than a week away. She'd shaken herself free of nervousness on the drive over, because she knew what she had to do and had a solid plan. Now she felt excited that she'd be able to tell her therapist that she'd done all the homework she'd requested.

When she knocked on the door, RJ answered it. Still dressed in his work uniform from Austin Power, he had a surprised look on his face. "Hey, sis. What are you doing here?"

She smiled. "I need to talk to you—can I come in?"

He shrugged and stepped aside. "Sure."

She entered the familiar confines of the house and headed straight for the sofa. She could hear the sounds of the girls' boisterous play emanating from the hallway, and she shook her head at their silliness. Clearing her throat, she said, "I don't like long introductions, so I'm just going to come out and say what I have to say. I'm leaving Austin."

His eyes widened as he sat on the sofa next to her. "What? When?"

"I still have some arrangements to make, but I expect to be out of here in less than a month."

"I don't understand. Why are you leaving in the first place, and why are you telling me so close to the time you expect to be gone?"

She placed her hands in her lap and laced her fingers together. "I could go into all the details of that, but I really don't see the point. Suffice it to say that you, Dad, and the girls need to know what it's like to live life without me being so accessible all the time."

His expression changed, his jaw tightening. "Hold on now. I don't think I like the way this is going. What are you trying to say? Do you think we ask too much of you?"

Peaches scoffed. "If you have to ask that question, the answer is obvious. Look, I don't expect you to see it, or validate it, or even understand where I'm coming from. What I do know is I'm exhausted, and it's time I dedicate some resources to focusing on myself and what I need."

He rolled his eyes. "I can't believe this. This whole thing is coming right out of left field. Your timing couldn't be worse. I anticipate taking on way more overtime and maybe even some weekend shifts until the company gets through this stupid tech transition."

"Lucky for you, you won't have to worry about childcare for the girls." Reaching into the back pocket of her jeans, she produced a business card and pressed it into her brother's hand. "I visited a nanny agency, and I hired you a mother's helper. She's flexible, she's well trained, has great recommendations, and can be here within thirty minutes of your call."

He sighed. "And just how much is this going to cost me? How do you know if I can afford a service like this, or if I'll even like this woman, or . . . ?"

She held up her index finger. "RJ, hush. You trusted me to handle things right up until five minutes ago, so just go with it. It's already taken care of, and if for some reason you don't like her, you can always get someone else that works for the same agency she does. And as far as the cost, that's not a worry, either, at least not yet. I've already prepaid her for her first twenty hours of service. After that, the bill is going to be your responsibility."

He looked at the card resting in his open palm, then directed his gaze back to her face. "You're serious, aren't you?"

She nodded. "Isn't that obvious?"

He shook his head slowly. "Wow. I had no idea you thought our family was a burden."

Dr. Jones warned me he might react this way, playing on my guilt in order to get me to do what he wants. Instead of taking the bait her brother was laying, Peaches smiled. "I never said that, but if you choose to believe that, that's on you. I'm doing what's best for me right now, and you're just going to have to deal with it. Just know that I love you no matter what."

He blew out an exasperated breath. "I love you too, though I must admit you have a funny way of showing your affection." He paused. "Wait a minute, what about Dad? I can't take off work to look after him, and I know that no matter how much you paid this mother's helper, she isn't going to be able to take care of him too."

"What? Do you think I forgot about Pops?" She pulled out her phone and sent him a text.

A moment later his phone dinged, and he grabbed it from the coffee table. "What did you just send me?"

"The electronic business card for our dad's on-call nurse."

He released a bitter chuckle. "Let me guess, you already paid for her too, huh?"

"Actually, no. Pop's long-term-care insurance is paying for her. I already went by Dad's house this morning, so he knows the deal and knows how to contact her if he needs anything. Now that you have the card, if you have any questions or concerns for her, you can reach out to her too."

He was silent for a moment, and he seemed to be thinking over everything he'd just heard. "Wow. Peaches, this is a lot to just spring on me like this."

"Is it really out of left field, RJ? Or have you just not been paying attention?"

"Huh?"

She shook her head. "Over the last few weeks, I started doing something I rarely did with you . . . saying no. You didn't notice that?"

He was quiet for a few moments, his gaze moving to some distant point beyond her face. "I . . . guess you're right. You've been working up to this."

She glanced behind her to the hallway. "I'm going to go in the back and talk to the girls and let you mull this over for a few minutes."

"Fine." He slumped back against the sofa cushions.

Peaches got up and walked through the kitchen, circling around the center island before entering the hallway beyond. The door to Olivia's room was open, and all three girls were sitting on the brightly colored braided rug beside her bed, surrounded by various and sundry plastic toys.

After entering the room, Peaches sat on the edge of Olivia's bed, holding out her arms as her nieces surrounded her.

"I didn't know you were coming over, Auntie," Ella said.

"It was a little surprise." Peaches smiled at the three of them. "I have some news for you, and I wanted to tell you in person."

"What is it, Auntie Peaches?" Olivia asked.

She took a deep breath. "Well, Auntie Peaches is going to be moving out of town pretty soon."

"Why?" Ella whined.

"Well, I finally think I found the right place to open up a second barbershop. It just so happens that that place isn't in Austin. So that means in order to make sure the new barbershop is successful, I need to move down there, at least long enough to get it started."

Reagan climbed into Peaches' lap. Throwing her tiny arms around her neck, she looked up at her with big doe eyes. "Don't go, Auntie."

It was all Peaches could do not to dissolve into tears. Taking another steadying breath, she spoke softly. "Listen, you girls are just about the best people in the whole wide world. And while I have to do this, I don't want you to think that it's going to change anything about our relationship. You're still welcome to come to Auntie's house anytime you want, and I'll be checking on you fairly often."

"Does that mean we can still have sleepovers?" Ella asked.

"Yep."

"And you'll still take us out for frozen yogurt?" That question came from Olivia.

She laughed. "Yes, sometimes when you least expect it. Everything is going to be fine, trust me. A nice lady named Nicole will come here to help your dad out when he needs a babysitter and I can't make it. Meanwhile I'm always just a phone call away. If anybody messes with y'all, I'm still going to come down here and box their ears." She held up her fist to emphasize the last three words.

That elicited giggles from all the girls, and soon enough, Peaches joined in their humor.

⌇

Keeping her eyes on the road, Jamie asked, "You doing okay?"

"Yeah, I'm good." Peaches shifted a bit in the passenger seat. "It's a little tight, but not as bad as I thought it would be."

Jamie chuckled. "That's good to hear. Since you drove the last two times, I thought it was only fair that I take a turn. Can't just be putting all the miles on your truck."

"I feel you." Peaches let the seat back a bit. "We just can't take any long road trips in your car. I mean, it's a decent size—I think I've just gotten used to all the space I have in the truck."

Jamie checked the GPS on her phone. "We'll be there in like thirty minutes."

"I can hang." Peaches let her head drop back. "It's way less hectic than a Saturday morning at the barbershop would be."

"Same for the nail salon." Jamie sighed. "I'm gonna miss that place. Barbara was a pretty cool boss, and I kinda hate that I won't be seeing my regulars anymore."

"Yeah. I feel the same way about my barbershop." Peaches ran a hand over her curls. "Anyway, we gotta look at the bright side. New city, new clients, building new relationships. Plus, it's a whole new life and career for you, Miss Scientist in Training."

She laughed. "You're right. I'm so excited to take a second look at this place with you. Here's hoping it's the one."

"I've got a good feeling about it. If the seller is willing to be flexible, I might jump on it today."

Jamie watched the open highway stretching out before them. It was a warm, humid May day, and fat, puffy clouds floated by in the bluish-gray sky above. Rain might come later, but she didn't care. Her mood was light and optimistic. She had her sweet, sexy girlfriend riding shotgun, and everything felt right.

She exited the highway and merged into the traffic on the Sam Houston Tollway. The area bustled with activity, and traffic only grew more tangled as they neared Town & Country Village, the location of Peaches' potential second barbershop.

Jamie parked the car as close as she could to the storefront and turned off the engine. "You ready?"

"Let me text the Realtor and see if she's here yet." Peaches pulled out her phone and began typing, then hit "Send." A few moments later, her phone dinged. "She says she'll be pulling up in the next five minutes."

When the black sedan arrived and parked across from them, Peaches unbuckled her seat belt. "That's her."

"Oh yeah." Jamie watched as the smartly dressed woman emerged from the car.

They met the Realtor, Grace, at the door to the storefront. The covered breezeway over the entrance provided a welcome respite from the hot Texas sun overhead. "Hello, Ms. Corbin, Ms. Hunt. You ladies ready for your second look?"

Peaches grinned. "Yes, ma'am." Grace used the key to unlock the door, then held it open so they could enter.

Inside, Jamie stood back and watched as Peaches explored the confines of the store.

"As I said before," Grace began, "you've got a nice amount of square footage in here to set up your shop." She walked around as she spoke, gesturing. "This space is twenty-one hundred square feet in total, with a narrow and deep thirty-foot-by-seventy-foot layout. Great storage space in the back, where you can keep your supplies, implements, whatever you need. And then you have a flex space you can use as an office or breakroom, along with the two restrooms."

"I see they finished up the painting that was going on last time we were here," Peaches remarked.

"Yes. They've given the walls this very modern slate gray that you see, and the chair rail and crown molding that extends around the entire main room has a fresh coat of white paint as well. It gives you a very nice contrast."

Peaches nodded. "I like it—it turned out really nice. And the electrical wiring and plumbing have been upgraded as well, right?"

"They have. The shopping center has been here since the sixties, but this space has been gutted and remodeled . . . It used to be a clothing store." Grace gestured to Peaches. "Come with me, and I'll open up the fuse box so you can have a look at it."

While they disappeared down the short corridor in the northwest corner, Jamie remained near the front, looking out the big picture window next to the door. There were plenty of cars in the parking lot, and lots of foot traffic moving up and down the breezeway. *I would never have guessed this center was that old; it's been kept up really well. There's that grocery store and the bookstore that anchor this shopping center. I think this is a good location . . . Peaches should have access to a nice pool of potential clients here.*

Peaches and Grace returned from the back, and Jamie turned her attention back to them.

"Everything looks really good here," Peaches said. "And the seller is still offering to pay closing costs?"

"Correct." Grace nodded. "The seller is very motivated. They sent me the reports from the final inspection to show that everything is up to code as well." She reached into the leather portfolio and handed a stack of papers to Peaches.

Perusing the documents, Peaches smiled. "I'm really pleased with everything I see." Walking over to Jamie with the papers still in hand, she asked, "What do you think, baby?"

I love that she wants my input on this. "I think this is the one. It's a great space, gets lot of traffic, and has all the things you need."

Peaches nodded. "Bet." Turning back to Grace, she announced, "I'm ready to put in my offer."

"Excellent. Let's move to the coffee shop two doors down, and we can do a little paperwork and reach out to the seller."

They left the coffee shop a couple of hours later, and Jamie could feel the buzz of excitement rolling off Peaches' body.

"Wow. I can't believe it. If they accept my offer, I'm finally gonna have a new Fresh Cutz location. It's been a long time coming."

Jamie nodded as she stopped at a red light. "Are you gonna keep that name? Like, call it Fresh Cutz Two or something like that?"

She shrugged. "I'm not sure. I've been so focused on securing the right property, I hadn't thought too much about the name." She rested her chin on her hand, appearing thoughtful. "I gotta think about it. Light's green, by the way."

Noting the teasing in Peaches' tone, Jamie accelerated through the intersection. "Anyway, are you hungry? Do you wanna grab lunch on the way to my place?"

"Yeah, I could eat. Let's grab a pizza or something." Peaches rested her palm on Jamie's bare thigh. "After we eat, I propose dessert."

"What are you thinking? Ice cream? Or maybe cupcakes from that place by the apartments?"

"Nah." Peaches chuckled and gave her thigh a squeeze. "The dessert I want is . . ." She let her hand drift between Jamie's legs.

Jamie's pulse raced, and she sucked her lower lip as Peaches' fingertip grazed her pussy through the layers of fabric. "Peaches!"

"C'mon, now. You leased your place like two weeks ago, and it still hasn't been properly christened." Peaches lingered there, circling her finger.

Jamie slapped her hand. "Not while I'm driving. You gonna make me run off the road, Miss Filthy McNasty."

Peaches laughed as she moved her hand back to Jamie's thigh. "Whatever. You know you like it."

After a quick stop at a local trattoria for pizza and salad, Jamie drove them to her apartment in the Addicks / Park Ten neighborhood. As they climbed the steps with their to-go cups, Peaches asked, "Why did you choose the upper floor again?"

"In the past, whenever I would get a downstairs unit, I would always end up beneath people who were really loud." Jamie took the carabiner holding her keys from the belt loop of her shorts to open the door. "The last time I lived under somebody, I could've sworn they ran an all-night bowling alley."

"Damn, was it really that bad?"

"Yes." After pushing the door open, she went inside, with Peaches close behind. "And during the day, they must have been practicing clogging or something."

Peaches snorted. "Not *Riverdance*."

"Wow. Memory unlocked on that one—haven't heard that in a minute." Jamie laughed. "But that was definitely the vibe. So you see why I go for the highest floor now. I don't rent at places with more than three levels, though. I'm not trying to be climbing stairs like that."

Peaches walked through the living room into the open kitchen, then set her cup on the edge of the center island. "I do the StairMaster at the gym . . . maybe once I move in here, I can do it for twenty minutes instead of thirty."

Jamie narrowed her eyes. "You really trying to be here with me full time like that?"

"I been told you that." Peaches walked over and grabbed her free hand, leading her back to the island. "I wasn't playing either. I mean, I guess we'll get a house eventually. Hopefully this deal goes through and I can start setting up my new barbershop. The only other thing Houston has that I'm interested in is you, shawty."

The sound of Peaches' ringing phone cut through the quiet. She reached into her pocket and answered. "Hey, Grace, what's up?"

Jamie watched Peaches' expression morph from curiosity to joy.

"Really? That's great! Tell them we can meet up at your office Monday. And thanks for your help, Grace." Peaches ended the call. "Baby, they accepted my offer . . . I got myself a barbershop!"

Jamie grabbed her face with both hands and planted a juicy kiss on her lips. "This is amazing. Congratulations, Daddy."

Peaches groaned. "Now, girl. You know how I get when you call me that."

"Oh, I know." Jamie hoisted herself up on the countertop. "We can go out for champagne later . . . but how about some celebratory dessert right now?"

Peaches licked her lips. "That's what I'm talking about." Her hands moved to undo the button of Jamie's shorts while she placed soft kisses along the column of her throat.

Jamie sighed, her head dropping back as she whispered, "I love you, Peaches." She parted her thighs.

"I love you too, baby." Peaches slid down the zipper and slipped her hand inside Jamie's shorts. As she pushed the thin fabric of Jamie's panties to the side and stroked her clit, the world fell away, and she dissolved into bliss.

EPILOGUE

Five Months Later

"I'm so glad y'all could make it up here for Friendsgiving."

Peaches looked up from her plate and smiled in Claudia's direction. "Hey, we haven't missed a game night since we moved to Houston." They were seated around the dining room table at Aiko and Summer's house, and the whole squad had assembled for the festivities.

"Right," Jamie added. She was sitting to Peaches' immediate right. "We definitely weren't about to miss this . . . especially when I heard Aiko say she got Elevated Soul to do the catering."

Aiko rubbed her hands together. "Thank you for recognizing my impeccable taste, Jamie."

Summer laughed and jabbed her wife with the handle of her fork. "How you gonna act like I didn't suggest them?"

"Okay, that's valid . . . but I did call in the order, though." Aiko winked, and that earned her another stab from the fork handle, followed by a kiss on the cheek from Summer.

That newlywed glow is still lingering. Peaches shook her head as she returned her attention to her food. "This is an amazing meal, so thanks to both of you." She dug into the baked mac and cheese and sighed as she chewed. The menu was bursting with all the good stuff: grilled lobster tails, rib eye steak, loaded baked potato casserole, and collard greens.

"Y'all save room for dessert," Summer announced. "I've got two pound cakes and two sweet potato pies in the kitchen."

"Whew." Taylor patted their belly. "I'm gonna try to save some space, but I can't make no promises. This food is hittin'."

Claudia laughed. "You right. I haven't eaten like this since Easter at my granny's place."

Conversation paused, and a comfortable quiet settled over the gathering as everyone focused on finishing up their meals. The sounds of silverware striking the Holts' wedding china, and ice clinking in the cut-crystal glasses, were the only noises in the room.

As they finished up dinner, Summer rose from her seat. "Let me start taking this stuff to the kitchen. I'll bring out the desserts in a minute."

Aiko was on her feet in a flash. "Let me help you, honey."

Peaches watched as her best friend snaked an arm around her wife's waist and placed a gentle kiss against her forehead. *These two are so damn cute. Is that how Jamie and I act now?* She turned toward Jamie then and found her looking at her with those big doe eyes and the softest smile.

Yep. That's exactly how we act. Leaning in, she brushed a few bread crumbs from Jamie's lips and gave her a kiss. *I'm cool with this.*

While Aiko and Summer floated around, collecting the dishes and the leftovers, Taylor made a fake gagging noise. "Not y'all too. C'mon now. Spare a thought for those of us still in the struggle."

Peaches snorted. "Taylor, are you saying you not enjoying the streets?"

"I ain't said all that," Taylor insisted. "I'm just missing out on all that lovey-dovey stuff. I mean, I'm surfing the apps and whatnot, and I got another very sexy enby in the DMs with major potential." They sighed. "Part of me wants to hit fast-forward so I can get where y'all at."

"What about you, Claudia? Anything happening in that department for you?" Jamie sipped from her glass of lemonade.

Claudia shook her head. "Girl, no. But that's on purpose. I'm still settling into my job at ACC Eastview. I love teaching, but there is way too much paperwork involved . . . perils of being assistant department head, I guess."

"You mean ain't nobody shooting their shot with you?" Peaches felt her brow hitch.

"I didn't say that. I get plenty of offers, and of course, I get way more attention than I want from men, especially since I want them to ignore my very existence." Claudia rolled her eyes. "But that's not the timing I'm on right now. I need to really get into the groove of this job, then maybe I'll throw my admirers a bone."

Peaches laughed. "You are such a mess. But I'm glad the new job is going well." She turned back to Taylor. "I get reports from Alonzo every week, but I know you have the real tea on everything happening at Fresh Cutz."

"You know I do, Peaches." Taylor started to say something but then paused as Aiko and Summer placed dessert plates in front of them and set a pie and pound cake in the center of the table.

Setting down the cake servers, Summer said, "Help yourselves to some sweets, people."

Taylor picked up one of the knives and cut themself a trim slice of pound cake. "So, like I was saying, it's going pretty good. Alonzo don't ask me dumb questions about my gender, or lack thereof, anymore. And I feel like Clyde is finally finding his groove within the complex social structure of the barbershop. We all went out for drinks about two weeks ago, and we invited the kid, even though he's barely of age." Nibbling a small piece of cake, they added, "Turns out Clyde's really funny."

"Let me find out you're crushing on Clyde," Jamie teased.

Taylor scoffed. "Please. You would have been the first to know if I was, duh."

Peaches nodded. "Sounds like things are going good. I know profits have been steady and stable, so I'm glad to hear everything is good inside the shop as well."

"You haven't told us much about the new shop," Claudia said. "All we know is that you named it Cuttin' Up."

She smiled. "Good name, right? I've been quiet about it because I didn't want to jinx anything, you know? I'm really happy with how things are going. It's just me and two other barbers right now, but business is picking up. Hopefully I can add one or two more barbers in the first quarter of next year."

"I'm proud of you, P," Aiko said around a mouthful of sweet potato pie. "It took you a while to get there, but you had a measured, thoughtful approach, and it looks like it's paying off."

"Thanks." She smiled at her best friend and threw her arm around Jamie's shoulders. "Houston is a good fit for me . . . for us."

"School is going pretty well—now that I've finished summer term and started a full semester, I feel way less rusty. But I love everything I'm learning, and having my baby at my side makes it even better." Jamie giggled. "We've been having a great time. And her nieces have been by to visit twice already. They are a handful, but it's so much fun when they come through."

"It really is." Peaches grinned as she thought of the girls. "It was touch and go that first weekend, but now that I've reminded them that they still can't jump on Auntie's sofa, even if it is in a different place, I think we're good. They'll be back when they get out of school for winter break."

"The whole break?" Aiko asked, wide eyed.

"Hell naw!" Peaches laughed. "I love my lil' homies, but I don't think I can hang for that long."

"You both sound real comfortable with having kids around," Claudia said, her tone and expression sly. "So . . . y'all 'bout to have some babies?"

Jamie shook her head. "Nope. I love my lil' nephew Levi, and the girls are hilarious. But I'm not cut out to be anybody's mama."

"Me either," Peaches added. "Being an aunt is fulfilling enough. We're just enjoying connecting on a deeper level, and that's all we need." She paused. "You should be asking them if they about to have some babies." She pointed at Summer and Aiko.

"Hold on, playa." Aiko held up both hands, palms out. "We may adopt in the next few years . . . but it's no rush, trust me."

"Seriously." Summer linked her arm through her wife's. "Y'all know I love kids—I made a career out of it. But I'm in no hurry to add to our peaceful little household."

Hours later, Peaches lay on her back in the bed in the guest room. Jamie lay next to her, with her bonnet-covered head resting on Peaches' chest. Staring up into the darkness, Peaches said, "This was so much fun. I'm glad we came."

Jamie sighed. "Yeah. It's almost like we still live in Austin—we're up here all the time. I'm not mad, though."

"Our squad is the best squad." Peaches draped her arm around Jamie, pulling her closer. "It was a little crazy of us to risk ruining this amazing found family the way we did, wasn't it?"

"It was," Jamie admitted softly. "But I'm so, so glad we did."

Peaches shifted so she could bring her face close to Jamie's. "So am I. We have so much lying ahead of us, and I'm excited for everything we're going to share." Resting her forehead against Jamie's, she whispered, "I love you, baby. So, so much."

"I love you too." Jamie tilted her head, bringing their lips together.

And there, shrouded in soothing darkness and the comfort of each other's arms, the two lovers did what lovers do best.

ABOUT THE AUTHOR

Photo © 2021 Kianna Alexander

Kianna Alexander has always been something of a dreamer. Raised among the Carolina pines, she routinely read fifteen or more books a week and was always thirsty for more. Her vivid imagination eventually led her to spin tales of her own. The author of *Can't Resist Her*, Kianna shows her passion for building empathy through fiction in her writing, and she truly believes literature can have a profound and positive impact on people's lives.

Kianna is also a mother of two; a dabbler in various crafts; and a lover of random trivia, music, white wine, and sunrises on the beach. She lives in the western US with her children, her partner, the world's highest-maintenance cat, and a precocious pup. For more information visit www.authorkiannaalexander.wordpress.com.